I0707561

IN SILENCE

A BLACK FALLS HIGH NOVEL

A DARK BULLY ROMANCE

K.G. REUSS

BOOK TWO

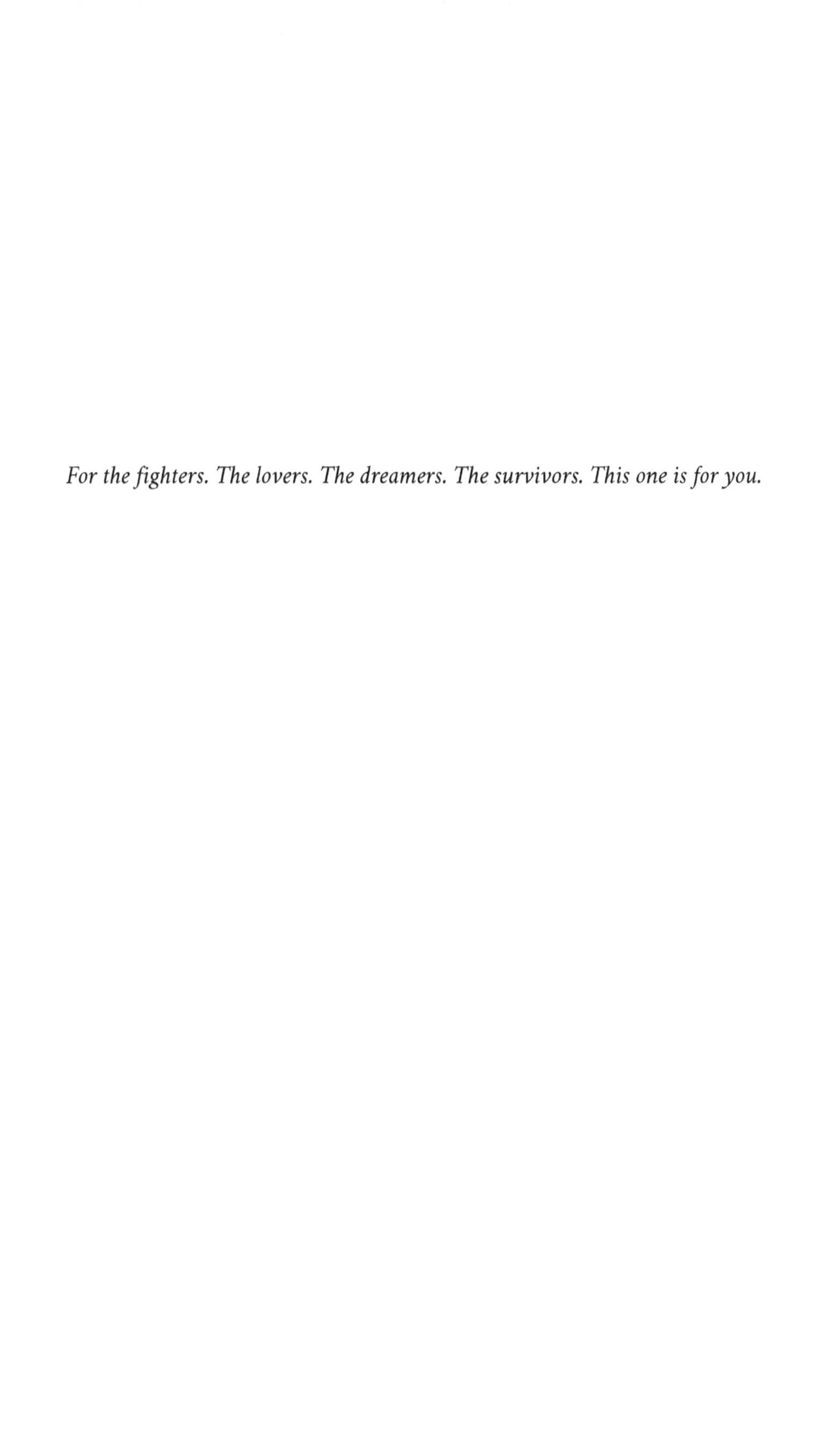

For the fighters. The lovers. The dreamers. The survivors. This one is for you.

Before You Embark On A Journey Of Revenge, Dig Two Graves

Confucius

FOREWORD

Dear Reader

This book isn't light and fluffy and filled with rainbows and butterflies. It's dark. There are dark themes, including violence and abuse in many ugly forms. Any chapter has the potential to trigger readers.

If you are easily triggered, or frown on the darker situations in life, I urge you to navigate away now. Once you start this book, there's no going back.

You have been warned.

Visit kgreuss.com for more content information.

-K

PROLOGUE

FOX

$\mathscr{I}$ fisted her hair, jerking her head back.

"Fox," she rasped, reaching out for me. "Please—"

"Don't touch me," I snarled, gripping her hair harder. She let out a whimper as she stared up at me with wild, lust-filled eyes. "You want me to fuck you?"

"Y-yes," she whimpered again.

I released her and tossed her roughly to the floor. The thought of burying myself inside her made me sick to my stomach. She was a fucking coffin for my dead soul. All I could think about was Rosalie. She hadn't spoken to me since shit went down with Juliet. She'd blocked me on social media. Threatened to call the cops on me if I kept pounding on her door. Wouldn't even look at me. And the guys? It took them a week to speak to me.

I fucked up. Bad.

I looked down at Juliet as she struggled to sit up, her mascara running, ugly black blotches on her cheeks, her breasts barely in her red bra.

"You going to fuck her or what?" Cole asked lazily from his leather chair in his living room as he sipped a glass of whiskey.

"You can," I grunted, going to the bar in the corner and pouring myself a drink.

Cole scoffed and sat forward, his blue eyes locked on Juliet. Ever since Rosie had left us, we'd made sure to stick to the bargain we had with Juliet: Fuck her and make her our queen over anyone else, and she'd keep all the stolen videos she had of Rosie tucked away. She wouldn't release them and ruin Rosie's life. As a bonus, she wouldn't release our notebook to the world and hurt the other girls. Pretty sure my full ride to Mayfair on a football scholarship would be ripped away from me if things got out. The disappointment at that alone would tear my old man to shreds.

I ground my teeth at the thought of all of it, especially Rosalie getting hurt. I'd been haunted by the look on her face since she walked away from me that day. Being blackmailed by Juliet seemed a fitting punishment for our atrocities. Who would've thought a bit of fun could ruin so many lives?

Looks like the tables have turned.

We were stuck between a rock and a hard place. We'd lost Rosie, but we could still preserve her innocence. We were helpless though, at least until we figured out what to do about Juliet. This feeling of utter uncertainty was well-deserved, considering we'd done it to Rosie weeks ago.

Guess that had backfired on us.

I'd made the stupid fucking mistake of breaking up with Juliet and not informing my dad. While I was at Cole's, she'd stopped by, citing she'd left her bag in my room. My dad, being a nice guy, allowed her into my room where I kept the backup videos of Rosalie. I didn't even know why I had them. Now, Juliet had everything that could ruin Rosalie.

I didn't give a shit about us being screwed over it. I worried for my girl. *My sweet Rosie.*

She didn't deserve any of this shit. I swore to protect her from the monsters, and there I was, becoming one. I hated myself for it. I hated the gnawing pain in my chest that wouldn't fucking go away. I hated I couldn't be with her. That I couldn't hold her or kiss her or get her to just listen to me. I wanted her to understand I didn't love Juliet. That she, Rosalie, had my heart. She was all I wanted. But to save her from my mistakes, I had to hurt her.

I had no intention of using those videos on her. I might have been an asshole to her initially, but I'd become a different person once I'd let my own shit go. I should've deleted the videos. It was a bad move on my part. Juliet copied them, and now, there we were in a whole heap of shit.

"Come here, you fucking bitch," Cole spat.

Juliet crawled across his floor to him, her eyes hooded. None of the guys wanted her. But she had to be queen at everything. She'd known about the notebook from the beginning. She knew we all wanted Rosalie. It drove her nuts knowing that someone like Rosie won our hearts instead of her.

And this was our punishment.

Juliet stopped at Cole's feet as Enzo, who'd been quiet the entire time, got to his feet.

Ethan quietly drank in the corner, looking down at the floor.

"You want my dick so bad, then fucking suck it," Cole snapped at her.

"Why are you such an asshole?" she huffed, rising to her knees and resting her hands on his thighs.

"You can't be that stupid," Cole snorted. "I could be buried in a tight pussy right now, instead all I have is you."

Juliet's cheeks flushed at Cole's crude words. This would be the first time we'd all be with her as per her demands. Hell, it would be my first time with her. She'd always held out on me when we'd dated, offering me weak blow jobs while I'd fingered her. Now I knew why. She wanted to be the one we worshipped. She'd been running her own game, the bitch.

I swallowed my glass of whiskey and took a hit from the joint I lit, my eyes focused on Cole as he stared at Juliet, disgust on his face. My heart went out to my friends. I'd gotten us into this mess with her and, in the process, had lost us Rosie.

It had hit us all hard. While I knew it fucked my world, it was Cole who'd lost his shit first.

I could still hear his anger now from that day a week ago ...

"What the fuck is the matter with you? How could you fuck us like this?" Cole snarled, his eyes wild. He fisted his hair as he stared helplessly at me.

"I trusted her—"

"It's fucking Juliet, you dumb fuck!" Cole shouted, his face red, spit flying from his mouth as he stormed around his living room.

Enzo looked on from his spot in the leather chair as Ethan chewed his thumbnail, his head down.

"The only thing you can trust about that bitch is that she'll royally fuck you over! How the hell did Rosalie even get the fucking notebook?" He stopped his angry march long enough to glare at me.

"I don't know. Whoever took it knew how to use it."

"We need to find out and beat the shit out of whoever it was," Cole spat. He kicked at an end table before grabbing it and pitching it across the room. It burst into splinters against the wall.

"Relax, Cole," Enzo called out. "We need to figure this shit out, not destroy the damn house."

"Fuck the house and fuck you," Cole shouted back, his face going from red to purple.

Ethan finally looked up, his eyes bloodshot. "You're not the only one who lost her, you know. We'll fix it."

My heart clenched. Ethan had legitimately given a damn about Rosie right from the start. He was a bleeding heart like that. Always kind. Always trying to find the bright side and make things better.

"You can't fix everything, Ethan! Not even you can with your fucking emotions and tears."

"Fuck you, Cole," Ethan snarled. "At least I have a grip on my shit."

"For now," Enzo murmured, glancing at Ethan. "But what are you going to do if this is permanent, and she won't talk to us?"

Ethan let out a sigh and looked away, a muscle thrumming along his jaw.

"That's what I thought." Cole let out a bark of deranged laughter, his blonde hair a mess.

He looked certifiably insane as his body shook.

"We need a plan," I said calmly. "We should try to talk to her."

"Oh, hey, you fucking genius. Let's see how that works." Cole stopped laughing and yanked his phone out and hit send on Rosalie's name. We all waited as he put it on speaker, the ringing like death knocking with every pulse.

"You've reached Rosalie. I'm not here right now, so leave a message!"

Cole ran his hand over his face and hung up only to hit redial. He did this several times before eventually his calls went straight to voicemail. With an angry snarl, he heaved his phone across the room where it shattered and fell to the floor.

"It's over," Cole breathed out, glaring at me.

"We'll fix it," I assured him, my throat tight. "Like Ethan said, you're not the only one who lost her—"

"Yeah? What the fuck are you going to do to fix it, Fox? You were so fucking eager to let her go in the beginning. Maybe this is just part of your mental fucking bullshit—"

"Fuck you," I snarled, shoving him.

He shoved me back. Enzo was on his feet, jumping between us.

"I've loved her for as long as I've known her." I glared at my friend, ready to beat his ass.

"Me too," Cole shot back, breathing hard. He walked away, fingers in his hair.

We all watched him for a moment before he stormed back, his face red. He let out a yell before his fist connected with the glass coffee table, shattering it. Blood streamed in angry red rivers down his arm as he glowered at me.

"Fucking fix it, Fox. I-I can't lose her."

I shook the memory out of my head. I hadn't known how much my love for Rosalie would grow. I hadn't anticipated any of this shit. I'd been careless, letting Juliet get too close. Trusting her when I knew I shouldn't. I'd been fighting my feelings for Rosie for years. Ever since my mom died. From the moment the earrings Rosalie had mentioned were given back to us with Mom's possessions. The whole reason Mom was out to begin with for Daniel Hall to hit while driving drunk. Because she went out to get Rosalie a special birthday present, Ian's dad was able to plow his car into her. She never saw it coming. Thankfully, Cole's dad was able to win a conviction, sending the asshole to prison for a few years. Unfortunately, he was up for parole in a few weeks and would be free to ruin someone else's life.

Life just wasn't fair sometimes.

For years, I'd blamed Rosalie for my mom's death. I took another hit from the joint and closed my eyes, seeing Rosie's pretty face in my mind's eye. Flawless porcelain skin. Bright green eyes surrounded by thick, black lashes. Full, pink, pouty lips. Lips I couldn't get enough of. Those large breasts and narrow waist which gave way to that sexy hip flair. I imagined twining my fingers through her thick, red curls. How she'd whisper my name, her nails in my back as I thrust inside her tight body.

"Give me some," Enzo grunted, taking the joint from me and inhaling deeply.

We were quiet for a moment. I tore my eyes away from Juliet who had her mouth around Cole's dick. His mouth was turned down into a frown as she bobbed up and down on him.

If we were grading her in the book, her dick sucking skills would be barely a one.

"Ethan, you cool?" Enzo called out.

Ethan didn't acknowledge him. He took another drink before pulling out a bottle of pills, spilling one into his waiting hand. He popped it into his mouth and washed it down with his whiskey. Ethan had anxiety and was a recovering addict. It wasn't a widely known fact by others, but we knew it. If Ethan was drinking and popping pills again, then something was seriously wrong because Ethan was always the straight-laced one of us. Falling back into his old ways was something he struggled to overcome. He had issues he didn't like to talk about. Issues we were aware of but didn't press him on.

"Want some of this?" Enzo tried again, offering Ethan the joint.

Ethan's green eyes flicked from Enzo's face to the joint before he shuffled to his feet and came to us, seizing what was offered and taking a hit.

"I'd rather *you* suck my dick than her," Ethan grunted, blowing out smoke, his eyes fixed on Cole and Juliet.

Cole had his phone out and was looking through it as Juliet continued her attempt at a blow job.

"If it got us out of this fucking nightmare, I'd slob your knob right now," Enzo answered, sneering in Juliet's direction.

Juliet released Cole's dick with a loud popping noise. He lifted a brow at her from over his phone.

"I can hear you," Juliet called out, looking over at us, her mouth set in a pout that may have worked on me months ago but did nothing for me now. "Maybe you should suck Ethan's dick, Enzo."

Enzo paled. Ethan shifted where he stood. Juliet got to her feet and sashayed over to us, a wicked glint in her dark eyes.

"I actually like that idea. You two sucking each other off."

"Juliet," I growled. "We're not gay."

She let out a soft laugh. "Prove it. Choke on Enzo's dick. Maybe I'll let you all off the hook early. If you don't, maybe I'll just send this video you guys so graciously took of Rosalie off to her daddy. I'm sure he'd love to see what his daughter has been up to. Heard he's a real prick."

"You're going too far, Juliet," I murmured. "We'll fuck you, but we aren't going to fuck one another."

"We could kill you and be done with it," Ethan snarled, his green eyes filled with storm clouds.

I stared at him. In that moment, he looked like he could rival me and Cole for dark thoughts.

"You're fucked up, Juliet," Enzo snapped.

"What's wrong, *Lorenzo*, you too insecure to suck off Ethan?" Juliet reached out and rubbed Ethan's crotch.

In a move that surprised me, Ethan shoved her hard. Ethan was the gentle one of us four. The caring one. The one Rosie had dubbed sweet. To see him get handsy meant he was pissed.

Juliet stumbled back and landed on her ass with a thump. Cole watched interestedly from his chair, a smirk on his lips. We didn't intervene when Ethan moved forward and fisted her hair, angling her head to the side. Juliet let out a gasp, wincing beneath his hold.

"You. *Disgust.* Me," Ethan hissed, tugging her hair harder. Tears filled Juliet's eyes as she stared up at him. "The fact you're trying to force us to *fuck you* makes you the vilest piece of shit I've ever dealt with."

"But you did it to other girls. You did it to Rosalie—"

"We never did *this* to girls. We played around. They were willing. Had they said no, then we'd have walked. We liked Rosalie too much to force her. She did what she wanted, when she wanted, with who the fuck she wanted." Ethan released her hair and moved his hands to her throat where he squeezed. Her eyes widened, her cheeks reddening from the pressure.

Enzo cast me a worried look. I took a step forward, not even sure if I wanted to stop Ethan from potentially choking her out. I cast a glance at Cole who wore a dark smile as he lazily drank his whiskey.

"And the difference between you and Rosalie is that we genuinely gave a shit about her. You? I'd enjoy watching the light fade from your eyes as you choked on my dick."

"Ethan," she rasped, reaching out for him as he tightened his grip.

"You're lucky I fucking love her," Ethan whispered, his breathing heavy as he squatted down to put his rage filled face in hers. "Or I'd have killed you already. Enjoy this while you can because once I figure out a solution, you're going to wish you didn't know me."

He released her and got to his feet as she sputtered, her eyes bloodshot from him choking her. He shot us an angry look before storming to the front door and slamming it closed behind him. The squealing of his tires, moments later, let us know he'd left.

"Well, looks like you pissed Ethan off." Cole laughed, breaking the silence. "Still want to suck some cock or is your throat sore?"

"Fuck you, Cole," Juliet rasped, her voice hoarse. Ethan's handprints were still on her throat.

"Nah. Not tonight. You ruined the mood. Get dressed and get the fuck out." Cole got to his feet and grabbed her shirt before tossing it at her. "We'll try again another time."

With her face flaming red, she put her shirt back on and got to her feet. "Fox?"

"Walk home," I said evenly.

"I'll release everything I have—"

"No, you won't," I said, stepping over to her and thumbing her bottom lip. "You know why?"

She leaned into my touch. "Why?"

"Because you're a pathetic bitch, and you need us. You like controlling us. Now get the fuck out like you were told." I dropped my hand from her face. She let out a throaty whimper that had me rolling my eyes. Her desire of us did nothing for me.

"Fox—"

I pressed my mouth to hers to silence her before shoving her away.

"Shut the fuck up and get the fuck out. Those are the only *fucks* you get today." I turned and walked away without looking back at her. A moment later, the front door opened and closed signaling her departure.

"We might have to kill her," Cole said softly, swirling his whiskey in his glass. "I'd rather fuck her dead body. Satisfaction in knowing she's gone and all."

Enzo chuckled. "Someone should call Ethan. I'm sure he has some ideas."

"I do too," was all I said before pouring another drink.

CHAPTER 1

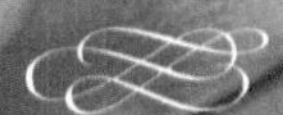

ROSALIE

I clutched the keyring in my palm, the cool metal keys poking through the spaces between my fingers as I crept through the night, one goal in mind: get to Cole's house. My car was parked a few streets over, and I had on my running shoes in case things went south.

Stopping just outside his house in the shadows, I let out a breath of relief. One of the only issues I'd anticipated was him having parked his pretty, red sports car in the garage. I didn't want to add breaking and entering to my list of things I shouldn't be doing. It'd go right beneath trying to fuck four guys at once.

This was nuts. Just weeks ago Cole had held me, his tongue dancing against my aching center, bringing me so much more pleasure than I thought was possible while Fox kissed me, his hands roaming all over my body.

Now, I stood outside Cole's house with the sole intention of destroying a little bit of his joy like he'd destroyed mine.

Hauling in a deep breath, I slunk through the shadows in my black outfit, my red hair tied back in a long braid, a hood pulled low over my face, a mask around my mouth and nose, and dark sunglasses on. I looked certifiably insane. But I'd have to be to be fucking with anything that belonged to Cole Scott.

I glanced around, making sure my getaway would be clear. I didn't need to trip over a trash bin or something in my bid for freedom.

If Cole caught me. . . My breath hitched. Cole was the dark one, the one who could cause so much devastation while wearing his beautiful smile, his blond hair perfect, his blue eyes glittering with the joy from the heartbreak. And he caused a lot. I'd know.

I imagined if I was caught, Cole would remind me what I was missing. Something about that sent tingles to my core. I'd be lying if I said I didn't enjoy how rough Cole could be. The only thing I didn't like about his roughness was when it played with my heart.

Which reminded me of the reason I was there. I owed him one. He had to pay.

I crept to his car and kneeled by the driver's side tire. I swallowed, drew in a calming breathing, and let the ugly memories take over. Fox and Juliet in bed together. The notebook. The lies. They'd all played with my feelings like a toy while I was falling for them. The pain of that just wouldn't leave my heart.

Fuck it.

The keys against the shiny, red paint of Cole's car gave me a wicked sense of satisfaction as they tore through the striking color in ugly, deep, jagged cuts. I moved faster, letting the keys dig into the paint job in unpredictable lines and uneven strokes. I ran them front to back and up and down, mesmerized as tiny bits of paint chipped off like week-old nail polish. I went all the way around the car, marking it up until it looked like it had fought a cougar and lost to its claws.

Satisfied, I smiled. I knew it was petty, but when it came to revenge, I was a bit of a novice. I figured I'd learn as I went. Everything I'd planned so far was petty and low but screw it. I'd hit each of them where it hurt before other ideas might come to me.

The back door of Cole's house banged open, making me swallow a squeak. I rushed through the darkness and hid behind one of the massive hedges on his property. I tried to flatten myself to the ground as much as possible, hoping to remain undetected if he decided to search for the culprit.

From my hiding spot, I watched as he walked to his car, his phone pressed to his ear. My heart stumbled in my chest. Cole looked good. So fucking good. His blond hair was a mess, like he'd been running his fingers through it. His designer jeans hung low, and his black t-shirt hugged his muscular torso. I swallowed hard as his car caught his attention. His mouth opened in an O of surprise as he slowly lowered the phone from his ear.

"What the fuck!" he shouted. His face turned red as he took in his torn-up beauty. I watched as he rushed to it, his hands running along the ugly grooves.

"Someone keyed my car… No, I don't see anyone." He looked around, the phone back against his ear. He nodded as he listened to whoever was on the other end of his phone call. A moment later, he pulled the phone away from his ear, snapped a few photos, and thumbed out a message.

I glanced behind me at the forest, wondering if I could make it there before he saw me. I hadn't planned on Cole coming out. I figured I'd be done and gone before he found out what happened.

This was a definite kink in my plan. Damn his ass for being a night owl. Guess I hadn't accounted for that.

"Well, look out your fucking window, Fox!" Cole snapped. "Is her fucking car home?"

Shit.

OK, so I wasn't a mastermind at this stuff. Another amateur mistake.

Cole stalked around the edge of his driveway, peering into the night, his brows crinkled. "It's her. I know it is. Who the fuck else would be brave enough or has such a vendetta?"

I peered around again, realizing Cole would need to go back inside for me to make my escape. It was open space between the bushes and the woods, and I wouldn't be fast enough to just make a break for it.

Shit. Shit. Shit.

"I swear to fuck if it's her, and I get my hands on her, she won't walk for a week. I know she's mad, but…" he sighed, his words trailing off.

I watched as he listened, his handsome face twisted into a mask of sadness. My heart clenched. In that moment, all I wanted to do was rush to him, tell him I hated him for what he'd done, and then hold him.

But this was war. And war had casualties, cars and hearts be damned.

I lay on the ground in silence for what felt like forever, all sorts of escape plots in my mind, but the truth was, there really wasn't one. I'd screwed up. Bad.

Tearing my gaze away from Cole, I sucked in a sharp breath as Fox's Jeep pulled into the driveway. I hadn't seen the guys since everything went down. Fox had pounded on my door a few times in the first few days, but after I threatened to call the cops, he'd stopped.

I'd been so sick over everything, I hadn't been to school since it happened. My parents thought I had the flu because of all the vomiting I'd done. That I was stressed. That I just needed a break. Dad tried to get me to go to classes last Wednesday, but I pulled the *I'm eighteen* card on him and asked him to leave my room. It hadn't gone well, but I didn't have it in me to look at the guys. My dad threatened to kick me out if I didn't return on Monday.

"I didn't see her car anywhere nearby. Her car wasn't home when I left," Fox's deep voice called out as he stepped from his Jeep. "But maybe it's not her. The garage doors were closed. Her car may have just been inside."

Cole shook his head. "Fuck it. Call Juliet. Tell her we aren't coming."

"We have to go."

"I don't *have* to do shit, Fox," Cole snarled. "She can be your fucking problem tonight, not mine."

"She's *ours*, Cole," Fox snapped back.

I winced at his mention of her being theirs. I had been theirs.

No, you weren't. You were a fucking joke.

"I'm not going. Tell her I'm fucking someone else tonight."

"I can't do that. You know that, man. If she starts shit—"

"Then I'll fucking finish it. All she needs to do is give me another reason. She's on my shit list right now," Cole growled.

"We can go to Rosie's after." I had to strain to hear Fox.

"And do what?"

"I don't know." Fox let out a sigh of frustration.

Cole ran his fingers through his hair again. "That shit is over too. We both know it. She's not even coming to school. Enzo said he cornered that bitch she called a friend tonight."

I bristled at his words. *Jamie.*

"Did she tell him anything?"

"No. She was too busy sucking face with that dickhead she's with. Enzo said Ethan nearly got into it with him. Shit's bad if Ethan is throwing hands. And you know as well as I do, he has his own issues to deal with right now."

A pang raced through my heart at the mention of Ethan. *My sweet Ethan.*

"Doesn't matter. None of it does," Cole muttered.

"Christ, Cole. I said to chill. She just needs time—"

"Fuck time!" Cole shoved Fox. My heart caught in my throat as Fox stumbled before shoving him back.

"I thought we were over this shit," Fox snarled. "What the fuck, man?"

"Over it?" Cole let out a bark of bitter laughter that made chills rush over my skin. "I'll *never* get over her. None of us will. If you didn't since you walked away the first time, what makes you think any of us will? Huh? Huh, Fox? Tell me how the fuck do I carry on without her," his voice cracked. "Yeah, she was a real fun fucking game to play, but I was playing to win that shit. But we fucking lost, man."

Tears threatened the edges of my eyes, and I hugged myself, trying to swallow down my sobs.

"She put a big fucking stain on my heart," he continued. "It doesn't matter what I do. I-I can't make it go away. Believe me, I'm trying. I-I just can't. I just don't *lose*. This shit has me going crazy."

"I'm sorry, man. I am. But let's just get through this, OK?" Fox reached for him, but Cole shoved his hand away.

"Fuck you, Fox. Go screw Juliet. I'm done."

"Cole—"

"I'm going to Rosalie's. I'll rip her right from her bed. She is *mine*. I'm not letting her go or getting over shit. She can call the cops. I'll fucking let them kill me because I won't go down without a fight," he vowed.

"You're being crazy."

"And you're being controlled by some dank pussy I can't even get off on. I fucking hate this. Even Ethan is losing his shit. Do you even know how bad shit has to be for *Ethan* to fucking lose it? He's come so far. He's going to slip further, man. We all know it. Then what?"

"Then we help him." Fox's voice was soft. "Just like before."

I had to strain to hear him. My heart thudded painfully in my chest at the mention of Ethan.

What was wrong with him?

I ground my teeth together, pushing away the ache that rushed through me.

I don't care what's wrong with him. He hurt me too. Get it together, Rosalie! This is war!

They deserve all the hurt. Cole just admitted it was a game. My heart was just a toy to them.

"Let's just get this night over with, OK? Take some of that anger out where it needs to be taken out."

Cole snorted. "I'll end up killing her."

Fox chuckled darkly and clapped him on the back. "Maybe I'll help."

I watched as the guys strode to Fox's Jeep and got inside. They sat there for a moment before the engine rumbled to life and they pulled out of the driveway. When Fox's taillights disappeared, I made a run for it into the woods and dashed down a jogging path until I came out the other side. My car was right where I'd left it. I hopped in and drove back to my place.

Luckily, wherever the guys were going wasn't to Fox's house because his driveway was empty, and the lights were out.

But it still hurt because deep down inside I knew where they were.

With her. Juliet.

I hastily wiped at the tears threatening my lashes, went inside, and got ready for bed. The hours passed by slowly as I lay beneath my covers, staring up at the shadows on my ceiling.

When I heard a car pull into Fox's driveway, I got up and stood in front of my window in my tank top and pajama bottoms. I'd left the curtain open and one of my lamps on. Maybe I was a glutton for punishment.

Obviously, or why would I do any of this?

The lamp on Fox's desk turned on as his dark figure emerged. I stared at him, waiting for him to snap his curtains closed on me like he always did. He looked tired. His mouth turned down into a deep frown as he removed his shirt, revealing all his glorious muscles. His black hair was a mess, sticking up in different directions.

My breath hitched in my chest as he looked up and locked eyes with me. His lips parted. My heart beat painfully in my chest as he took a step closer to his window. I couldn't move. I was frozen in place as he stared out at me, so much pain and devastation on his face it made nausea churn in my guts.

He reached out and rested his hand on the pane of glass, his brows crinkled. Mesmerized, I watched as he blew onto the window, his breath fogging it. He scratched out some letters and then looked back at me.

I'm sorry.

When I didn't respond, he wiped the letters away and tried again.

I miss you. Please come back to me.

Why I was even entertaining the interaction was beyond me. But it set the stage for the cruelty which had taken up residence in my heart. I took a step forward and blew onto the window and wrote my return message to him.

Never.

I backed away and watched as his face crumbled as he read my words. To twist the knife further, I pulled my shirt off and tossed it aside along with my pajama bottoms. I settled in bed, leaving the curtains open so he could see what he was missing.

When I peered through my lashes at him, he hadn't moved. Only one thing had changed. There were now tears running down his cheeks.

CHAPTER 2

od. Can you imagine being Rosalie Bishop right now?" Mary Santos asked, staring into the mirror in the third-floor girls' bathroom at lunch on Monday.

I'd only just returned, and already my morning had been shit. I'd arrived early to avoid seeing the guys. The rumors and whispers followed me everywhere. People snickered as I passed by. One of the guys on the lacrosse team elbowed me so hard I'd gone sailing into a locker. He'd laughed at me and called me a slut.

So the bathroom seemed like the best place for me during lunch.

From my haven within the locked stall, I swallowed thickly and peeked through the crack in the door, seeing them, Jenna Andrews and Macy Stein. My stomach churned as they continued to talk.

"I can't even! I saw Fox this morning with Juliet. That's gotta be a burn." Jenna popped her lips, surveying her lip gloss. "And all the shit people are saying." She shook her head.

"Did you guys hear about Juliet cornering Rosalie and writing *freakshow* on her forehead in permanent marker right before all this shit went down?" Macy asked with a giggle.

I ground my teeth, trying to keep my breathing calm and even.

"Heard it? I saw it! Word is Rosalie screwed around with Fox after

21

he and Juliet had the short breakup. Can you imagine? Poor Juliet!" Mary shook her head sadly and capped her mascara. I dug my nails so deep into my palm I drew blood.

"Poor Juliet?" Jenna scoffed. "She's a bitch. You know she is. I'm Team Rosalie on this one. If Fox and the horsemen looked twice at me, I would've jumped their bones too."

"She's a slut." Macy snapped her gum. "There are even rumors about her and Ian Hall, and he's with Jamie. That's probably where their falling out came from. Rosalie was probably trying to get with him too. Pathetic."

"Ian is hot. I wouldn't kick him out of bed, but oh my god Enzo De Luca!" Jenna squealed. "You know they say his dad is the biggest crime boss this side of the country. Like serious mafia ties. That screams bad boy. I bet he's fire between the sheets. Cammy Woods said he's hung like a freaking horse. And I heard he's set to take over the family business. So. Hot!"

The girls let out a peal of giggles at her words.

They weren't wrong about how hot Enzo was, but that wasn't what I focused on then. I frowned at the info about his mafia ties. I'd heard the rumors before but hadn't thought much of them until that moment. People talked. It didn't always mean shit. But it made sense. I'd seen Enzo get into blacked out vehicles often, a man about my father's age behind the wheel in a dark suit. Sometimes other men were in the car. If Enzo was set to take over for his dad at some point, that was scary but expected, if it was all true.

Enzo had that wild, dark streak in him despite his playful demeanor. I knew if he ever snapped, shit would hit the fan. Thinking that beneath the surface of the sexy jokester was probably the heart of a killer made me uncomfortable, but not necessarily in a bad way. *It turned me on.* Mortification filled me at the heat low in my belly.

I'm so fucked up. I might need therapy.

I logged that away as I thought of how all the guys seemed to have a dark streak, considering the sort of shit they were into. Cole was the only one who didn't bother to hide it.

"Do you think Enzo really fucked Rosalie? He doesn't seem like her type. She's, like, a total loser, and he's, well, *Enzo De Luca*." Mary planted a hand on her hip and surveyed the girls.

"Can you imagine what she must be thinking right now? Like what would she say if she knew everyone was talking shit about her?" Macy let out a cackle that had me seeing red.

"God, how could she *not* know? Everyone is talking." Jenna looked at the girls through the mirror's reflection.

I'd had enough. I kicked the stall door open and walked out. The girls stared wide-eyed at me as I strode forward.

"I'd say if you're going to talk shit, at least make sure no one else is in the bathroom with you," I said calmly, turning the water on and washing my hands. The girls said nothing as I moved to wipe my hands on a paper towel. I pitched the used paper into the trash bin.

"Oh, and I didn't screw the horsemen. Just Fox, although Enzo *did* taste delicious. And Ian never got any either. Get it right next time." I walked out to their gasps, my head held high. I trembled on the inside, but it wasn't from anything but anger.

I was sick of this shit. The guys were still gods. *And me?* I was slut shamed. Luckily, I hadn't seen the guys yet. At the rate I was going, I'd probably punch each of them in the face. Apparently, they hadn't tried to quell the rumors since they raged like wildfire. But what did I expect from four assholes who'd used me as a joke? I shoved down any feelings I had for them, letting my anger rule.

The bathroom was once again my sanctuary and even that had been penetrated now.

Sighing, I walked down the hall, wishing like hell I could go home. I had revenge to exact. I just didn't know how I was going to do it yet. Cole's car had been a jumping off point, but hell, now what? Everything else seemed dim in comparison, and I certainly didn't know what to do about Juliet. But I wanted that bitch to pay.

I let out a squeak of air as someone tugged me into a dark classroom.

"Ian," I choked out, gazing into the eyes of the guy I thought was my friend only to find out he'd drugged me and tried to fuck me all while making threats that if I didn't finish what had started, he'd hurt

Jamie, my best friend and the girl he was dating. Well, maybe *former* best friend was a better description. She still wasn't talking to me.

"Hey there," Ian greeted me. "Been a minute, huh, Rosalie?"

"Not nearly long enough," I answered back, gritting my teeth.

He rolled his eyes at me. "Enough with your innocent monologue. You know why we're doing this—"

"How could I forget? You want me to wet your dick." Ian had threatened to tell Jamie about everything that had gone down between him and me at Cole's party months ago. How I'd made out with him. Touched him. How he'd touched me. How we'd almost had sex. The only problem was, he'd drugged my ass and I'd thought he was Fox because I was some whacked out lovesick bitch who couldn't get over losing her best friend five years ago when his mom died and he'd cut me loose from our friendship.

I'd been avoiding Ian ever since, hoping he'd leave me the hell alone. Those hopes were dashed as we stared one another down.

"Such a foul mouth, Rosalie," he admonished. "I thought getting fucked over by the horsemen might light a fire beneath you. I'm not disappointed."

I didn't have the time or patience for his shit. "Say I fuck you, Ian... Then what? You get off, I compare you to Fox, you *fall short*, and then you still tell Jamie. So the only *fuck* you're going to get from me is this one." I raised my middle finger at him.

His cheeks reddened. I let out a whimper as he struck me across the face, knocking me to the ground. I landed with a painful thud, crying out. He was on me in an instant, pushing me flat on my back, positioned between my legs. I winced as his hard-on brushed my center.

"Get the fuck off me," I snarled as he pinned my hands over my head.

He grinned, grinding his dick against me. "If you were wearing a dress, and we had five more minutes, that pussy would already be mine," he breathed out, rubbing against me once more.

"Ian, get off me," I repeated, glaring up at him. "I'll scream. I fucking swear I will."

"Rosalie, come on. We both know your voice is silent at this school. You're just a slut, after all. No one cares about your shouts for help. They'll just keep ignoring them like they always have. Besides, you can't scream if you can't breathe," he said, grasping my hands with one of his and using his other hand to cover my mouth. I struggled beneath him, but he was far stronger than I was.

"Listen, Rosalie," he said conversationally. "I got you out of trouble with your *boyfriends*. I fucking *saved* you. I'd say that at least earns me your pretty mouth on my cock. Don't you think?"

I shook my head furiously beneath his hold. He pressed his hand harder on my face, cutting off my air.

"I'm going to kill you and fuck your corpse if you don't start taking this seriously. Meet me at my place tomorrow night. I'm tired of playing. I let you have your little vacation. Now, let's settle this." He removed his hand from my nose and mouth, and I gulped a mouthful of air greedily.

"Do we have a deal?"

"No. Fuck you, Ian," I snarled at him.

"You know I fingered Jamie's pussy? I thought about you the whole time."

"You're sick," I choked out.

"Tomorrow. Meet me."

"I'm not meeting you at your place. No fucking way."

He smiled down at me and cocked his head. "Fine. Tomorrow. Rocky's parking lot. Nine o'clock. Deal?"

I stared up at him, wishing he'd get hit by a bus. "Fine."

He moved off me, leaving me on the floor. He walked to the door before turning around. "You should ice that." He pointed to his eye and winced. "I hit you a little hard. It's swelling."

And with that he opened the door and walked out.

I TRUDGED to my car after school the next day with my head down. I'd been arriving to school thirty minutes early to avoid the guys. Leaving wasn't so bad because they had football practice after school, so I could easily avoid them. Two days in and I hadn't seen any of them. I counted that as a small victory.

My skin tingled with the sensation of being watched, so I looked to my left. The guys were next to Fox's Jeep. My heart jolted in my chest at the sight of them. They should've been at football practice. At least Juliet wasn't around. My eyes locked on Cole's then Fox's. Both stared back at me with pain etched on their faces. I couldn't bear to look at Enzo and Ethan.

Falling for their games wasn't going to happen again. I steeled my heart and kept walking. I couldn't even trust that their wounded expressions were real. Maybe the bonus round to their game was tricking me again. Regardless, the tears on Fox's face the night I saw him in his bedroom still haunted me.

Somehow, I managed to get into my car and locked the doors. I'd barely gotten my seatbelt on when my phone buzzed. I lifted it and saw Ethan's name on the screen with a text.

I licked my lips, my curiosity wild. Maybe I needed to know what he said so I could hate them all a little more.

Against my better judgement, I opened the text.

Ethan: I miss you.

I took that moment to look up. Bad idea. I locked eyes on Ethan's. My heart broke once again. He'd been the kind, sweet one. He took a step forward, his green eyes wide. *Pleading.* He was usually so put together. Always smiling. But this Ethan looked sick. Exhausted. Not that beautiful guy I remembered.

I miss you too!

I just couldn't...

I ground my teeth and forced myself to avert my gaze before driving off.

SIX HOURS LATER, I sat in the parking lot of Rocky's, the local hangout, waiting for Ian. My cheek was still swollen from him hitting me. I'd put ice on it, but it hadn't done much good.

A knock on my passenger side window jolted me from my thoughts. Glancing over, I saw Ian standing there. I unlocked the door and waited for him to get in.

"You're late," I muttered as he closed the door.

"Sorry. I was trying to teach Jamie how to give a blow job. She sucks, and not in a good way."

I scowled at him. "I don't want to *fucking* hear it. Say what you came here to say, so I can go take a shower and wash the filth off me."

Ian shot me a withering look before speaking. "You want revenge on the horsemen?"

"I want revenge on your weasel ass," I snarled at him.

He had the audacity to smirk at me. "Yeah, but Rosalie, I didn't actually fuck you. And in my defense, you weren't telling me no. It was you rubbing my cock. I didn't force you."

"You drugged me, you skeeve!"

Ian scoffed and shook his head. "Not really. It was barely anything. You're just a lightweight. I didn't even give you a full hit. I just wanted to test the waters."

"How many others have you done that to?" I demanded. "How many girls fucked you because they couldn't run away?"

Ian shrugged and looked down to his lap. "This isn't about me. My numbers aren't important."

I surveyed him with disgust. "So what? You thought you'd get lucky with me and fuck me?"

"I wasn't really thinking, Rosalie. I don't make it a point to drug every chick I like. I do have *some* class. I just knew I fucking wanted you. Seeing you with Cole pissed me off. I fucking hate him. Taking you from him would be one of my biggest victories."

I scoffed at his use of *class*. "Why? Because you can't *be* him?"

A muscle popped along his jaw as he stared out the window. "Like I'd want to. Cole's old man is the guy who put my dad in prison."

"What?" I crinkled my brows at the information.

Ian looked at me, his mouth set in a firm line. "My dad is Daniel Hall. He's the guy who got drunk and killed Fox's mom. Cole's dad was the lawyer on the case. My dad has been in prison for the last five years. So I have to take care of my mom and little brother. I do what I have to. Drug bitches, fuck, steal, run shit for bigger fish."

My heart stumbled in my chest at the information. Revulsion washed over me. I'd known the man who killed Amy was named Daniel, but I hadn't made the connection to Ian. Ian never spoke of his dad. He'd said his parents were divorced, and we never pushed the subject since it seemed to be a touchy one. And I knew Ian did odd jobs. *But what the actual hell?*

"Your boys didn't tell you that?"

I shook my head and stared straight out the windshield.

"My family was torn apart over this shit."

"So was Fox's," I whispered.

"My dad is a murderer. At least Fox's mom isn't suffering like the rest of us. Amen for that."

"You're unbelievable, Ian. *Amy is dead*, and you're sitting here playing the victim?"

"Yeah, she's fucking dead! She's gone. She doesn't need to deal with this shit. You have no idea how fucked up my life is because of this, Rosalie!"

"It doesn't give you the right to be a piece of shit, Ian," I snapped back, shooting him a glare. "You're blackmailing me. You're hurting Jamie. You're doing unconscionable things to people. Just because your dad is a grade-A screw up doesn't mean you need to follow in his footsteps!"

A squeak of air left me as Ian lunged forward and shoved me against my door, his forearm in my throat, cutting off my air. I fumbled trying to grasp the door handle, but Ian, sensing I was up to something, pushed harder on my throat, causing tiny stars to blip through my vision.

"I have it all, Rosalie," he hissed, his eyes raking over my face. I clawed at his arms as I tried to breathe.

"The videos? I have every single one they made of you. There's more than one. More than two. They watched you for a long time. They recorded *everything*." His hot breath blew over my face, his eyes wild. "It's more than me being able to tell Jamie. I have *everything* that could ruin you. Cole eating your pussy in that dark corner at school with Fox's tongue down your throat because they were so careless. Enzo and Cole in Enzo's basement. You and me at Cole's. I have *everything*, Rosalie. They gave it all to me with their carelessness. You know that saying, keep your friends close and your enemies closer? They fucked up."

He released me. I coughed and sputtered, gulping in air. My guts twisted at the information he'd given me. "H-how?"

"Did you think I'd let them beat me and get away with it? That I'd let them *humiliate* me? Cole and Fox ruin anything they touch. My family is torn apart because of them." He let out a dark laugh that made me flinch. *He was crazy.* Telling him that it wasn't Cole and Fox's fault wouldn't do anything but provoke him, so I sat there, my hand inching closer to the door handle.

"The one thing they want more than anything is *you*. At first, I wanted you because you're so fucking beautiful. And smart. And funny. The fact you don't even realize these things about yourself is a huge turn on. But then I saw you with Cole. He soiled you by touching you. As the days wore on, it became about more than just wanting you for myself. The more I saw them pulling you in, the angrier I got. They always get what they want." He laughed again and shook his head before glaring at me. I flinched away from him as he took my hand in his.

"I watched too. *I'm good at watching.* I took a page out of their book and used a camera. I recorded you with them that day when Cole made you come on his face behind the school. Figured a little extra insurance never hurt anyone." He brushed a curl away from my face.

I flinched at his nearness, so disgusted by what a piece of shit he was that my stomach roiled.

"Now, you're the piece I need to take them down. And it just so happens, they fucked you over too. You're the school slut. They fucked you in more ways than one, Rosalie. You want revenge so bad I can *smell* it on you. We can play a little game. What do you say?"

Ian was right. I did want revenge. But the thought of teaming up with him revolted me. "Let me put it to you this way. I have all the videos because I knew I'd need them. I enlisted help to get them—"

"Who?" I rasped, wincing at the pain in my throat. "Who did you get them from?"

Ian chuckled softly and cradled my face in his hand. "Someone who wanted what you had, Rosalie. Someone *you* stole from."

"Juliet," I whispered.

Ian nodded, smirking. "We all want something at the end of the day. It's all part of the game, baby. You're just the fucking pawn for us to get what we want."

I shook beneath his touch, bile clawing its way up my throat.

"But I can offer you revenge. They hate me. *Be with me.* It'll save Jamie too, a minor victory."

"She'll hate me forever." A tear slid down my cheek. Ian thumbed it away before pressing a kiss to the edge of my lips.

"But you'll be a hero. And she already hates you. Trust me." Ian trailed his lips along my jawline before he whispered in my ear, sending shivers coursing through my stiff body, "I'm all you have left, Rosalie. I'm the way to either save you or doom you. How much does your future matter to you?"

I swallowed down a sob as Ian's hand moved to cup one of my breasts through my shirt, his lips still at my ear.

"Unfortunately, I'll need an answer tonight. No more waiting around. What will it be? All I have to do is hit send on this outgoing message and everything you've struggled for is gone. Yes or no. What will *Rosie* decide?

His lips moved to my neck. I squeezed my eyes closed, trying to control my breathing as tears slid down my cheeks. Everything. Scholarships. College. Respect from my parents.

Friendships. My entire life, wiped out with one foul swing.

But then, a thought swept into my head. Revenge. Power.

Keep your friends close and your enemies closer.

I'd bring all the fuckers down, Ian included, so I said the only word I knew how to say now.

"Yes."

CHAPTER 3

I stared at myself in my bedroom mirror the next morning. Ian said he was going to break up with Jamie last night after our meeting. Worry gnawed at me for my friend. She'd be devastated. It didn't matter that she hated me right now. As far as I was concerned, she was still my friend. I hated I was doing this to her. Reasoning that this was the best way to keep her safe was my only solace. I had to save her from heartache by breaking her heart.

How screwed up was that?

Ian promised to keep what happened between us a secret. But at this point in the game, I didn't know if it mattered. The only thing that kept me hoping she never found out was that she'd hate me even more, making our friendship unsalvageable. There'd be no way to come back from it if she found out.

Sighing, I went downstairs to find my parents at the table eating breakfast.

"Morning, hon," Mom greeted me as she buttered her toast. Dad didn't look up as he sipped his coffee.

"Morning," I mumbled, grabbing a pancake and placing it on my plate.

"What's going on with Fox?" Mom asked after a moment.

I paused, my fork halfway to mouth. Dad glanced at me, a brow raised. "What do you mean?" I swallowed thickly.

"I mean, he was here this morning looking for you. We didn't know you guys were friends again."

"I thought we were, but it was a mistake." I finally took a bite of my pancake.

"Fox is a good kid. Damn good kid," Dad said, spearing a sausage. "They did a write-up on him in the paper this week." For emphasis, Dad pushed the paper at me, Fox's face smiling at me. My stomach clenched.

"They're going to be state champs this year. Everyone is talking about Fox's arm. Kid has a rocket. Says he's got a full ride to Mayfair in the fall. The only problem I see is Kurt said he wants to major in writing. All that talent, and the kid wants to be a writer." Dad snorted and shook his head.

I stared down at my plate. I hadn't known that was what Fox planned on doing. Memories of all his stories from when we were kids washed over me, making nausea twist low in my guts. I ground my teeth as the image of him and Juliet together in his bed swept through my mind, erasing all those fond recollections. My resolve was reinforced, and I blew out the deep breath I'd hauled in to steady myself.

"That's nice," was all I said, taking another bite of my pancake.

"We should invite him over for dinner," Mom called out brightly. "It's been so long since he's been here. Maybe you and him can talk, Rosalie—"

"I'm good. Thanks."

Mom frowned and looked to Dad who only shrugged as he sipped his coffee.

"Rosalie, what's going on with you at school?"

I ground my teeth. I hated when Dad wanted to get conversational. Tryouts were coming up for the musical. I'd tossed out the song I'd worked on with the guys, vowing to never look at it or sing it again. After roles were cast, the drama department would start promoting it.

I was tired of hiding it. But I knew Dad. It would have to be a secret until it wasn't an option.

"Nothing. Just homework."

"Jamie hasn't been around much," Mom commented. "Is everything OK with her?"

"She got a boyfriend. I don't like him." I frowned, the nausea returning. "We're better off not talking right now."

"I see," Mom said softly. "Well, maybe you girls can work it out. Have you tried talking to her about it?"

"No." I gave her a tight smile. "I'm not that great at communication. It's something I need to work on."

Mom patted my hand reassuringly. "You'll figure it out. Boys come and go, but best friends are forever."

Right. Just like Fox. I'd believe that when I saw it.

"I need to get to school." I rose from my seat.

Dad looked down at his watch. "Why so early? You've been leaving a half hour early lately."

"Just like going to the library and getting a jump on things. I stay focused better when I do," I lied through my teeth.

Dad nodded his approval. "That's my girl. You know how important your future is. I admire how dedicated you are, Rosalie. You make Mom and me very proud."

That nausea in my stomach twisted around my heart as I offered my parents a smile. "I'll see you guys tonight."

Once I was out of their sight, I snatched my backpack and went to my car. I'd tried not to look at Fox's place since the Juliet incident. But sometimes I failed. Today was one of those days as I found myself glancing at his driveway. His black Jeep wasn't there. Something about that bothered me. Every morning I made a mad dash to school to avoid him, and today he wasn't home.

It doesn't matter. Get to school and get through this nightmare.

I PARKED my car in my usual spot in the back of the lot and got out. Going around to the back door, I opened it and yanked out my backpack. When I turned around, I came face to face with Fox.

A squeak of surprise left me as I stared up at him. His blue eyes were sad, black circles rimming them. His lips, lips I missed so much, were turned down into a deep frown. His leather jacket, white V-neck t-shirt and low-slung ripped jeans made him look like the incredibly sexy bad boy he was.

"Rosie," he said in a hoarse voice.

"What are you doing here?" I answered, peering around the lot for signs of the other guys or Juliet. "Why were you at my house this morning? I told you I'd call the cops if you came back."

He reached out and started to tuck a loose strand of hair behind my ear. His lips parted, a pained expression crossing his face as I flinched away from him. "I wanted to talk."

"We have nothing left to say to one another, Fox."

"You know that's a lie," he murmured, reaching for me again, this time in an attempt to hold me at the waist.

I shoved him away. "I said *no*, Fox. I know it's not a word you're used to hearing, but fucking learn it."

A muscle thrummed along his jaw as he stared back at me.

"Let me explain everything. Enough time has passed, Rosalie. You've had time to cool off. We both have. Now let's talk."

"How about you kiss my ass?" I snapped, shoving past him, my heart racing. "I told you to leave me the hell alone."

He caught me by the arm and tugged me back against my car, his body pressed against mine.

"I'd love to do a whole host of things to your ass, but right now, I need you to listen to me." His warm breath blew over my face. I tried to steady my trembling body. "Juliet doesn't mean *shit* to me. *You do.* We fucking miss you, Rosie. Please. Meet me tonight at the treehouse." He leaned in, his lips brushing against the shell of my ear as he gave my waist a gentle squeeze. "Let me fix everything."

I closed my eyes as he rubbed against me, his hard length apparent through his jeans. My fury took over. *He thought sex was how to fix everything?* The betrayal and heartache rose to the top of my heart and bubbled over.

Fuck him. Even if I did miss him. Fuck him.

"I'm seeing someone."

He stilled against me, his body tensing. I waited for his reaction, hoping the news hurt like hell. He deserved it. This was only the beginning of what I had in store for him. But then I remembered I was just a game to him and the guys. The only thing this did was put a damper on the bonus round for them.

"Who?" he growled in my ear, his hold on my waist tightening enough to make me wince.

"None of your damn business."

He moved a hand to my face and cradled it, a dark look in his eyes. "You belong to me... To Cole, Enzo, Ethan. I want to know who it is. Tell me."

"I *belong* to no one," I hissed at him. "Least of all any of you. You all made that perfectly clear." I tried to push him away from me, but he held fast.

"You will *always* belong to me, Rosie. It doesn't matter who you're fucking. In the end, I'll win."

"That's not how this works, Fox. You don't get to call the shots. *I do.*" I cupped his manhood in my hand, giving it a squeeze that made him wince. "You don't have shit I want. Not anymore. Not even *this.*"

This time when I shoved at him, he released me, his cheeks flushed pink.

"Rosalie!" he called out to my retreating back. I paused, breathing hard from the encounter. I didn't look back at him as I waited for him to speak. "We're playing for keeps. You're the prize, and we never lose."

"First time for everything," I answered before walking away.

Operation *Takedown the Horsemen* was off to a rocky start. First was Fox's sudden appearance at my car. Then before lunch, I opened my locker to find a red rose inside with a handwritten message.

Lunch on the bleachers? -Ethan

I ground my teeth, crumpled the note, and pitched the rose into the trash. A thorn caught my finger, making me wince as a bead of blood ballooned out.

Even their damn flowers hurt.

"You're a hard girl to track down," Ian said, falling in step beside me.

"Good. Then my plan is working."

He let out a dark chuckle before he snaked his arm around my waist. I stiffened beneath his touch. If he noticed, he made no mention of it.

"I broke it off with Jamie for you. She cried and cried. Begged me to reconsider." He steered me down the hall. "Pathetic, really."

I hated that he tried to make it like this was all my fault. *Prick.*

"Is she OK?" I murmured, glancing around to find curious looks aimed in our direction. I ducked my head as we stopped at his locker.

He lifted my chin with a finger. "I don't really give a fuck if she is or not."

"Ian," I hissed angrily.

He rolled his eyes. "I'm sure she'll be fine. It's not like she put out anyway. I had to beg for any action and even that wasn't as much or as good as I wanted."

I shook my head and ground my teeth as I turned away from him.

"You're mine now," Ian said softly as his hand rested on my lower back.

I stilled, my chest aching.

"And you're going to do *all* the things she wouldn't." His lips brushed against my ear as he spoke, "Turn around."

Clenching my teeth, I turned to face him. He smiled down at me as he cradled my face in his hand. Out of the corner of my eye, I saw Jamie come around the corner. He glanced in her direction, his lips turning up into a slow, wicked smile.

"Kiss me," Ian said, turning back to me.

I shook my head at him, bile burning my throat.

"Rosalie," he growled. A warning. A threat. "We have a deal. Remember? *Pay up.*"

Everything within me fought my next move. I'd saved Jamie. Maybe she'd never know it.

Maybe she'd hate me forever, but I'd saved her from him.

In the process, I'd broken myself, trying to take over places maybe I shouldn't tread in. In only moments, everyone would know. I'd be the talk of the town. More gossip. More rumors. But I was going to take all of them down. Each one who'd hurt me would suffer. I'd do what I had to do. Willingly.

For Jamie. For revenge. To rule.

I leaned in and pressed my lips to Ian's. He pulled me close, his tongue sweeping against mine.

If it wasn't with Ian, I'd have said the kiss was decent. Nowhere near the caliber of anything the guys could do, but not terrible. If I didn't hate him so much, I may have even enjoyed it.

After a few seconds, I broke the kiss off and wiped at my mouth.

"Rosalie?" Jamie choked out mere feet from us. Her face had gone white. She trembled where she stood, her eyes darting between me and Ian. "Ian?"

"Hey, Jamie," Ian greeted her brightly.

"You said you needed space," she croaked, tears snaking down her cheeks. People stared at us as they slowed in the hallway to watch. "You said there wasn't anyone else."

Ian shrugged and glanced at me, his arm still around my waist. "Guess I lied."

She opened her mouth, more tears trailing down her cheeks as she turned her glare on me. I held my breath as she approached me.

"You're supposed to be my best friend, Rosalie," she choked out. "Why would you do this to me?"

I stared back at her, wordless.

"You had the elite. You had the *fucking horsemen*! I guess when they were done fucking you, you decided to keep up your whore persona," she continued, her voice rising. We were drawing a crowd. "Is that it? Figured you'd fuck your way through the entire school before graduation?"

"It's not like that, Jamie," I answered softly.

Ian chuckled beside me.

I closed my eyes for a moment to compose myself.

"It's really not, Jamie," Ian broke in. She moved her gaze from me to Ian. "The night of the party—"

"Ian, no." I widened my eyes at him.

"*Baby*, she knows we're together now. It doesn't make any sense to hide the truth," he cooed.

"Ian, *please*. You promised—"

"She *deserves* to know. What sort of friend would you be if you didn't tell her?" He gave me a Cheshire smile before he turned back to Jamie. "I fucked her that night. That's why I was upset with her. She wouldn't talk to me after. You kept asking me long after it happened. Now you know."

"You asshole," I snapped at Ian.

He pressed a kiss to my temple and dug his fingers painfully into my side.

"Fucking slut," Jamie breathed out. One moment she was in front of us, the next she was swinging at me. What little bit of self-preservation I had left kicked in as I avoided her hit. It grazed my shoulder before her fingers tangled in my hair. A hiss escaped my lips as she fisted a mass of my red curls and gave a tug.

Instinct took over as she pulled my hair, calling me every name imaginable. People gathered around us, cheering.

With as much strength as I had, I shoved her. She tumbled to the floor, and I was on her in an instant, pinning her arms.

"It's not like what he says. I'm trying to save you, Jamie," I whispered, frantic and breathless. "You wouldn't let me explain. You *have* to let me tell you. He's bad, Jamie. He lies. He was going to hurt—"

"You're a fucking slut," she sobbed, the fight leaving her body. She twisted her head away from me, my words falling on deaf ears. She wasn't going to listen. Not here. Not now.

"Maybe," I murmured, releasing her arms. "But not this time. Not with Ian. I'm doing this for you. *Please.* I-I need you to talk to me, Jamie."

She wept harder as she lay on the floor, covering her face with her hands. Warm hands brought me to my feet. It took all the willpower I had not to burst into tears.

"Come on. It's over," Ian said, steering me away from a sobbing Jamie. The crowd parted for us, and we walked through it.

And then, there they were. The horsemen. Fox. Cole. Enzo. Ethan. Staring from me to Ian to Jamie then back to me, disbelief on their faces. *And anger.* So much anger I flinched, drawing my body away from them and closer to Ian.

"What have you done, Sunshine?" Enzo murmured as we passed by.

"What I had to," I answered, holding my head up.

This moment would be the last piece in a puzzle of definition, defining the woman I had to become.

And I would take no prisoners to finish this.

Revenge was a bitch. Or maybe I was. It was open for debate.

CHAPTER 4

Sometimes you have to eat shit to get ahead in life. To win. To come out on top.

I rinsed my mouth out in the bathroom, practically gagging as I thought about what the hell I'd gotten myself into. I could've walked away. I could've let it all go. But I was so tired of being on the bottom rung, with everyone using me as a foothold to gain dominance. I wanted to take over. *I* wanted to be on top for a change. And so, I ate shit.

God, I was a fucking mess. *This* was a mess. But I'd done it to myself and to everyone else.

This was me at the edge. I felt like I was going to finally break. I couldn't let them win. *I couldn't.* That was why I was doing everything.

But at the cost of my dignity. At the cost of losing myself in a game where no one could win. Maybe that was the appeal. The challenge. To take over in a place I never belonged. To prove I had what it took to be... hell, I didn't know. Something. *Anything* more than what I was.

I stared at myself in the mirror.

"What a mess," I muttered at my reflection before wiping my mouth and grabbing my bag. I left the room, the door slamming closed behind me. I had one class left, and then I could go home. It offered me some semblance of comfort.

"Hey, Rosalie," Cam, one of the guys on the football team, called out to me.

"Hey," I muttered, walking past him.

"I have a message for you."

I stopped and turned back, wondering what the hell he could want. I narrowed my eyes at him. He approached, the students in the hall jostling past. "What's the message?"

He leaned down and spoke quickly. "Bleachers or your place. Choose wisely."

I swallowed thickly. "Thanks for that. Tell whoever sent you I've chosen my place. Alone."

Cam frowned, nodding. "Right. Then I have a second message for you."

"And what's that?" I asked dryly.

"Don't go to war if you aren't prepared to lose everything." He backed away as I glared at him, his hands held high in surrender. "Don't shoot the messenger," he called out before joining the throng of students.

"Jerk," I muttered, turning and going to my classroom.

Let them show up at my place. Hell, I was prepared for war, so their threats held no weight. They'd broken my heart. I wouldn't let them break my spirit. I knew going into this there'd be casualties. There always were in a war. Jamie. Myself. Even the guys. I'd accepted the painful reality of it and had solidified the nightmare moments ago in the bathroom.

Words Cole said to me when this first started with all of us flashed in my mind.

I like the torment.

He'd better hope he did because that was what he and the guys were going to get. Whatever the cost, I'd pay it because that was just how deep the anger ran in my body.

~

"MY PLACE. TONIGHT," Ian said, winding his arm around my waist as I walked through the parking lot later that afternoon.

"How about *no, kiss my ass?*" I shot back.

"Rosalie, you're not a good girlfriend. How am I supposed to fuck you if you keep fighting me on it?"

We made it to my car. I spun and glared at him.

"Listen, I'm going to let you in on a little secret. I didn't fuck the horsemen. I messed around with a couple of them, but I didn't just lie back and spread my legs. If I didn't do it for them, then I sure as hell won't do it for you. You want it from me?"

He stared down at me, hunger in his eyes.

"*Work for it.* I'm not your warm hole for nesting in. Treat me with respect. I'm not going to just fuck you, Ian."

"I get where you're coming from, Rosalie." He reached out and clutched my waist, drawing me to him. "But I want what I want. And that's your warm hole."

"Pig," I snarled at him.

He let out a dark chuckle. "You're a fucking whore, Rosalie. *My* whore. I know the extent you went to just to get your pussy eaten, not by one guy. But by *multiple.* Just consider me another notch."

"The only thing I consider you, Ian, is another bitch to take down." I leaned into him, my hand on his chest.

He held me tighter, both hands on my waist.

My lips skimmed across the shell of his ear at my next words. "Trust me. If you want me to *fuck you,* it'll happen." *Just not in the way you think.*

"You're right. You will." His lips crashed against mine, making me wince as his tongue infiltrated my mouth, stealing my breath, and not in a good way. I didn't stop him when his hands cupped my ass or when he deepened the kiss, his erection pressing against my hip.

I kissed him with my eyes open, looking at a point over his shoulder.

Fox and Juliet. Together.

She went up on her tiptoes and planted a kiss on his lips. Nausea took my guts hostage. I broke off the kiss with Ian and moved to open my car door.

"He doesn't love you," Ian called out, glancing over his shoulder at Fox who'd been joined by Cole.

"I know," I snapped, my hands shaking. I told myself I wouldn't react to them. But damnit. I still had a long way to go.

"Would you look at that," Ian mused as Juliet leaned in and kissed Cole.

I saw red. My body trembled. I dropped my keys.

"Looks like she took your spot. Being replaced like that has got to hurt. Maybe I'm trying to fuck the wrong girl. Maybe Juliet is the one I should bury myself in. Seems she's the top pick."

"Eat shit, Ian," I spat, snatching my keys off the pavement and opening my door.

Ian grabbed the keys from my hand. "I'm driving."

I would've argued, but Enzo showed up, and just like Cole, Juliet kissed him too. All I wanted was to get the hell out of there.

The leather seats burned my thighs as I slid onto the passenger's seat.

"By the way..." Ian glanced at me as he pulled out of my parking spot. "We're going to my place."

I didn't even bother telling him no. I was too busy watching the guys who were now looking at me. Juliet gave me a smile and wave.

I gave her one back with my middle finger held high.

"I NEED CHAPTER SIX DONE, and I need notes taken." Ian nodded to his homework on his desk.

I flopped down onto his desk chair, but he was quick to haul me to my feet. He sat in the chair and pulled me onto his lap.

"I'd prefer to work like this," he murmured, his hand high on my thigh.

I swallowed thickly and opened his history book so I could begin his chapter outline.

"I've been thinking," he continued, his hand moving higher. I ground my teeth but kept working on the first section. "I want to take this slow too. Make it a real relationship where we build up into fucking. I think I'll enjoy it more."

"Good for you," I muttered, my pencil scratching across the white notebook paper.

"I mean, I want to taste your pussy tonight, but I won't fuck you."

I tensed as he let out a soft chuckle, his hand fully beneath my skirt, skimming the edge of my panties.

"Or maybe you can suck my dick. How does that sound?"

"Like you might lose your dick tonight," I grunted, penciling in a new section on the paper.

Ian laughed. "Fine." He kissed along my neck, both hands under my skirt. His erection poked me in the back. "I have an idea."

"Let's hear it, Brainiac."

"How about your get my homework done first, then I'll show you."

"Or how about you just sit there and shut the hell up so I can?"

I let out a whimper of pain as he pinched my side. The ache raced up my ribs, and tears sprung to my eyes.

"Spread your legs."

When I didn't, he shifted, adjusting his knees between my legs and pried them apart. I winced.

His fingers threatened the edge of my panties again. His breathing grew heavy and ragged as his fingers burrowed beneath the cotton.

"Ian," I choked out.

"Understand something, Rosalie." He slid his finger through my folds and wrapped his arm around my waist and cinched me to him, locking me in place. His finger slid deeper and hooked inside me, pressing against a spot I'd reserved only for the guys. "You belong to me now, and when I want to play, no amount of begging is going to stop me."

"I hate you," I snarled. "I fucking hate you."

"Good. That makes this more exciting." He pushed another finger into me. I winced, my back pressed to his front as his fingers moved in and out of me. "Now give me what I want."

I squeezed my eyes closed, trying to block out the way my body began to tingle as his fingers moved faster. Of how he sounded as he made quick work of taking what I'd willingly given to the guys.

I forced myself to imagine the guys with Juliet. How they chose her over me. The anger burned my chest as I relaxed against Ian's chest, his hot breath in my ear. It made this moment easier. I spread my legs wider, eager to give to Ian what they wanted from me, even if I did fucking hate him with every ounce of my being. I reminded myself I was also saving Jamie from his abuse.

I'd take them all down. They thought they were winning as they all put their dicks in places they didn't belong.

Ian pushed harder and deeper into my tight channel, making me cringe. He certainly wasn't gentle as he rammed his fingers in and out of me. I gripped his jean-clad thighs as he continued his onslaught. I squeezed my eyelids closed so tightly that tiny sparkles lit up the darkness.

This was what I'd wanted. *Play dangerous games, win dangerous prizes.* And Ian was a danger to society. I was definitely saving Jamie and whoever else he'd target.

I was his. For now. I'd play the part. To win, I'd play the part. When the tingles grew into a sweeping heat, I didn't fight it. I came undone on Ian's fingers, old memories being replaced by new, ugly ones.

But this was war. And war had casualties. I knew that. I accepted that. I'd wanted the torment. Even this. It wasn't no. It was an ugly victory, even if it broke me inside.

"Good girl." Ian withdrew his fingers from me and shoved me to the floor. I winced as he reached down and fisted my ponytail.

"Now finish my homework. I'll let you off for tonight. But the next time we do this, you play along a little better. I don't like when I have to hurt you. Got it?"

"Yes," I answered, sitting up.

He smirked down at me before padding to his bathroom.

My phone buzzed in my pocket. I took it out and stared down at the screen. A picture of mine and Fox's old treehouse greeted me with a message.

Fox: I'm waiting for you, Rosie.

THE MOMENT I GOT HOME, I showered, my body trembling. Between my legs was tender from Ian's less than gentle touches. I grimaced as I washed, hating my life.

When I got out my phone buzzed again.

Enzo: Why him?

I stared down at the message, my chest aching. I hadn't replied to the guys since everything fell apart, but this seemed like a good time to. Anger coursed through me. Hatred. Remorse. Vengeance. I'd already stepped into the ring. To back out now meant defeat.

Rosalie: Because he's not you.

I hit send, readying the game. Enzo's message came through quickly.

Enzo: Don't do this, Sunshine. You're breaking my heart.

I stared down at the text, my heart in my throat, my guts twisting in agony from his words. But they'd hurt me, and they'd continue to hurt me. They'd lied. No amount of words from them now would ever fix it. It was an ugly truth none of us could run from. I'd *seen* them with Juliet. The betrayal was too much. I'd return it tenfold. It was one of the reasons why I'd agreed to Ian's demands. That was why I was sore between my legs. That was why my heart fucking hurt and my mind ached. I'd finish this one way or the other.

This. Was. WAR.

So I said the only thing I could say.

Rosalie: Good.

CHAPTER 5

I didn't know what the hell I was doing. I was a mess. It only seemed to get worse as the hours ticked by. Maybe that was why after my shitty day I was once again dressed in all black lurking in a driveway. Enzo's message ate at me. It seemed like every time I started to calm down, one of the horsemen would pop back up like a bad fucking news bear and mess with me. I needed to take that anger out on something.

This time I was at Fox's. He loved his damn Jeep as much as Cole loved his sports car. The jars of Vaseline and rolls of toilet paper thumped against my waist in the bag they were in as I did my best to ninja over to his Jeep. My entire plan was risky, but to hell with it.

I crept to the passenger side door and said a silent prayer that it was unlocked. When it opened, I grinned and slid onto the passenger's seat. I made quick work of turning his stereo up to full volume and inserting a CD of farm animal noises and a little sassy song from an old audiobook I'd had when I was younger. I promptly popped off his volume knobs and power button. I snickered before sliding one of my mom's uncooked salmon fillets under the seat. When I was done with the interior handiwork, I got out and closed the door quietly, ready for the exterior.

Telling myself Fox could go to hell, I dipped my hand in the Vaseline and slathered it up and down his Jeep, leaving behind big chunks of the thick, oily substance. I went through a few containers before I was satisfied. Then, I applied the pink streamers and toilet paper over the slimy mess. I wrapped it in cling wrap the best I could before standing back to admire my handiwork.

Good enough. He'll love it. And once he gets the mess off and fixes his stereo, it'll be about the time the fish starts stinking.

I rushed across the street and dropped the empty containers and remnants into Mrs. Ames's trash bin before sneaking back into my house and putting my pajamas on.

Maybe I should change my middle name to *Petty Bitch* because that was exactly what the hell I was. Attacking the guys' rides seemed childish, but I was new to this. I had to cut myself some slack. Ideas on how to fuck with them weren't just streaming out of my head.

I knew Enzo would be a problem. He lived in a gated community. I'd probably have to catch him during school hours. Maybe I'd get his locker or something. But that didn't seem big enough. I'd sleep on it.

But whatever I came up with, really had to screw him over.

I awoke the following morning to the sounds of loud swearing and banging coming from outside. Quickly, I went to my bedroom window to see Fox standing outside his Jeep, cursing up a storm and kicking his tires. Enzo wheeled into his driveway. He and Cole got out. I could see them talking but had no idea what they were saying.

With a grin, I whirled from my window and got dressed in the new clothes I'd picked out. Since I'd decided to play the part, I dragged on a pleated, plum purple skirt and tight, black scooped neck blouse. I added black, high heeled boots that went to my knees. Then I straightened my red waves until they hung in a sheet of fire down my back. I'd never straightened it before. It was a hell of a look for me.

Thick, black mascara and black eyeliner with the cherry lip gloss

Cole loved so much on my lips had me looking like a whole other person. And I had to be if I was going to keep up the shit I was doing. Old Rosalie had died that night in Fox's bedroom, and a new Rosalie had risen from the ashes. Not that I was new and improved. Just. . . different.

All this work put me a little behind schedule, making me leave at my old time. Luckily, my dad had to leave early for work, and it was Mom's cardio day, so she was out on a run with the other neighborhood women. I grabbed an apple and granola bar then went outside to my car.

The guys seemed to have left with Enzo, which was just as well. Fox's Jeep looked horrible. I'd really outdone myself with it.

Grinning at my accomplishment, I got into my car and drove to school, my music blaring. The inkling Fox might corner me had me nearing a panic attack as I arrived at school. I didn't know if he'd gone to school, but I had this vision of him storming across the parking lot to beat my ass red.

Instead of him finding me, it was Ian.

"Great," I grumbled, shutting the car off as Ian strode to me.

He pulled my door open and led me out.

"Nice. I like this," he said, nodding his head. I only smiled back at him. He draped his arm over my shoulder and steered me to school.

And just like old times, the guys stood on the sidewalk. They all stared at me and Ian as we walked. When our feet hit the sidewalk, it was Ian who spoke, "Was it worth it?"

Cole took a dangerous step forward, but Enzo grabbed his arm.

"Was what worth it?" Fox growled, his eyes locked on me as we slowed our steps.

Ian was milking it.

"All of it. I've got your girl now. That's gotta suck to know it's me buried in her, especially knowing my dad killed your mom."

Fox moved like lightening, his hands colliding with Ian's chest and shoving him hard. Ian stumbled back but was quick to shove Fox back, a wild, excited look in his eyes.

"Ian, stop!" I shouted, moving forward to get between them. I wasn't sure why. Part of me wanted them to beat each other to bloody pulps, the other part wanted to protect Fox. *I hated that part.* But today wasn't the day to mess with Fox. I'd screwed with his Jeep. I was sure he was seeing red from that alone.

Ethan's arm snaked around my waist and dragged me back, his lips at my ear. "Let them, sweetheart."

I thought Fox was going to kill Ian. Before he could land the first punch, Juliet was at his side, talking him down.

"Fox," she called out, wrapping her fingers around his arm and pulling him away from Ian who he was chest to chest with. "No, *baby.* He's not worth it. *She's* not worth it. She's fucking the guy whose father killed your mom. They vandalized your car because that's how pathetic they are. Let it go. Let the trash join its dumpster fire."

I ground my teeth, my eyes narrowed at her. I couldn't wait until I could sink my claws into her eyes.

"Easy, sweetheart," Ethan murmured in my ear as I tensed in his hold. "She's the one who's not worth it."

"Says the guy fucking her," I hissed back, elbowing him hard in the ribs. "What's that make you?"

He let out a soft grunt and released me.

Enzo glanced at me, his lips parting like he wanted to say something. Instead, it was Cole who made a move.

He seized my arm, his grip so tight I winced. "What the *fuck* are you doing, Rosebud?" His voice was so low in my ear I had to strain to hear him.

I tried to pull away, but he only tightened his hold.

"I asked you a question," he snarled, giving me a shake.

"Don't fucking touch her." Ian shoved Cole away from me, tugging me to his chest like a shield. *Asshole.* I knew it was so Cole wouldn't launch himself at Ian and beat him half to death. Ian planted a kiss to my temple, his arm around my waist, binding me to his front. "She's with me now. She's *my* girl."

Fox's gaze locked on mine. There was so much torment in it I had to look away, my guts clenching with nausea.

"Hey, Cole," Ian called out, backing away with me still in front of him. Cole's icy blue gaze leveled on Ian. "How are those sloppy seconds of Fox's?"

"How are mine?" Cole growled back.

"Fucking delicious." Ian let out a bark of laughter.

"You're dead," Ethan snarled, his fists clenched at his sides. He took a step forward as Ian pulled me back. Ethan still looked rough. If possible, the circles beneath his eyes had grown darker. His once brilliant green eyes were glassy and unfocused.

Enzo grabbed Ethan, stopping him from whatever he planned on doing. I'd never seen Ethan look so menacing before, but in that moment, I believed his threat.

"You're making a big mistake," Enzo called out. I wasn't sure if he was talking to me or Ian, but it didn't matter.

"You see that? Your fuck boys are nuts," Ian grumbled as he gripped my arm tightly and yanked me along.

"Where are we going?" I demanded, trying to get him to release my arm. His grip tightened.

"They made a threat. We aren't going to sit back and let them get away with it."

"We? There is no *we*, Ian. It's me. And it's them. You barely register as human on my radar."

He pulled me to a hard stop and caged me between his arms at my locker.

"There is a *we*, baby girl. In fact, I've been thinking. Wouldn't it be fan-fucking-tastic if I put a baby inside you? Imagine that. Together forever."

I couldn't control myself. I spit in his face. In a move so fast, he had me jerked into the girls' bathroom, locking the door behind us.

In all my time knowing Ian, I never thought he had a mean bone in his body. His recent highlights had changed that. If there was any doubt of what sort of monster he was before, his painful shove which had me crumpled on the floor confirmed he was a complete prick, and nothing he'd done previously had been out of desperation. He really was an asshole.

"Oh god!" Tears rolled down my cheeks as he landed a hard kick to my ribs.

With a hiss, he fisted my hair and pulled my face up. "Don't fuck with me, Rosalie. I'm not a fucking pushover. You are *not* in control here, understand?" His eyes flashed before he full on spit in my face.

"Fuck you," I choked out. "I'll fucking bury you, Ian. I hate you. I'm going to call the cops —"

He responded by slamming my face to the tiles, pushing so hard I saw stars.

"I'll kill your fuck boys. I'll kill Jamie. I'll kill your parents and even your fucking cat. Go ahead and try me, Rosalie. I will tear your whole world apart and make you watch. Is that what you want? Huh?" He backed up a bit.

"No," I sobbed. "N-No."

"Then do what the fuck I tell you to do. Be a good girl for me so I don't have to do those things." I flinched as he reached out to touch me. A look of frustration crossed his face before he tried again. This time I let him, my body stiff and aching.

He cradled my face, his gaze sweeping over me. "You're so fucking beautiful when you cry."

I squeezed my eyelids tight as he pressed his lips to mine in a tender kiss, a kiss completely uncharacteristic of the man who'd just kicked me in the ribs and threatened the lives of people I knew.

"Mm," he sighed, pulling away. "Definitely love it when you cry. Your lips are so soft and salty from your tears. It's the best taste in the world."

I shivered as he brushed his knuckles across my cheek.

"I'll be sure not to hurt your face. But the rest of you..." He let out a soft, dark laugh. "Is fair game. Stop making me do it."

I believed every word he said as he lifted me to my feet and pressed one more kiss to my lips.

"I hate that lip gloss. Don't wear it again. Got it?"

I nodded numbly, my ribs aching as I tried to control my choked breathing, my body desperate to breathe normal again.

"Get cleaned up. You look like shit."

And with those words, he left me standing in the bathroom realizing I had a bigger problem than the horsemen and wanting revenge. I'd enlisted the fucking devil as an ally.

CHAPTER 6

By lunch time, I was trying to find a new hiding spot to stay away from Ian and the guys. Deciding maybe the bathroom was still my best bet, I headed in that direction. I stepped inside and sighed.

The clicking of the lock had me whirling around to see Cole standing there, an eyebrow raised at me.

"What are you doing?" I choked out.

"I figured you'd come back to your old stomping grounds." He peered around. "Gotta admit, you girls have a nice place for a bathroom."

Determining I wasn't going to stick around to talk to him, I started to move past him, but he stepped in front of me.

"Un-uh-uh," he tutted softly. "You're not going anywhere, Rosebud."

"Cole, let me leave."

He reached out and thumbed my trembling bottom lip. "I know you're the one who keyed my car. I know you fucked with Fox's Jeep."

I swallowed thickly. "Prove it."

He chuckled softly. "I don't need to. We both know it. I'm not mad. Neither is Fox. Not really, anyway."

I stared up at him, my body quaking.

"In fact, it only turns me on to know you went to such extreme measures to get our attention."

"Trust me when I say your attention is the last thing I want."

"Oh, babe. Don't play me like that." He reached out and grabbed me before whirling me around and pushing me against the wall. He leveled his body against mine. "You look fucking beautiful today."

I remained silent as he stared down at me, hunger burning in his baby blues.

"Your hair. You have me mesmerized, Rosebud." He reached out and ran his fingers through my hair, his lips parted. I swallowed thickly and stared up at the impossibly beautiful devil before me.

"You think you're playing us. You think this is a fucking game, don't you, beautiful?" His warm breath caressed my face. "Did you forget who I am, babe?"

"The fucking devil," I whispered back.

"I'm *your* devil." He shifted, his hands finding their way beneath my shirt. I winced slightly as he touched my injured ribs. My heart slammed against my chest as he stared down at me. "And it doesn't matter to me how hard you try to avoid me. To avoid *us*. You're only playing a dangerous game of cat and mouse. It fucking makes my cock hard knowing the lengths you're going to in order to make me jealous."

His hand moved to my breast where he dipped inside my bra before pulling it free. I whimpered as he rolled my nipple between his fingers, but I made no move to stop him. My brain flooded with want.

Taking note of that, he moved his hand lower. My breathing came in short gasps as our eyes remained locked on one another's. When he lifted my skirt, I didn't move or try to stop him. I'd gone temporarily paralyzed.

"Oh," I gasped as he cupped my ass before trailing his hand to my panties. He moved my panties aside and ran his finger along my wet slit. I whimpered and flinched at his touch. I was still tender down there from Ian hurting me in his room.

Cole crinkled his brows at me. "What did he do, Rosebud?"

I shook my head, choking down my cry as Cole ran his finger along me again.

"Did he hurt you?"

I squeezed my eyes closed as Cole teased me.

"I'll kill him if he hurt you." He kissed the corner of my lips before he darted his tongue out and ran it along the seam of them. I parted my lips on instinct.

"My favorite lip gloss," he murmured, running his finger faster over the slit between my legs. "I can still taste it on your lips." He'd nearly snaked between my folds, coming dangerously close to my clit.

"Say yes," he whispered against my lips.

I shook as he continued to touch me.

"Say it, and I'll make all your dreams come true."

As much as I wanted to say it, I held back. I'd never give him the satisfaction. Not after what he'd done to hurt me. It didn't matter how much I ached for his touch. I wouldn't give in.

"Say it, Rosalie," he commanded, his voice a low growl. "Fucking tell me you want it. Tell me you want me."

I remained silent, eyes locked on his. A muscle popped along his jaw.

"Fucking say it!" he shouted, his eyes becoming wild. His voice echoed. He removed his hand from between my legs and wrapped his fingers around my throat.

I quivered beneath his hold but didn't look away.

"Stop *fucking* playing with me, Rosalie." His hold on my throat tightened. "You're going to unleash the ugly side of me. I don't want that to happen because I don't think I can control myself once it's fucking free."

I stared back at him, noting the darkness lurking behind his pretty blue eyes. I knew Cole hid his true self from the world. With the exception of me and the horsemen, people knew him as the blue-eyed, blond-haired heartthrob. But Cole Scott could give the devil a run for his money.

"This isn't over, Rosebud. The next time you're alone with me, I'm going to fuck you so hard you won't remember that piece of shit's name you're with." His lips crashed against mine.

I didn't kiss him back. It took everything I had not to. He pressed his lips harder to mine, his hand tightening around my throat as he tried to force the kiss from my mouth.

When he realized it wasn't going to happen, he broke it off and rested his forehead against mine, his breathing heavy.

"This isn't over," he repeated, his voice shaking. "I'll kill that piece of shit before I let him take you from me." He pressed a fierce kiss to my forehead. "Don't go anywhere alone, Rosebud. Because I'll find you and lay claim to what's mine."

He stepped away from me, his distance leaving a wake of cold behind. He turned, sauntered to the door, and unlocked it, pausing as he opened it and looked back at me.

I still leaned against the wall, trembling from his intensity.

"I got you something," he called out softly. "It's in the bag on the sink." With those words, he left me alone, the door banging shut behind him. It took me a moment to compose myself. On shaking legs, I went to the brown paper bag on the sink and opened it to find a sandwich inside, a bottle of water, and a note written in Cole's scrawl.

Eat. You're going to need your strength for the next time. XO-Cole

I stared down at the note. He knew I'd deny him, and yet, he tried anyway.

But I'd gotten to him. I counted that as a victory. It was my concern of how he'd gotten to me that scared me.

WHEN I WAS FIRST FORMULATING my plan, I figured I'd forego trying out for the musical to focus on disrupting the lives of the horsemen. It wasn't like it was some Broadway musical. It was something a former drama teacher had written before he'd retired. He'd had mild success in the theater world, so the school liked to perform some of the plays and musicals he'd written.

I'd been back and forth on the idea for too long. Mostly, I wanted to avoid getting screamed at by my father. And I desperately wanted to go to Mayfair. But after my encounter with Cole, I decided I needed the play as a means to take my mind off everything and to keep me busy and away from them as I tried to figure out what to do next.

It was also a way to escape Ian. The past week with him had been practically unbearable with his shitty attitude and demands for sex.

Another week down. Another week safe. Being part of the play would mean less time around him too. At least that was what I'd told myself.

A week later, I stood in the auditorium, a pop song memorized. I vowed to never sing the song I'd worked on with Fox and Enzo again.

"Rosalie Bishop!" Mr. Dennison called out my name, making me jump. I'd been so absorbed in thinking about how the hell to avoid my new nightmare that I'd spaced out on my current reality.

Shuffling to my feet, I made my way to the stage.

"What are you singing for us today?" Mr. Dennison asked.

I took in the small panel before me. Mr. Dennison, the director and current drama club teacher, Mrs. Adams, the vocal teacher, and a handful of students working on the show for extra credit.

And Jamie. She averted her eyes from me and stared down at her clipboard.

"Uh, I'm going to do 'Dangerous Woman.'" My voice wasn't nearly as loud or as strong as I'd intended. A few chuckles sounded out around me. I shielded my eyes from stage lights and peered out at the crowd. I sucked in a sharp breath. Fox and the guys were settling into seats near the middle, and Ian had taken up one near the front.

Fuck my life. I couldn't get away from shit. Ever.

"Excellent. And for your monologue?" Mr. Dennison lifted a dark brow at me.

I cleared my throat. "Um, I'll be doing a monologue of Helena's from *A Midsummer Night's Dream.*"

He gave me a nod.

The track for "Dangerous Woman" started playing. Fear seized me as I stared at the guys. Fox locked eyes on mine. He leaned forward.

Cole narrowed his eyes. Enzo gave me a thumbs up. And Ethan...just a smile.

Shit. They played this game better than me.

"Miss Bishop?" Mr. Dennison called out to me.

"S-Sorry. C-Can I restart?"

He let out a sigh and nodded. The music started again. This time I saw Jamie. Her brows crinkled as she stared back at me. It was her worried look. I swallowed hard. My gaze shifted to Ian who snapped a photo of me and winked. It would probably end up in the school paper with the headline *Rosalie Bishop Chokes Again. . . This Time, Not on Cock.*

I missed my cue again. Laughter echoed around me from other students scattered throughout the auditorium.

"Miss Bishop, if you aren't prepared—" Mr. Dennison started.

"I-I am. I'm sorry." I shook my head and drew in a deep breath.

"Come on, Rosebud!" Cole shouted.

"Yeah. You've got this, Sunshine!" Enzo joined in.

Mr. Dennison turned around and shook his head.

My face heated at their cheers, anger coursing through me. *Who the hell did they think they were coming in and ruining more of my shit?*

"Thank you, Mr. Scott and Mr. De Luca," Mr. Dennison called out, shaking his head, a tiny smirk on his lips. Mr. Dennison spun back to face me. Fox had disappeared at some point. But I couldn't focus on that.

Once more, the music started. And once again, I failed.

Shit.

My palms were sweaty. My pulse thundered in my ears. I shielded my eyes from the bright lights, everything sounding like a dull roar around me.

"Miss Bishop, how about you come back when you're actually ready to perform for us—"

"She's ready." A warm hand pressed against the small of my back. Fox was at my side, his guitar in hand. "We're going to do a different song though. It's called 'All of Me'. It's an original Rosalie wrote."

Mr. Dennison sighed and gestured for us to continue.

"What are you doing?" I squeaked out softly.

"Helping you, Rosie. Just sing, OK? Like we practiced. Close your eyes. It's only us."

I gawked out helplessly at everyone waiting on me. I knew if I shoved Fox off stage, I'd follow since all my chances were used up.

I nodded.

Fox gave me an encouraging smile and strummed the intro to my song.

So much for never singing that damn song again.

I hauled in a deep breath and closed my eyes, the words falling from my mouth as I sang my heart out. When we reached the chorus, Fox joined in, his voice perfectly pitched with mine. I opened my eyes and locked them on him as we sang together.

I wasn't sure how I managed to get through it, but I did. Our final note hung in the air.

Stunned silence greeted us. I tore my gaze from Fox's and peered out at Mr. Dennison and Mrs. Adams.

Mrs. Adams sat forward, a glint in her eyes.

"Rosalie, why aren't you in any of our vocal classes? Choir? Glee?"

I shrugged my shoulders. "I-My dad doesn't like me to sing," I finally mumbled. "I only got to be in it freshman year."

"That's a damn shame." She sat back in her seat, shaking her head. I glanced at Jamie, but she was focused on her clipboard again.

"And Fox Evans." A smile curved Mrs. Adams's lips up. "Let me guess? You aren't in my vocal classes because of football?"

Fox chuckled. "You're correct, but I could make an exception."

She shook her head, still smiling at his flirtatious comeback, and looked to Mr. Dennison.

"Mr. Evans, can I safely assume you're available for a part in this production and that your song with Miss Bishop can be considered a dual tryout?"

Fox didn't look at me as he answered, "Yes, sir."

I gaped at him, my mouth falling open. Fox didn't do drama, at least this kind. *What the hell was he thinking?* He had to keep up grades for football and his scholarship to Mayfair.

"Very well. Miss Bishop, let's hear that monologue," Mr. Dennison said, clearing his throat.

When my attention shifted from Fox, all I could see was Cole and Enzo grinning at me from their seats. Ethan simply stared back at me like he couldn't believe what he was seeing. Wanting nothing more than to get the hell out of there, I launched into my monologue, putting everything I had into my performance.

"Nicely done, Rosalie. Nicely done." Mr. Dennison nodded. "We'll have everything posted sometime next week. Try to enjoy your weekend. As for you, Fox, what monologue are you going to do?"

I didn't stop to listen to Fox's answer. I rushed off the stage, my body trembling.

Ian greeted me at the bottom of the steps.

"Good job, babe." He wrapped his arm around me, his voice gruff. "Didn't know you could sing like that."

"Thanks," I mumbled. The feelings I expected to feel weren't there. I thought I'd be giddy and excited. Instead, I felt hollow. Empty. Lonely. I thought Ian might say something about Fox, but he didn't.

"Let's celebrate."

"Celebrate what?"

"You're going to get the lead."

We strolled to my locker where I gathered my books for the weekend.

"Ian, I'd really rather just go home—"

"Not happening."

"Please?" I didn't want to whine, but I needed to be alone with my thoughts.

"No. Come suck my dick, and I'll let you go home early."

"You're such a piece of shit," I seethed at him.

He smirked. "You wanted this."

"I never wanted *this*—"

"Rosalie! Hey!"

I spun to see Jamie coming toward me. My heart leaped into my throat, my body tensing.

If she wanted to fight, I wasn't in the mood.

"You were really great." She stopped a few feet from us.

I frowned, wondering what the hell alternate universe I'd stumbled into.

"Thanks?" It was more of a question than anything else. Ian wound his arm more tightly around my waist. Jamie flinched slightly but kept a smile fixed on her face.

"For what it's worth, I think you got it."

"Thanks, Jamie. Rosalie was worried." Ian smiled down at me and pressed a kiss to my cheek.

"We're going to get going. Rosalie and I have plans in my bedroom." Ian tugged me, but I pushed him away.

"Jamie—"

"It's fine. Go do...whatever." The pain in her voice was clear.

"It's not like that, Jamie—"

"Rosalie," Ian snapped. Both Jamie and I flinched at his tone. "Now."

"I-I gotta go. Text me?" I called out hopefully as Ian dragged me away. Jamie's eyes flickered from Ian to me, a frown on her face.

I never got to hear her answer because Ian had me out the door before she could speak. I snatched my arm away from him, but he grabbed it again, this time harder, and tugged me to the car.

"Stop it. Ian, stop! You're hurting me!" I finally got my arm away from him, but it was a bad idea. He shoved me against my car, his eyes flashing with anger.

"You will *not* talk to her. Do you understand me?"

"What?"

"You fucking heard me, Rosalie. You and Jamie are not friends. She hates you. And quite frankly, I don't want to have to see the bitch."

"I don't know who the hell you think you are, but you aren't going to tell me who I can and cannot be friends with," my voice rang out.

Ian clamped his hand over my mouth, making me bite my tongue.

"I'm the guy in charge. That's who the hell I am. You belong to me. No one else. I swear to god, Rosalie, if I catch you even looking at anyone but me, I'll make you the sorriest you've ever been. If Evans makes it into that play, you'll quit. Or I swear to fuck, you'll regret it.

Get me?" He moved his hand away from my mouth and gave me a stern look.

"You can't do this, Ian. If I make that play, it's all I have—"

"Baby, *I* can do anything I want. *I* make the rules. *Not* you. I have the power here. I have the videos. It's by my will alone I don't spread them around like wildfire. Plus, you'll have me. All of me if you'll just fucking fall in line."

"Please," I whispered, reaching out for him. "What do you want from me?"

"The same thing you want from me. Revenge."

I shook my head. "Not at the risk of losing my freedom, Ian. I don't want that."

"Then be a better girlfriend, Rosalie. All you had to do for the horsemen was lie on your back and spread your legs, and you fucked that up. It's all I really need from you to make this work more smoothly. Give me what I want, and I'll give you what you want. It's that simple."

"Why is everything about sex with you, Ian? What the hell is your problem?"

"My problem is we had a deal, and you aren't holding up your end of the bargain. I've gotten about as far with you as I did with Jamie. That's not going to cut it. If you want, I can walk right back in that school and tell her how stupid I was for letting her go. I can say all sorts of shit she'll lap up. I never lost her, Rosalie. You know that. The girl is head over heels for me still."

"You're a narcissistic pig."

His hands came out lightning fast and landed on my waist. I let out a whimper as he pinched my sides. My eyes watered as he twisted. His mouth turned down into an ugly snarl.

"And you're a fucking bitch. Guess we both have a few things that need to be worked on." His lips brushed against my cheek. "And if I so much as catch you talking to the horsemen, I'll put you through the worst hell imaginable. You'll think of these moments as just a fucking warm up. Their little cheering section only pissed me off. And guess who pays the price for that?"

"Me," I choked out.

"That's right, baby. *You.*"

Ian kissed me, his tongue deep in my mouth. I kissed him back, nausea roiling in my guts. This wasn't part of the plan. Or it was, and it just wasn't working. Bad planning on my part. This was all meant to keep Jamie safe, but he'd already spilled the secret to her. Now, it was about hurting Fox and the guys by me being with Ian. Not to mention he had the videos. Once again, I'd landed myself in another shitty situation.

Despair washed over me. My ribs still ached from him kicking me days ago in the bathroom. Ugly bruises adorned my side, a reminder of my bad ideas.

"Sad how fast you moved on," Enzo called out.

I broke away from Ian.

Enzo stood a few feet away, his dark eyes wavering. "Thought we meant a little more to you, Sunshine."

"Tell him to fuck off, Rosalie," Ian murmured so only I could hear him.

Truth be told, I wanted to tell all of them to fuck off. Hauling in a deep breath, I readied myself. "You're screwing Juliet, Enzo. You were even before you were after me," my voice shook, my sides aching from Ian's pinches.

Enzo scoffed. "Is that what you think?"

I ignored Ian still holding me as I pulled myself together and shouted at Enzo. "It's what I know! I saw Fox in bed with her! I saw the notebook."

Enzo took a step forward, but Ian shifted in front of me, his back to my front.

"Face it, De Luca. You played a dangerous game you couldn't win. Walk away with some dignity." Ian chuckled softly.

"Fuck you, you fucking weasel," Enzo hissed, his hands balled into fists. "You're a dead man and don't even know it yet."

"Let me tell you something." Ian took a step forward, so he and Enzo were nearly chest to chest. "Your daddy and your money and your fucking supposed *mob* ties won't get you shit here. *They don't fucking matter.* I'm not afraid of you, De Luca, and you aren't going to win her back. She hates you. She hates you so much, she *came to me.* And tonight, she's going to *come* for me. *Again.*"

Enzo's body vibrated with anger.

I wanted to step forward and stop Ian but seeing Enzo's reaction was what I'd been longing for. I wanted him angry. Hurting. Sick with stress because I was sick. *I was so fucking sick.* If I wasn't, I wouldn't be doing the shit I was doing. If anyone was playing a game they had no business playing, it was me.

"That's right, De Luca. Those little moans and her trembling body are mine now. And all because you and the horsemen didn't know how to play the game. *Amateurs.*"

"If you fucking touch her—"

Ian let out a soft laugh. "*If?* Too late. It's more like *when* I touch her."

"Ian." I reached out for him and took his hand. "Let's go. Please."

Ian backed away from Enzo, a smirk on his face. "Don't you just love it when she begs?"

"I meant what I said, Hall. You touch her, you're dead." Enzo peered past him and locked eyes with me. "I can help you, Rosalie. You know how to reach me. We have a lot to talk about." He turned and strode away, his head down.

"What a bitch," Ian snorted.

I swallowed hard and stared at Enzo's back, wondering if maybe I should start listening. But I was in too deep. This was a hole with no way out. I needed new tactics.

CHAPTER 7

I woke with a groan, a heavy arm over my midsection. I lay beneath Ian's arm, staring at the ceiling, my head throbbing. No other pain from his violent touches greeted me. Not even the slap.

After we'd gotten to his place, he'd launched himself into a rage about Enzo, ending it by slapping me across the face before getting me an ice pack and turning on the television. I almost wished his mother would come home, but she worked nights. His younger brother was at a friend's place.

But I'd lucked out and only suffered from his heavy hand and not the other things he was capable of.

Guilt greeted me with the sun.

And hatred. Anger. More despair.

A tear slipped out of the corner of my eye. I reached for my phone on Ian's dresser. I'd told my parents I was staying at a new friend's house. I didn't say who. But I was Rosalie, Daddy's little girl. They would suspect nothing. And if they did, fuck it. Eighteen meant something to me.

My dress still hugged my body. My panties were in place. I shook my head. I'd gotten off easy last night.

I unlocked my phone screen to find a message from Fox.

Fox: Not him, Rosie. Anyone but him. I'm begging you.

I bit my lip and snapped a picture of me and Ian in bed and sent it to him, feeling like the biggest, pettiest bitch in the world. *Let's see how he liked me in bed with someone else.* I hoped it hurt like hell, just like it had for me when I'd seen him and Juliet together.

His answer didn't take long.

Fox: Rosie, why?

Rosalie: It hurts, doesn't it?

Fox: I only did what I did to protect you, Rosie. Never to hurt you. I never wanted to hurt you!

Rosalie: But you did. You were never honest with me. I was just a game to you. How does it feel to lose?

I waited for his answer. It took a few minutes for it to come.

Fox: Meet me tonight at the treehouse. I'll wait for you. Alone.

I darkened the screen, my heart in my throat. Ian shifted beside me, his naked torso pressing against me. I held my breath as he reached out and rubbed my breast through my dress.

"You're a nice sight to wake up to," he mumbled, tugging me close.

"I need to go."

"No, you don't."

"Ian, I really do. Please."

He sat up on his elbow and loomed over me, his dark hair a mess. If I didn't hate him so much, I might have swooned. Ian wasn't bad to look at, but damn, my hatred canceled everything else out.

"Last night wasn't much fun, Rosalie."

I crinkled my brows at him.

"I can offer you the escape you need. I know you're afraid to go all the way with me. One tiny pill. If you want it, it's yours. But that's not how I want to take you. I want you to tell me you want it."

"I thought getting me high was how you'd prefer it." I glared up at him.

"If that's how you want to do things, I'll do it, but I won't be satis-fied until you climb on me and say you want me. That's the only time it'll count."

"So you've grown a conscience?" I snorted. "Date rape isn't doing it for you anymore?"

I let out a strangled cry as he gripped my throat. I thrashed against him as his hold tightened, making me wheeze. The way he could snap in heartbeat was terrifying.

"I've put up with your mouth long enough. I think you're beautiful, Rosalie. But if you keep it up, I'll fucking kill you and bury you in a place no one will find your body. Stop. Fucking. Testing. My. Patience." Each punctuated word brought on a tighter squeeze around my neck until I clawed at him, kicking my legs because my ability to breathe was gone.

Stars dotted my vision. Tingles shot through my body, the loss of oxygen weakening me as he held on. He cocked his head and stared down at me.

"You'll make a beautiful corpse someday. I can only imagine how much *that* would hurt the horsemen. I hate them too, you know. Fox and Cole are the reason I have no father. Well, Fox couldn't really help it, but then he had to try to take you. Such a bad idea."

I tapped frantically at Ian's arm.

"It hurts, doesn't it? Not being able to breathe. I bet your lungs ache right now." He squeezed harder.

Darkness blotted my vision. Ian was going to kill me.

"I'm curious how long you can last."

I swatted at him with a final burst of energy. I caught him in the nose. He shoved me hard, releasing me, and I tumbled out of his bed onto the cold, hardwood floor. I scrambled, choking in oxygen, to get away from him, but he was on me in an instant, fisting my hair in a painful hold.

"The more you fight me, the more I enjoy it. Fall. In. Line." He smashed my face down onto the floor.

"Fuck you. Kill me, you fucking pussy," I rasped as he put pressure on my head. I barely had a voice. I imagined I'd have bruises along my neck to match the ones on my ribs.

He let out a ferocious snarl and smacked my head off the floor again.

"You can't even do it, can you? Can you?" My voice broke, coming out barely above a whisper.

He let out another snarl and lifted me to my feet before shoving me down again. His foot met my ribs, and I buckled beneath the pain. I got to my hands and knees again and let out a laugh. And once again, he kicked me. I fell once more, crawling away from him.

His foot came down on my lower back, knocking me to my stomach. The weight of his body straddling me made me wince, his hard length pressed against my ass.

I let out a choked sob as his hand closed around my throat again, his other hand pulling my head painfully up by my hair.

"Is *this* what you want? You want me to hurt you? Huh?" His voice was a low growl. He released my neck and fumbled with my dress, jerking it up. I let out a cry as the warmth from his dick pressed against my center.

"I could fuck you right now," he growled in my ear, breathless. "Is that what you want me to do?"

"No," I choked out. "Stop."

He released me and moved away.

I let out a sob, my throat and body aching.

"*Fucking bitch.* This is all your fault. You make me this insane monster. God damn it!" He rammed his fist into the wall, creating a crater in the plaster. He breathed hard, his fingers tugging at his hair. A moment later, he turned to me.

I let out a squeak as he hauled me into his arms and held me.

"I don't *want* to hurt you. I've never hurt anyone like that before. Fuck, Rosalie. Fuck!"

I wept softly.

He peppered kisses on my forehead and cheek. "Forgive me."

He squeezed me hard when I didn't answer.

"Tell me you forgive me."

"I-I can't."

He pushed me away, and I tumbled onto my back on the floor, his large form looming over me again.

"Go home before I end up killing you." He turned away from me and went to his bedroom window and gazed out. I didn't waste any time getting to my feet and stumbling out, leaving my shoes behind.

If it meant I got to live long enough to bring him down, I'd say it was worth the cost of a pair of twenty-dollar sandals.

CHAPTER 8

urtlenecks and jeans were going to be my wardrobe for the next few days as I healed from Ian's onslaught. I sat in my bedroom later that night and stared at myself in the mirror. Dark circles rimmed my eyes. Ugly bruises peppered my neck. My ribs were a purple disaster. Ian messed me up bad.

I looked down at my phone as it buzzed on my vanity.

Fox: I'm waiting. I'll wait all night.

I stared at his message, my heart aching as much as my body.

I dabbed on foundation, covering the bruises on my cheek and eye. The purple eyeshadow helped, blending anything I missed. I did up my entire face until I barely looked like myself.

Hauling myself to my feet, I winced and grabbed a dark turtleneck and jeans. I put them on. Then I slipped on a pair of chucks before heading to the door.

The clock read just after eleven at night. My parents went to bed an hour before. The walk to the treehouse was long and dark. I didn't know what the hell I was doing or why I was doing it. Maybe I needed to see Fox's face just so I could gain more fuel for my quickly dwindling rage fire.

When I reached the treehouse, I stood at the bottom and stared up at it. A lantern was lit inside, casting a dim glow. I climbed the ladder and knocked on the door.

"You came," Fox breathed out as he closed the tattered notebook he'd carried around with him for years, tucking the pencil inside it. He looked like the night, dressed in all black. Even his beanie was black. It seemed like he wanted to pull me into his arms. If this was any other time, I would've loved for him to hold me. But I knew he'd been holding Juliet in those same arms. The thought disgusted me.

"What did you need?" I stepped inside and glanced around. I hadn't been in there since we were kids. The same blue and pink bean bags were still on the floor. I swallowed hard and turned away from them.

"I miss you."

"So?" I met his gaze.

"Rosie, please."

"Please, *what*, Fox? What do you want from me?"

"I want nothing but your forgiveness."

"Just my forgiveness?" I scoffed.

"No. I want your love as well."

I let out a laugh and shook my head. "And what? I love you while you fuck Juliet? No thanks. Played that game. Won a stupid prize."

"Rosie, it's not like that with Juliet."

"Are you fucking her?"

A muscle popped along his jaw. "Yes."

My heart jackknifed in my chest. I already knew he was. Hell, I'd seen it.

What did I expect his answer to be?

"But I don't love her. None of us do."

"Then why do it?" I choked out.

"I don't have a choice. She owns me at this point."

"Nice," I snorted. "I sympathize."

"Rosalie, I'm being honest. I don't love her. I fucking hate her, matter of fact. It's you I think about—"

"Don't even finish that sentence, Fox. It's disgusting."

He hung his head and nodded. "I'm sorry."

"I'm tired. Like *really* tired. Tell me why you wanted me to trek out here."

"You look beautiful," he murmured, moving to reach out to me.

I pulled away from him, not knowing if I could handle him touching me. He dropped his hand back to his side, his blue eyes wavering as he stared back at me.

"I wanted to tell you I'm sorry. We all are. The book was a stupid game. We did it to get girls. We never made them do anything they didn't want to do. We may have had dirt on them, but we weren't big enough dicks to use it. We genuinely wanted them to like us. It was just a way to get them to be close to us in the beginning."

"And me? Were you going to do that to me?"

Fox licked his lips and looked away. "I-I had issues, Rosalie. I blamed you for my mom. She went and bought you those fucking earrings you wanted. That's why she was out the night she died. Getting you a gift. So I blamed you." A tear snaked down his cheek as he handed me a small, velvet box. "Take it. She wanted you to have them."

My hands trembled as I opened the box and stared down at the tiny earrings. A tear trickled its way out.

"They'll look beautiful on you," Fox murmured.

I hurriedly wiped at my eyes, my throat tight.

"I lost my mom, Rosie. Then I fucked up and lost you. My life has been shit ever since that day. I drink too much. I get high too much. I fuck around too much. I hate everything. I make stupid fucking choices that lead to even bigger mistakes."

He wiped his eyes, his Adam's apple bobbing. I had to look away, my throat growing tighter from trying not to cry with him.

"I *thought* I was going to do that to you. I intended on it. I hated you, but I loved you so fucking much more. I kept denying it. Cole knew I loved you. He rode my ass about it. Ethan talked about you so much ever since the day he bumped into you in the hall last year. Drove us nuts with all his talk about wanting to get to know you. To ask you out. To even just gain your friendship. Enzo...well, the moment he saw you on your knees, he was done for. You were the perfect girl for us all. Even me with all my bullshit. But I couldn't get past it. Then I saw the video of you kissing Enzo and Cole. You said you wanted it." He blew out a breath. "Then in my bedroom. I-I tried to resist. I did. But I failed on that too. I kissed you. I tasted you. I fell so fucking deep with you, I knew there was no way out. And I was beginning to be OK with that."

"But then you tripped, and your dick fell into Juliet." I turned and glared at him. "Were you even broken up with her when you were with me?"

"Yes! I *never* cheated on you, Rosie! Never! My heart was *always* with you." He took a step forward and reached for me.

I pulled away, backing up until I bumped against the wall. He didn't stop. He came forward and stood in front of me, caging me between his arms.

"Then what did I walk in on?" I whispered, staring into his pretty blue eyes.

"You walked in on me making a deal with Juliet to keep you safe."

"You had to *fuck* that bitch to keep me safe?" I let out a raspy laugh.

Fox frowned. "What's wrong with your voice? It's all low and crackly."

I swallowed hard, the ache from my throat searing through my neck as I peered up at him. "Ian's dick is too big for my mouth. Guess it gives me a sore throat."

Fox's face darkened, his lips turning down into a frown. "Why are you torturing me, Rosie?"

"You tortured me for five years, Fox. I'd say you deserve everything I give to you."

"Even fucking the guy whose dad killed my mom?" His words held no anger, only a sadness so deep and dark it cinched around my heart like a vice. "Is that your revenge? Hurting me like that? Or is it fucking up my Jeep?"

"I don't know what you're talking about."

"Right. I'm sure you don't. But hey, let's pretend like you do. Maybe you can tell me why you decided to leave a fucking fish under my seat. That was disgustingly creative but not as good as taking the stereo knobs and the other buttons off so I'm stuck listening to farm animals fuck themselves at the highest volume." His blue eyes glinted.

I couldn't stop the soft chuckle that bubbled out of me at how absurd it sounded coming from his mouth. "Let's pretend like I did do it then. If I did, know that it's only the beginning, Fox."

"Don't let it be, Rosalie. Let's fix this." He reached out and pulled me to him. I let out a whimper at his firm hold on me, my ribs screaming for distance.

"What's wrong?" He gave me a searching look, the annoyance leaving his face. He switched gears so fast. One minute he was an asshole, the next he was concerned. "You're hurt. What's hurting, baby?"

I shook my head, his term of endearment making both desire and anger course through me. "N-Nothing."

"Don't lie to me. *Please.* I know you. You blink when you lie. Your cheeks turn pink. Your lips part." He reached out and thumbed my bottom lip, a hungry look in his eyes. "Tell me so I can make it better."

I steeled myself. "There's nothing to tell. I like it rough. Ian just tries to accommodate it. Probably have Cole to thank for that."

"Liar," Fox growled. "You hate Ian."

"I hate you too, and yet here we are."

"You don't hate me, Rosie." Fox ran his nose along mine. "Baby, you love me right back. You're just mad."

"No, I really hate you, Fox," I whispered. "So much."

"Please don't."

"Then make Juliet go away. Stop seeing her. Start telling me the truth."

"I can't. Not yet."

If he loved me, he'd let her go. He'd tell me the truth.

"She owns me. For just a little bit longer. I swear to you I don't feel shit for her. It's your name on my lips. Your face I see. It's you that I kiss. Not her. *Never* her."

I cried out as he squeezed me. His eyes swept over me, his brows crinkled.

"He's not good for you. He's hurting you. Tell me he is, and I'll fucking kill him, Rosalie."

"It's you who's hurting me. It's always been you, Fox."

"I don't want to hurt you. I don't mean to."

"But you keep doing it. If you say you're sorry and then continue to do the same things you said you're sorry for, how does anyone ever believe you? *Leave her, Fox.*"

"Leave Ian," he countered. "Stop fucking the guy whose dad took my mom."

I flinched at the anger behind his words.

"You wanted to hurt me. You got me, Rosie. You broke my fucking heart, but I love you so much I can push past the betrayal."

"Guess that makes one of us."

I shifted to push him away, but his mouth crashed against mine, his tongue sweeping inside. Heat pooled between my legs as he kissed me. Tingles shot through my body. His arms wound around me, causing pain to shoot through me.

I let out a cry against his lips, trembling in his arms.

"What's wrong?" Concern darkened his features as he asked for the third time. He released me, his eyes wide. "Tell me, Rosalie. Let me help you. Let me fix it. He's not good for you."

I shook my head. "This isn't going to work. Coming here was a mistake."

"The mistake would be walking out—"

"And if I stayed?" I wiped at the tears falling down my cheeks. *Damnit. I didn't want to cry in front of him.* "You fuck me then fuck Juliet in the morning? You get both of us? Or do you want her to join us all like some big screwed up harem?"

"I don't want her near you," Fox snarled. "And I'll continue to fuck her until I know she's not a threat to you anymore."

"Nice," I choked out. "Real nice, Fox. You're a real piece of shit."

"I'm really not," he breathed out. "I'm just a guy in love with his best friend who is stuck in a really shitty situation."

"You love me?" I zeroed in on his words. "*Really* love me?"

"So fucking much, Rosie. Just...let me, baby." He reached out and cradled my face in his hands. "I *need* you. You don't even realize how much. When this is over, you'll belong to me for good. To all of us."

"I don't want you." I hated the whispered lie. I hated myself more for the way I wanted to cave in and belong to him and the others. I couldn't stop now though. "I-I love Ian."

Liar! I love you, Fox.

Fuck.

"Ian is a fucking dumpster fire, Rosalie. He only wants one thing from you. You already know that."

I shook my head, grinding my teeth as his hands fell away.

"If he touches you, I really will kill him." His words sent a shiver down my spine. "If you had any sense, you'd tell me what's going on so I can save you."

"I don't need you to save me, Fox," I snapped, pushing him away from me. "I've made it this long without you. I don't need your help now."

"So you admit you need help," he murmured.

I shook my head and looked at a spot over his shoulder.

"I'll save you," he whispered. "I promise to keep the monsters away."

Tears stung my eyes again. "What if you're the monster?"

His bottom lip trembled. "Just ask for help, Rosie."

"I can handle myself."

He sighed. "Then pick someone else! Fuck Brandon. Cam. *Anyone* but Ian. If you want to make me and the guys suffer, then pick anyone else."

"What if I pick only *one* of you?" The idea sprang up in my mind, a devious plan forming.

"We all care for you, Rosie, but we have an agreement. It's all or nothing. Those are our rules."

"Rules were made to be broken."

"Not with us. *Never* with us."

"I bet Cole would take me up on that offer without much convincing on my part. We could have a dirty, little secret."

A muscle popped along Fox's jaw again as he gritted his teeth. "Don't even think about it."

I shrugged.

"Rosalie, I'm serious. T-That's not playing fair."

"All's fair in love and war. Besides, don't you trust the guys?" I cocked my head at him, the tears gone.

"I trust them with my life."

"Then I guess there's nothing for you to worry about then, huh?"

He shook his head at me. "I love you, Rosalie. With my entire heart and soul, I love you." My heart clenched, but I shoved the feelings away. I swallowed down my answer, hating that it was on the tip of my tongue, wrestling to make itself known.

"I hate you, Fox," my voice cracked as I spoke.

"You blinked," he whispered. "Your cheeks are pink."

I let out a soft laugh as I backed away from him.

"Stay the night, Rosie. Don't go."

"I don't want to intrude. I'm sure you'll need to check in with your girlfriend."

"You're my girlfriend."

"No, I'm Ian's girlfriend. I'm just the girl you fucked." I stepped out the door, taking in the pained expression on his face. "Stay away from me, Fox. We're over. I mean it."

He stood in the center of the treehouse, his eyes shimmering with unshed tears. "I really do love you. Please believe me, Rosie."

I turned, unable to bear looking at him anymore. If I didn't leave then, I knew I'd stay the night. And nothing good ever came from giving in.

He gave me the fuel I needed to push forward.

CHAPTER 9

The following Monday, I stuffed my clothes into my locker in the locker room and set the combination.

"What's wrong, sweetie? Missing someone?" Juliet called out to me.

I turned to face her, surprised she was without her minions. "Just the silence you interrupted."

"Cute." She tossed her hair over her shoulder. "Guess where I was Saturday night."

"Judging by what I know of you, about asshole deep in a shit ton of cocks."

"Usually I'd laugh, but in this instance, you're right. I was with the horsemen. *All* of them. We finally made it official."

"Really? What time was that?"

"Around eleven."

I laughed softly. "You couldn't have been with Fox since I was with him around eleven. Try again."

Her cheeks flamed red before she pulled her phone out and thumbed through it quickly.

She shoved it in my face a moment later.

"Take it. See for yourself."

I took her phone and stared down at the group message.

Cole: Christ, Juliet, get your ass over here already.

Juliet: I'm coming ;)

Enzo: Just hurry. We've been waiting.

Cole: Is Fox with you?

Juliet: No. He said he'd meet me at your house.

Fox: I'm just finishing up something. I'll be there in a few minutes.

I looked at the time stamp of Fox's message. Eleven thirty-seven. Right after I'd talked to him. *The bastard.*

"Look at the next picture."

I did as she instructed. Bile burned my throat as I stared down at a photo of her draped over Fox. Enzo was beside her. It was a selfie, so the angle only showed the three of them. But there were definitely clothes missing.

"Why do you think I need to see this?" I asked softly, doing everything in my power to control my fury.

"In case you had any ideas about trying to win the guys back. Figured you should see what's really going on."

I nodded, my jaw tight. "Do you have videos of me? Are you black-mailing the horsemen, Juliet?"

She crinkled her brows at me, looking confused at the question. "No. I've known about the notebook since the beginning. Fox never really participated in it unless we were broken up. But then they said they wanted to fuck with you. Since I can't stand you, I thought it was a good idea. I went with it and did as I was told. If they told you differently, they're lying."

"I see." I gripped her pretty, pink phone tightly.

"So you can stop your secret meetings with Fox. You can stop talking to any of them. They're trying for the lightning round. It's a game, sweetie. They just want to break you so they can fuck me harder. It gets them off to hurt girls. I'm the only one they care about. If they cared about you, they wouldn't lie to you and then fuck me after. Think about it."

"Right." I nodded. "So all four are fucking you now then?"

"Yep." She popped the p on the word and smiled smugly at me.

"And you knew about this thing the whole time and have been in on it? And Fox and the guys are lying trying to see if they can get me a second time?"

"Pretty messed up, huh?"

"And what about you having the videos? Ian said you did. He even told me a similar story that the guys told me."

"Well, Ian wants you. He approached me with the idea. I agreed because the guys had gotten in too deep. I stole the notebook and gave it to Ian who made sure it got into your hands. We're all working together in this. Although, I think Ian actually *does* want your ass."

"So everything has been a lie? All the begging, messages, calls, meetings, all of it. Lies."

"They're good, aren't they?" She reached for her phone.

Hatred raced through me as I pulled away, her phone still in my hand. "It's still a fucking game. I'm just a fucking joke to you all."

"It's not even a big deal. It's just a bit of fun. I thought we should end it though, which is why I'm here telling you. Just let it go and move on."

"Who has the videos?"

"Ian." Her answer was automatic. "And Fox has copies somewhere. I gave my copies to Ian in exchange for his help on this. So he's probably telling you the truth when he says he has the goods."

I squeezed her phone tighter, trying to control myself.

"But the game is over. Walk away before you really do get hurt. I don't want you to have to watch your back all the time. Plus, I might take Ian from you too. Just a little warning and advice, *girl to girl*. I mean, he *is* cute." She giggled and tossed her hair over her shoulder again.

"Girl to girl, go fuck yourself, you dumb bitch." I reared my arm back and threw her phone as hard as I could. It crashed against the brick wall and shattered on the way down. She stared in horror at her phone for a moment before turning her glare on me. It didn't last long because I was ready.

I full on punched her in the face, knocking her back. She fell on her ass, grabbing her bleeding nose.

"It's not me who should watch her back," I snarled down at her as I fisted her hair. She let out a screech, her bloody hands flailing as she tried to reach me.

"It's you because I'm going to set fire to your fucked-up world and dance in the ashes. Keep your boys close because I'm coming for them. And once I'm done, you're next."

I punched her again before landing a decent kick to her side. I was just about to smash her ass to the floor when arms wound through mine and tugged me back. Feeling my revenge could come later since I'd pretty much gave it to her good, I let the fight leave me.

"That's enough," Jamie said. "Come on."

She dragged me a few steps from Juliet who sat sobbing on the floor, her blood coating her hands and gym clothes.

"Say one thing to the principal or anyone else, and I swear to god, I won't stop next time. Fucking try me, Juliet. I'd lose everything just to watch you fucking burn, you evil bitch."

She didn't answer me, only cried harder. I let Jamie lead me out of the locker room. We didn't bother stopping to go to class. When we made it to my locker in the hall, I finally turned to look at her.

"Why?" I asked.

"I heard what she said," Jamie answered softly. "I-I didn't know any of this happened to you, Rosalie. I'm sorry."

I nodded, my throat tight. "It's my fault. I should've just told you in the beginning."

"We suck." Jamie laughed softly, her brows crinkling in worry.

"And Ian, he swore he'd hurt you if I didn't agree to be his. I never had sex with him, Jamie. He lied. He's been one of my biggest tormentors."

"Oh, Rosalie." Jamie wrapped her arms around me. We hugged it out in the hall, both of us crying softly.

When we pulled away from one another, I gave her a watery smile. "I have to finish this. My way."

Jamie nodded. "But Rosalie, we could just get the authorities involved—"

"Maybe, but not yet. I need more proof. If I'm sending Ian away, he needs to be gone for a long ass time. He's dangerous. I-I don't think he's ever going to let me go." I swallowed hard at the realization.

"God, Rosalie. What do you need me to do?"

"Stay away from me. He doesn't want me around you. He already told me. Just let me figure this out—"

"I'm not going to let you do this alone. You never should've been alone to start with. I'm the worst friend. I don't even know how you'll ever forgive me—"

"Jamie, I was never mad at you. There's nothing to forgive."

She sniffled and hugged herself. "Thank you, Rosalie. I'm sorry for everything." Her gaze swept over me quickly. "You should wash up. Juliet's blood is all over your hands."

A tear slipped out of my eye. The adrenaline had worn off, and my body shook.

"What happened?" Cole's voice boomed out. He jogged toward me with Enzo in tow. "Rosalie, what happened? Are you OK?"

"I'm fine. Your bitch isn't though. Maybe you should go check on her before she bleeds out on the locker room floor."

"We already know," Enzo murmured, reaching for me.

I took a step away from him. "Don't even think about it, De Luca. *Get. Fucked.*"

Enzo's brows crinkled as he stared back at me. "Rosalie, we're here because Juliet came and got us—"

"Then here I am. She sent her dogs. Do your fucking worst, but I guarantee it's nothing compared to what I'll do back." I stared defiantly up at Enzo who still wore a look of confusion on his face.

"Easy, Rosebud. Why the fuck would you think we're here to hurt you? And on Juliet's orders. That bitch doesn't own me." Cole's gaze darkened as he stared at me.

"Just your cock, right?" I looked from Cole to Enzo. "After all, you're *all* fucking her."

"It's not like that, Sunshine—"

"Oh, shove it up your ass, Enzo! I just talked to Juliet. She told me everything I needed to know. I know how you wanted to break me. I know she knew from the beginning. I know *everything*. Even how you were with her over the weekend. I saw the fucking selfie."

For the first time ever, both guys visibly paled in front of me.

"I was just a fun, little game, huh?"

"Things changed, Rosalie," Cole growled.

"Did they?" I cocked my head at him.

"They did," Enzo whispered.

"Do you deny anything I just said? Do you deny being with Juliet?"

"No," Cole answered in a monotone.

Enzo hung his head as he ran his fingers through his black hair, his rings glinting beneath the fluorescent lights of the hallway.

My heart plummeted to my knees. I didn't know what to expect. Maybe a pretty little lie to make the pain stop. But no.

Cole looked me in the eyes and confirmed what Juliet said. "But we did it to keep you safe —"

"The only one I need to be kept safe from is you guys." I took a step toward them. I reached out and cradled both their faces in my hands.

They leaned into my touch, both of them with hunger burning in their eyes.

"Mark my words, horsemen, the only one you should be worried about keeping safe is yourselves. Because I'm coming for all of you. And I swear I won't stop until you're nothing but a steaming puddle of shit beneath my feet."

"Don't go to war with us, Rosalie," Enzo whispered in a choked voice. "*Don't*. I'm asking you to not do this."

I smiled at him and rested my hands on his chest. He stared down at me with his dark eyes, turmoil burning deep within them.

I went up on my tiptoes and whispered in his ear as his hands landed on my waist, "I'm not afraid of you, Lorenzo De Luca. Not even your mafia daddy frightens me. Death would be a welcomed vacation from my life right now. So if you're going to retaliate, kill me. I'll hand you the fucking weapon." I pulled away from him.

His Adam's apple bobbed in his throat.

"You're making a mistake, Rosalie." Cole grabbed my hand as I turned to leave.

Jamie stood silently behind me the entire time, not moving.

"The only mistake I made was ever letting you anywhere near me, you fucking twisted animal."

"Is that how it's going to be, Rosebud?" Cole's bottom lip trembled. Whether it was from his suppressed rage or something else, I didn't know. Nor did I want to explore it.

"That's how it *is*." I glared at him.

He released my hand and gave me a tight nod. "Then bring it, little girl. But don't be surprised when we fight back. We care for you, but we won't let you ruin us."

"Of course you won't." I smiled at him as I backed away. "You'll fight the entire way down, but that only makes it hotter. I do, after all, *like the torment*." I winked at him before turning on my heel and strutting away, my head held high.

Jamie was at my side in a moment. But it was the look in Cole's eyes that made my throat tight.

Cole didn't fuck around. If I was going to bring it, I'd have my work cut out for me. I needed to tear them apart from the inside out.

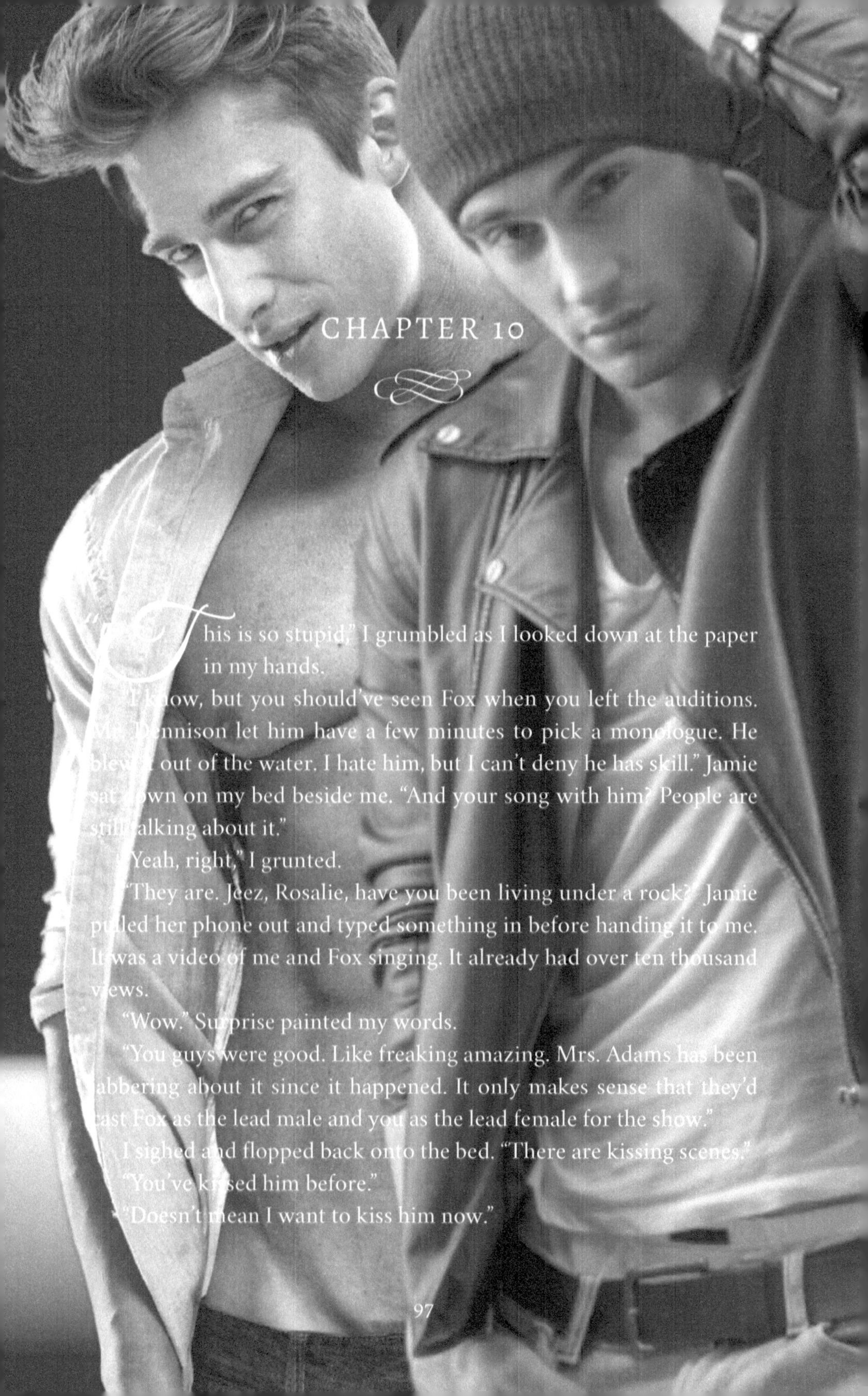

CHAPTER 10

This is so stupid," I grumbled as I looked down at the paper in my hands.

"I know, but you should've seen Fox when you left the auditions. Mr. Dennison let him have a few minutes to pick a monologue. He blew it out of the water. I hate him, but I can't deny he has skill." Jamie sat down on my bed beside me. "And your song with him? People are still talking about it."

"Yeah, right," I grunted.

"They are. Jeez, Rosalie, have you been living under a rock?" Jamie pulled her phone out and typed something in before handing it to me. It was a video of me and Fox singing. It already had over ten thousand views.

"Wow." Surprise painted my words.

"You guys were good. Like freaking amazing. Mrs. Adams has been jabbering about it since it happened. It only makes sense that they'd cast Fox as the lead male and you as the lead female for the show."

I sighed and flopped back onto the bed. "There are kissing scenes."

"You've kissed him before."

"Doesn't mean I want to kiss him now."

"Well, it's going to tear Juliet apart because she auditioned for the lead and didn't get cast at all."

"Silver lining."

"Definitely. They were going to give her a role as an extra, but she pitched a fit about it. So, Mrs. Adams said that was fine and she wouldn't be needed. I honestly think Juliet thought she'd be a shoo-in, but you upended her."

"Bitch can eat shit," I muttered, peeking over at Fox's house. His room was dark. But it was a Friday night, and they had a game. It would be starting within the hour.

Jamie grew quiet for a moment before clearing her throat. "What time do you have to meet Ian?"

"He wants me to meet him before the game." I sat up and took in her reaction.

She nodded and gave me a weak smile. "Is he mean to you?"

I nodded and gave her hand a squeeze. "He's not a nice guy."

"He got really short with me a few times. I just blamed it on stress and stuff. I know his dad is getting out soon."

I nodded again.

"He hits you, doesn't he?" her words were barely above a whisper.

"Sometimes," I murmured.

"Does he. . .make you do things?"

"Sometimes." I released her hand and wiped at my eyes.

"Rosalie, you have to tell someone—"

"I can handle it. I *will* handle it. I just need to get him in a position where he can't run from what he's done."

"He might really hurt you before then—"

"That's why I need to figure it out sooner rather than later."

"Then what's the plan? Let me help."

"I honestly don't have one yet. I figure once I decide what I'm going to do with the horsemen, Ian will fall into place."

"You said you want to tear them apart from the inside, right?"

"I do."

"Do you have any ideas?"

"Actually..." I got to my feet and paced for a moment before turning to her. "I do. The guys are all really tough. The only one I think I can break is Ethan. He's the sweet one. I genuinely think he gave a damn."

"Makes sense. I heard someone say they don't think he's in on it with Juliet."

"Really?"

Jamie nodded. "Think about it. Have you ever seen him with her like the others? He's always off to the side. And seriously, have you looked at him lately? He looks rough. Like he's sick."

"I have," I murmured, thinking about how sad and tired he looked the last time I saw him. "I heard Cole and Fox say there was something wrong with him. I wonder what it is."

"Maybe he has depression or something. Maybe he did love you and is taking this hard. Maybe he doesn't want to be part of the harem Juliet has and can't leave because they're holding something over his head."

"Maybe." I frowned. "He might be my in."

"I say go for it. He misses classes a lot. He's in my calculus class. He hasn't been there in a few days."

"He hates calculus." I smiled at the memory of helping him. How he'd been so eager to learn. How he'd caught on quickly when I'd tutored him.

"I think you should talk to Ethan. Maybe break him away from them."

"Steal him," I said softly, my heart thudding at the possibilities of Ethan being mine. He was gorgeous. Sweet. Funny. Caring. He was the sort of guy any girl would be lucky to have. Minus the bullshit that came with him, of course.

"Do it. I know for a fact he hangs out in the library at lunch. He's always in the nook. I wanted to go in there the other day for some quiet time away from all the rumors." She cleared her throat. "I found him in there."

"Did he talk to you?" The nook was a small, secluded area of the library no one visited because it was dedicated to philosophy books and things of the like. It was all the way in the back through the maze of shelves. It had two large, leather armchairs and a small table. There wasn't much room for anything else.

"He did." She bit her bottom lip.

I sat down at my desk and looked eagerly at her. I cared deeply for Ethan. I couldn't deny it. While I cared for all the guys more than I should, I always felt like Ethan had *earned* my feelings, rather than demanded or stolen them.

"He told me how much I meant to you. He said we should talk. It's one of the reasons I came after you when you finished your audition. I missed you." She gave me a quick smile and blew out a breath. "But I think he was doing drugs or had done drugs. He looked high. I mean, he even acted high. His words were a little slurred, and his eyes looked strange."

I frowned at the information.

"Maybe that's what the guys were talking about with him. Maybe he's smoking too much. Or worse."

"I hope not," I whispered, my heart clenching. My phone buzzed in my pocket. I pulled it out and looked down at the message.

Ian: I'm coming to pick you up. Be ready in ten.

"Shit," I hissed, jumping up. "Ian's on his way."

Jamie didn't need telling twice. She was on her feet and grabbing her stuff.

"Call me if you need me, Rosalie," she said breathlessly as we rushed downstairs.

I yanked open the door, and we hugged for a moment before she ran to her car and got in. I watched as she pulled out of the driveway, driving in the wrong direction. It was a good idea since Ian would be coming in from the opposite side.

I managed to make it upstairs and was in my closet trying to find something to wear when I felt like I was being watched. A yelp left my mouth as I saw Ian leaning against the doorframe to my walk-in closet. I hadn't even heard him come in. My parents weren't home.

Should've locked the damn door!

"You look hot as fuck," Ian commented, his gaze traveling over me in my bra and panties.

I immediately snatched a shirt and tried to cover myself, but he stepped into the room, grabbed it from my hands, and tossed it to the floor.

"I like you like this. All *vulnerable*." His lips brushed against my jaw. "Where are your parents?"

"They'll be back soon."

He chuckled as he dropped his hands to my waist.

"Not soon enough for you, I'm afraid." He pressed his lips to mine, letting me know exactly what he meant by it.

CHAPTER 11

winced as Ian dragged me along the sidelines, his camera
in hand. Being the editor of the school paper, Ian liked to
do the sports photos for the teams. The area between my legs was sore
from his earlier assault of rough fingers and a not-so-gentle mouth.

"Come on," he snapped at me, tugging my arm roughly.

I trotted to keep up and was grateful when we stopped near the
team. Ian snapped some photos, completely losing interest in me. I
shifted awkwardly and looked around. Ethan sat on the bench, his
head hanging. Cole tapped him on the shoulder and said something to
him, but Ethan shoved him away. Cole seemed angry because he
threw up his hands as Fox moved toward them. Enzo stood back and
shook his head. I couldn't see their faces because of their helmets.
Except Ethan. He wasn't wearing one.

Coach called them to a huddle, but Ethan didn't bother moving
from his spot. They ran out onto the field a moment later, Ethan
remaining where he sat. He finally lifted his head and looked behind
him, scanning the crowd. Then his gaze landed on me.

I wasn't far from him at all. His eyes shone, unnaturally bright. His
lips parted. I could almost hear him saying my name as they formed

the word without sound. His dark hair was a hot mess. It stuck up in various directions. Dark circles rimmed his bloodshot eyes.

Ethan looked like hell.

I took a step toward him, not even thinking. His gaze darted from me to someone behind me.

"Get the fuck over here," Ian growled in my ear as he wrapped his arm around my waist and pulled me closer. Ian reached out and turned my face toward him, kissing me deeply, his tongue in my mouth. He winked at me when we broke apart before giving my ass a squeeze.

"Don't even think about it, Rosalie," he whispered before turning back to the game.

I glanced at Ethan to see the devastation on his face. He got to his feet and swayed before he took a stumbling step forward. Enzo saw him first. He slapped Cole on the chest as Ethan shuffled forward, shoving through people to reach me.

"Shit," I choked out.

"Sweetheart," he slurred, reaching for me before he staggered and stumbled, falling forward.

I caught him to my body as he tried to keep himself upright.

"*My Rosalie.*"

"Ethan." I held onto him as Fox and the guys stared in our direction. Even the coach looked confused.

"Get the fuck off my girlfriend," Ian snarled, grabbing hold of Ethan and making to shove him away.

Ethan caught his arm and pushed him hard.

Oh no.

"Fucking piece of shit," Ethan snarled, his face morphing into a mask of hatred and rage. "She's not your girl. She's *mine.*"

I didn't know what the hell to do. There were whistles blowing and people surging forward to try to separate the two as Ethan shoved me roughly aside. I lost my footing and fell to the ground as Ethan punched Ian. Ian hit him back. They tore into one another, fists flying, until they were both on the ground with Ethan on top.

"You stole her. You fucking took her from me!" Ethan shouted through a sob as he pulled back to hit Ian.

Ian moved his head just before Ethan's fist hit the ground. Fox reached them first. He tore Ethan off Ian. Cole and Enzo and half the team tried to hold him back. A few of the players got behind Ian and helped him up but hovered nearby in case he attacked again.

"I don't know what the hell is happening here, but it ends now, Masters. Get the hell off the field. And you..." Coach pointed a finger at Ian. "Don't come onto my field if you're going to fight."

"He attacked me. I defended myself," Ian spat.

Coach nodded tightly before looking to Ethan whose chest was heaving, his wild-eyed gaze locked on me.

"Off the field, Masters. Now."

"Rosalie. Come with me." Ethan tried to step forward, but Enzo and Fox held him in place. He shoved at them, trying to break free, but they held fast. He threw a punch which landed on Fox's helmet.

"Masters!" Coach shouted. A couple assistant coaches moved forward and took hold of Ethan, trying to drag him off the field.

"Rosalie! Please," Ethan shouted. "I need you. I fucking *need* you!"

I stared at him, my heart breaking. Whoever that guy was, he wasn't Ethan. I took a step forward, but Ian reached out and wrapped his hand around my arm.

"Do it and fucking pay, Rosalie."

I tore my arm out of his hold. "Eat shit, Ian."

I ran away from him and toward where they'd led Ethan. I passed by the guys who didn't say a damn word to me. My heart was in my throat. I knew I'd pay for my disobedience to Ian but screw it. Ethan needed me. Something wasn't right.

I had no clue where they'd taken him. I checked the bathrooms first before looking at the building where the crow's nest was for the announcer. I knew there was a sitting area there. Maybe they made him sit there. When I didn't find him, I ran into the locker room, breathless. He was seated on the bench, sobbing alone.

"Ethan," I murmured, approaching him carefully.

His head snapped up, his eyes unfocused. His pads were gone, and he sat in trackpants and a white t-shirt.

"Rosalie?"

"Hey." I kneeled in front of him.

He let out a soft laugh, his eyes unable to focus on me. "You came."

"I did. Are you OK?"

"*Are you?* I pushed you. I didn't mean to." His words came out in a slur as he cradled my face. "I'm sorry, sweetheart. I didn't mean it. I didn't mean any of it. I don't ever want to hurt you."

"Shh," I murmured. "I'm fine." I rested my hands over his.

He gave me a tired smile. "Will you go home with me, Rosalie? I want to keep you forever."

My heart clenched. "I can't."

"You hate me." He released me and stumbled to his feet. "You fucking hate me. *I* hate me."

I watched in horror as he punched a locker, denting it. He did it again and again until the door barely hung.

"Ethan. Ethan, stop!" I called out, terrified of the man before me.

He turned to me, his chest heaving, his eyes dark.

"Let me help you. Will you let me?" I reached out to him.

He stumbled to me, his lips parted. When he reached for me, I closed the distance and drew him into my arms. Ethan towered over me by a foot and outweighed me by a lot, but I held him as he sobbed into my neck.

"I'm not OK, Rosalie. I'm sick. I'm so fucking sick."

"It's OK," I mumbled in a choked voice. "It's OK."

We stood like that for a long time before my body shook, growing weak from his weight on me.

"Can I take you home?" I asked gently. I could smell the alcohol on him. He nodded and lifted his head up.

I cradled his face in both hands. "Where are your keys?"

"My bag," he mumbled.

"Do you need anything else?"

"Just you," he answered in a slur.

"Well, I'm here."

He smiled, his eyes barely open. "Then I'm fine."

I led him out of the locker room and to the parking lot, my body quaking from trying to hold up his weight. When we reached his car, I unlocked it, worried Ian was going to come charging at me. I hurriedly helped Ethan into the passenger's seat and buckled him in before getting in on the driver's side.

As quickly as I could, I pulled out of the parking lot and drove to Ethan's house. He mumbled incoherently in his seat as I clutched the steering wheel. *This was so screwed up.* He was messed up beyond anything I'd ever seen before.

When I pulled into his driveway, I cut the engine and turned to him. His eyes were closed, his lips parted. Sighing, I got out and went to his side.

"Ethan, come on. Let's get you inside."

He grunted and opened his eyes as I tried to shuffle him out of the car. When I got him standing again, we made our way to his front door.

"Keys are on the keyring," he mumbled.

I fumbled for a moment with the keys before getting one of the three on the ring into the lock.

"Are your parents here?"

He shook his head no.

Thank god.

I'd never been in Ethan's house before. It was a cute ranch style, thankfully. I wasn't so sure I could get him upstairs on my own. After a few moments, I finally found his room. Breathlessly, I released him onto his bed.

I dropped to my knees and took his shoes off then helped him onto his side.

"Don't go," he called out weakly as I started to move away to get him some water and aspirin.

"I'm only getting you some water."

He grew quiet. I grabbed him a glass of water from the faucet in his bathroom and stared at myself in the mirror. I looked tired.

And scared. Definitely scared.

Ian was going to kill me. As if sensing my thoughts, my phone vibrated in my pocket.

Ian: You better hope he doesn't touch you. I'll kill him.

I swallowed thickly and stuffed my phone back into my pocket. I rummaged through Ethan's medicine cabinet. A couple bottles of pills fell from the shelf into the sink. I turned them over and read the labels.

Xanax. Ativan. Valium. Morphine. Methadone. Ambien.

"What the actual fuck," I whispered, staring down at the pill bottles. Only a few had pills left in them, and they certainly weren't many.

"Rosalie? Rose?" Ethan's garbled voice called out for me.

I quickly pushed the bottles back into the cupboard before snagging a bottle of aspirin. It was still sealed, so it at least had that going for it. I went back to his room and placed the water and pills on his bedside table.

"Hey." Ethan reached out for me.

"Hey," I answered, taking his hand and sitting on the edge of his bed.

"Are you really here or am I completely fucked?"

"I'm really here."

He smiled, his eyes barely open. "I'm happy."

"I'm glad." My heart ached as I stared down at such a beautiful disaster. I ran my fingers through his dark hair, the silky strands tickling my fingers.

"I like that," he mumbled. "I like when you touch me, Rosalie."

I swallowed the lump in my throat. "Here. Drink this."

I held the water to his lips and watched as he slurped it down.

"Will you stay with me?"

"I-I can't, Ethan."

I let out a squeak as he jolted out of bed, his eyes wild. "You can't leave me. Rosalie. Don't go. Please." His breathing changed, coming out in short gasps.

"Ethan. Hey. Calm down—"

"Rosalie, please. Stay with me. *Please.* You're the only one." A tear slipped from his eye. "I don't sleep. I need you. Don't leave me."

"OK. OK, Ethan. I'll stay," I whispered, pushing my shoes off. Ethan lay down, his breathing still coming in gasps.

Quickly, I moved to lay beside him. I pulled the blanket over us and rested my head on his chest. His arms immediately snaked around me, and his breathing slowed. I listened as his heart hammered hard and fast before it slowed with his breathing.

"You should lie on your side, Ethan."

"I like it this way with you in my arms. It feels good."

I didn't say anything as he twined his fingers through mine and rested them low on his abdomen.

"This is the best dream," he murmured sleepily. "No monsters. No devils. Just me and my angel."

I squeezed his hand, tears prickling my eyes. Ethan's world was nothing like I thought it was. He had his own monsters to battle.

"Can I tell you something?" he called out thickly, his voice heavy with sleep.

"Yes," I whispered.

"I'm sick, sweetheart. It's going to kill me."

My heart clenched at his words. "You can't die on me, Ethan," I said softly into the darkness. "I won't let you."

"Because you're my guardian angel, here to save me." His words were still slurred and jumbled. He grew quiet, not elaborating.

I didn't say anything else, just listening as his breathing became deeper and more even before he let out a soft snore. I simply lay in his arms until sleep took over. Just an angel with her devil.

And tomorrow there'd be hell to pay.

CHAPTER 12

Light barely filtered through Ethan's blinds as I opened my eyes. The first thing I did was look at him. His chest rose and fell with each breath. He looked so beautiful as he lay there. But I couldn't stay. Seeing him like that last night nearly killed me. It opened up my heart but darkened my soul. I hated seeing him the way he was. And his words. . .

I quickly, but gently, untangled myself from him and pressed a soft kiss to his cheek. He murmured my name softly as he rolled over and hugged his pillow.

My heart jerked in my chest, but I kept moving. I pulled my shoes onto my feet and left his room as quietly as I could. I'd just rounded the hallway when I ran into someone.

A hand was placed over my mouth before I could scream.

Enzo.

"Good morning, Sunshine." He removed his hand and smirked down at me.

"What the hell are you doing?" I whispered, my heart still jack hammering in my chest.

"I could ask you the same thing."

"I stayed to make sure Ethan was OK." I shoved past him.

He followed me to the living room. I was grateful there was no one else there.

"And is he?"

"Obviously."

"You're wrong. He's got problems only you can solve."

I stopped and turned to Enzo. "What's going on?"

"What isn't?" Enzo muttered. He moved to the couch and sank down onto it.

I hesitated for a moment before going and sitting in the chair next to it. Enzo gave me his dashing smile.

"Just tell me."

Enzo sighed. "It's better if I tell you at my place. I don't need him waking up and finding out I'm divulging all his secrets."

I surveyed him for a moment before giving him a nod. There was no way I wasn't going to get some damn answers. "Fine. When?"

"Now?" Enzo raised his brows at me. "As long as Prince Charming is safely tucked away in bed."

"He is."

"Good." Enzo got to his feet and nodded to the door. "Come on."

I followed him out to his car. He opened the passenger side door for me, and I slid onto the leather seat. After he closed me in and got behind the wheel, he slid his dark sunglasses on and fired up the engine.

We were on the road before either of us spoke. He was the first to break the silence. "I'm surprised you went after Ethan last night."

"Imagine my surprise to find you in his house when I woke up. Did you stay there?"

Enzo nodded and turned onto another street. "Sure did. I beat the other two in a coin toss for the position."

"I guess it's good you're all so eager to look out for him."

"Oh, Sunshine." He shook his head and gave a wry chuckle. "Baby girl, you know as well as I do it was more about getting you alone. No one is all that eager to go through this hell with Ethan. We do it because we love him, but it's fucking rough. You're just the silver lining to the shitty situation."

"And what's the shitty situation? Why is he spiraling?"

Enzo sighed but didn't answer because his phone rang. "Yeah?"

He grew quiet for a moment. "He's fine. Sleeping it off... Yeah. She was there all night." I glanced at him out of the corner of my eye as he chuckled into the phone. "No. Not yet, Cole. I'm working on it... Dude, eat shit. I'll tell you later."

He shook his head and dropped his phone into his lap before turning into his driveway.

"Come on." Quickly, he got out of the car and was at my side in moments, opening the door to help me out.

I took the hand he offered, my heart racing. Something about his touch did crazy things to my insides.

Keep it together, Rosalie! Enzo is smooth. You know this.

He tugged his sunglasses off, tossed them onto the seat, and shot me a wink. I stared stonily back at him, not wanting him to think my anger was gone. He didn't say a word as he led me into his house.

"Where are your parents?" I asked as we stepped inside.

Enzo's house was big. He lived in one of the gated communities the rich lived in. It wasn't a mansion, but it was big enough.

"Out." He didn't elaborate beyond that.

Instead of going to his basement, he led me upstairs to a room on the left. I followed him in and stood awkwardly in his bedroom. I'd never been in his room before. Any time I'd been with him was in the basement.

"We could've talked in the living room," I said, glancing around at his space. It was clean. Not as clean as Cole's room was, but definitely well taken care of. So far, the guys had impressed me in that area. None of them seemed to be slobs.

"And miss the opportunity to have you on my bed?" He winked at me. "Never."

He gestured for me to take a seat on his made bed. I rolled my eyes at him and sat in his computer chair. The move made him smirk.

He dropped the green canvas designer jacket he'd been wearing onto his dresser before he passed in front of me. He ran his fingers through his black hair. I shifted uncomfortably as his cologne wafted over me. It took everything I had not to breathe him in deeply. But hell. Lorenzo De Luca smelled divine. Like cloves and spice and every damn thing nice.

Reel it in, Rosalie!

"So..." I cleared my throat, noting how it shook as Enzo took a seat on the edge of his bed. *Damn it.* "Tell me what's going on."

"Give me what I want first, and I'll tell you anything you want to know. Within reason, of course."

I narrowed my eyes at him as we locked gazes. "What do you want?"

"Come sit beside me."

"Enzo, seriously—"

He shrugged and scooted back a bit on the bed, his gaze still fixed on me. Sighing, I got up and moved to sit beside him.

"Fine. I'm here. Tell me."

"Kiss me first."

"What? Why?" I sputtered, my heart knocking against my rib cage.

He took my hand in his, lifted it to his lips, and pressed a warm kiss to my knuckles.

"Because I miss the way you taste, Sunshine."

His lips brushed my knuckles again.

"Did I tell you how fucking hot it was to hear about you kicking Juliet's ass?"

"I figured you'd be mad I hurt your girlfriend."

He let out a soft chuckle. "It turned me on thinking of you drawing blood."

"Let me guess. You fucked her after to help soothe the ache."

"No." He smiled and pulled his phone from his pocket. He thumbed through it quickly before showing me a still shot of me from the video he'd made of me with him and Cole in his basement. I was straddling Enzo's lap in my bra, his hands all over me.

"Why do you have that?" I asked in a throaty whisper.

"Because...it helps me when I miss you. When my cock aches to be inside you, I look at this picture. When I come, it's always to you."

My cheeks heated with his dirty words.

"What about Juliet?"

"She can't hold a candle in the darkness when compared to you." He cradled my face in his hands and leaned in. "Kiss me, Sunshine. Give me something else to think about when I hold my cock in my hand."

"It doesn't mean anything, Lorenzo," I whispered, my resolve cracking.

Mother fucking damn it! Everything about Enzo pulled me in. He was the perfect monster. I hauled in a calming breathe. "I just want to know what's wrong with Ethan."

"I'll tell you, babe. Just give me this. I won't tell anyone."

I knew he meant Ian because there was no way Lorenzo De Luca would go behind the backs of his best friends with me. But knowing he might tell them made me smile on the inside.

That could work in my favor. Cole and Fox wouldn't be able to stand me alone with Enzo while they got nothing.

I nodded. A glint of victory flashed in his eyes as he leaned in. *Silly boy, thinking he was winning.* I was simply tightening the reins on my own game. I was taking what was Juliet's. *This* was winning. At least that was what I told myself.

I didn't close my eyes. If I did, I knew I'd fall into that deep, dark hole I'd been clawing my way out of.

Enzo's lips pressed to mine, sending a flurry of butterflies crashing through my insides. I parted my lips, fighting to keep my eyes open. But he won when he deepened the kiss, his tongue caressing mine. I closed my eyes, letting him in, relishing in how he felt against my mouth.

It's OK to want. It's OK to feel. This is OK because you're going to win. I repeated the words over and over in my head as our breathing grew heavier.

He kissed me hard, yet his mouth stayed tender. There was so much fury and demand in the kiss, I couldn't stop myself from raking my fingers through his hair. We both moaned, eating the pleasure, as our hands acted on their own accord, traversing one another's bodies.

The hard planes of Enzo's abdominal muscles flexed beneath my fingers as he pulled me down on top of him. I pushed reason out of my head, completely lost in the guy dubbed the Italian Stallion as he ground his erection against my aching center.

I shamelessly rubbed myself on his hard, jean-clad length, both of us breathless. When his hands slid inside my pants, I didn't stop him. In fact, I unbuttoned his jeans and took his thick cock into my hand.

A moan left my lips as his fingers pushed inside my wet channel. He was far gentler than Ian was. But more demanding. Experienced. He worked me, his thumb on my clit as his fingers moved in and out of me. I ran my hand up and down his dick, keeping pace with his movements.

A sputter of protest fell out of my mouth as he traversed away from my aching center. I thought he might leave me wanting. Instead, he shoved my pants down in a fluid movement, and I, being a glutton for punishment and completely under his spell, kicked them the rest of the way off. I shoved reason out of my head, telling myself this was just another part of the game. It meant nothing.

When his pants and shirt came off, I ran my hands over his hard body. My shirt was gone a moment later followed by my bra and panties. His lips molded to mine, barely breaking away as he devoured my mouth with his hot kisses. The rattle of a package tickled my ears. *Condom. He's going to fuck me.*

My head was cloudy with desire as he expertly rolled the condom on his cock without breaking his lips from mine.

Love drunk. Lust drunk. Totally fucked as he rolled me onto my back, his bulging head at my entrance.

"I'm going to fuck you so hard you won't remember fuck boy's name," he growled, shoving inside me in one fluid motion. I let out a cry as he filled me with his thickness, whimpering beneath the pain and intense pressure. His mouth found one of my nipples, and he sucked it, his tongue whirling around it as he massaged my other breast, his cock moving in and out of me in slow, deliberate motions.

"Oh god," I choked out.

"That's it." He shoved into me hard, making me arch my back. "Fuck, you're tight." He moved faster, pistoning so quickly it felt like he'd started a fire inside me from the friction of his dick against my trembling walls.

I clung to him, breathing hard and moaning as I raked my nails down his back and brought my pelvis up to meet his rough thrusts. He gripped my hips as he went to his knees and pulled me to his waist, burrowing so deeply inside me I moaned out his name.

"That's it, Sunshine." He hammered faster into me, the sound of our flesh meeting filling the room. "Tell me you like this."

"Mm," I whimpered.

"Fucking tell me, Rosalie." He slammed harder into me, his grip tightening. "I won't stop torturing this sweet pussy until you tell me what I want to hear."

"I like it," I cried out. I reached out for him.

He wasted no time in snatching me up and pulling me onto his lap, his dick still buried deep inside me.

"Fuck me," he demanded, nipping at my earlobe. "Ride my cock."

I rocked on his dick, not giving one damn about what the hell we were doing. Enzo was wild, and he brought out the carefree side in me. I was living in the moment, convincing myself I deserved this. I deserved to feel good. I was taking from him. From Juliet. I was the one winning.

His lips met mine in a frenzied kiss, both of us sweating, our bodies sliding against each other as I rode him hard.

"Like this?" I whispered breathlessly against his lips.

"Fucking just like that, beautiful," he breathed out, moving his head down to kiss along my breasts as he helped lift me up and down on his dick. "Fuck, I love your pussy. So fucking good."

The sweeping heat of my impending orgasm gripped me, and I let out a moan of pleasure, throwing my head back. Enzo shoved into me harder, the pain he gave mixed with pleasure as I crashed around him, his groans of ecstasy filling my ears. His cock pulsed inside me as he came down from his high. We both held on to each other, breathing hard.

He traced his fingers lightly over my back, making goosebumps pop along my skin. His lips pressed to mine in a soft kiss.

Realization set in at what I'd done. I hadn't meant to take it that far. *Sane me* knew it was wrong. *Crazy me* wanted it. Both were at war with one another.

I pushed away from his lips and stared at him, horrified.

"Don't look at me like that, Sunshine," he murmured. "We both needed it. We both wanted it. *I won't tell anyone.*"

"Ian will kill me," I choked out. This was definitely fodder to fuck with me. And knowing Enzo the way I did based on past experiences with him and the horsemen, this was fuel for their fire. If they told Ian I screwed Enzo, they probably figured they'd be fucking me over and ruining what I had, thus freeing me up for them. What they didn't know is that he'd probably kill me. For real.

I'd let my lust and desire make my decisions. I'd really screwed this up.

"I *won't* say a word, Rosalie." I was acutely aware of how he was still buried deep within me. "I promise."

"What's the catch?" My voice shook. *There was always a catch.*

"There is none. You have my word." He kissed my palm, his dark eyes locked on mine.

"You won't tell Ian?" My voice shook.

"Never," he murmured, kissing my fingertips. His gaze roamed from mine, and I swallowed hard as he reached out and brushed his fingers against the dull purple bruises on my neck. He said nothing as he crinkled his brows.

"I'll never say a word," he whispered again.

I searched him and found there wasn't an ounce of dishonesty on his face. Feeling slightly more satisfied, I shifted off him and sat on the edge of the bed. Wordlessly, he got to his feet and disappeared into his bathroom. Taking the opportunity, I quickly put my bra and shirt back on, already worried he'd seen the damage on my ribs from Ian. He returned before I had my panties on, his dick free of the condom. I averted my eyes from his equipment as he approached me.

"Lie back," he murmured, giving me a gentle shove.

I went onto my back, and he pushed my legs apart. His eyes darkened as he took in the bruises. With trembling hands, he swept a warm washcloth up my tender center before leaning down and pressing his lips to the sore area. He saw the evidence of what Ian had done to me, but he didn't say anything.

"You're beautiful, Sunshine," he whispered, his gaze locked on mine from between my legs as I bit my bottom lip, worry coursing through me. "Don't worry."

He moved away and helped me to sit up. I didn't say a word as I pulled the remainder of my clothes on. Enzo did the same. When we were both fully dressed, he sat beside me and reached out and thumbed my bottom lip until I released it from my teeth. He cupped my cheek and gave me a sweet smile.

"Ask me what you want to know."

Trying to get past what we'd just done was difficult, but Ethan was more important than another one of my fuck ups. "What's wrong with Ethan? Is he sick?" My voice was hoarse and shaky.

"He is, but not in the way you think. Ethan has a rough past. I don't want to tell you about it since it's his story, not mine, but he's under a lot of stress. It's made him slip into some of his old ways."

"Drugs," I said softly.

Enzo nodded and dropped his hand from my face. "He was doing good for so long. He only hit weed every now and then. Then all this shit happened. He's not handling it well. We'll get him better. We've done it before."

"I'm scared."

"I am too. But I know him. He's trying. He just needs time."

I nodded. "Is it my fault?"

"No, Sunshine. He's haunted by his own demons."

"But he was fine before all this." I gestured around, tears stinging my eyes.

Enzo looked down at his hands and sighed. "Don't blame yourself. Ethan was happiest when you were with us. He's just going through some shit. Breakups are hard." He looked up and gave me a sad smile.

His phone rang before I could say anything. He pulled it out of his pocket and looked down at the screen, Juliet's name on it. He sighed and denied the call.

"I should go." I got to my feet and winced. I was definitely sore.

Enzo grabbed my hand, a sad look blanketing his face. "I'll drive you home."

I nodded and followed him out to the car. Once again, he opened my door for me and made sure I was safely inside before shutting me in and climbing behind the wheel.

We rode in silence to my house, his hands tight on the wheel. When I cast a glance at him, I noticed a muscle thrumming along his jaw. His brow was furrowed.

What's wrong with him? Is he really that upset about Ethan? Or is it what we did together? Is he going to tell? Oh god. What if he recorded it? But he didn't have his phone out. In fact, it was in his pocket on the floor after we stripped naked.

He pulled into my yard and put the car in park. The thoughts rolling around in my head were shoved to the side as we both sat. We were silent for a beat before he spoke.

"I miss you, Sunshine."

"Yeah, well, Juliet seems to be keeping you busy. You'll forget about me soon enough." My words were laced with sadness.

He reached over and wrapped his arms around me in a fierce hug. "I'll never forget about you. You're my first love. My last love. We'll be together again."

Tears burned my eyes at his words. I pushed away from him and opened the door. The guys sure knew how to play this game. I'd have asked for pointers if I thought it wouldn't show my weakness.

Enzo didn't try to stop me from getting out, and I didn't turn around as I closed the door and stepped into the sunshine.

CHAPTER 13

"Did you fuck him?" Ian seethed at me as I sat on his bed the next day. I couldn't get Ethan and Enzo out of my head. I hadn't heard from either one of them since Enzo had dropped me off at home.

"No."

"Lying bitch," Ian roared, lunging forward and pushing me onto my back. He hovered over me, his mouth twisted into an angry frown. "Don't fucking lie to me."

"I didn't fuck Ethan, Ian. I swear it," I whispered, omitting everything about Enzo. "I-I didn't do anything with Ethan. He didn't even try."

Ian glared down at me. I thought he was going to hit me, but instead he let out deep breath and rested his forehead against mine.

"I believe you. You'd be a fucking idiot to go behind my back."

A breath of relief escaped my lips, but that relief was soon replaced by fear of the monster hovering over me.

"Just don't fucking embarrass me like that again. Do you know how it looked to have my girlfriend running off to take care of her ex?"

"I'm sorry." It was a lie. Remorse was the last thing I felt for going to Ethan, and I certainly didn't give a shit how it made Ian feel.

He kissed me, his hands moving beneath my shirt.

"Ian," I managed to say between his kisses.

"Mm?"

"I have to work on memorizing my lines for the musical."

"Fuck the musical. You're not in it."

I shoved at him, anger taking over.

He frowned down at me. "What?"

"This is something I want, Ian. I need it. I'm trying to get into Mayfair. They're going to have college reps at the show."

"Are you majoring in music? I thought you were going to be a doctor or some shit."

"I want a career in music. *Please*. Don't ruin this for me. It's my dream."

His frown deepened as he stared down at me. "I don't want you around Evans."

"Ian, I want nothing more than to bring him down. You don't have to even concern yourself with what he wants."

"Prove it."

"What?"

"Show me how much you want it. Prove you're mine."

I tried not to spit in his face as he kissed along my jaw. While Ian hadn't tried to actually fuck me, he'd hinted that was his goal. Today would be just another time he wouldn't get his way, but I was willing to do anything besides that to get him off my case.

"What do you want me to do?"

"Surprise me," he answered, nipping at my ear lobe.

I knew where this was going, but there was no way I was going to have sex with him.

Instead, I pulled his face back to mine and kissed him like I meant it, thinking about Enzo the entire time.

It helped substantially.

Envisioning Enzo's hands on me, his tongue against mine, the way he thrust his dick deep into my body had me pawing at Ian. Ian returned my affections in full force, his hands squeezing my breasts, his tongue in my mouth. I reached down, trying to keep the image of Enzo forefront in my mind, and unbuttoned Ian's pants and pushed them down his hips.

I sat up, our mouths never parting, and managed to get on top. I yanked my shirt off and straddled his waist.

"Fuck," he growled. If playing this ugly role kept Ian off my ass for any amount of time, I'd do what I could without spreading my legs for him.

He let out a breath, his Adam's apple bobbing in his throat as I stared down at him. He cupped my lace covered breasts, his lips parted. I kept imagining it was Enzo. His hands. His breathing.

I moved farther down Ian's body and tugged his boxers down. He went up on his elbows, his eyes wide, as I took his length in my hand. I hated I was doing this. But survival was the name of the game with Ian, and I had to live. With my eyes locked on his, I sucked him into my mouth. A first for us.

"Fucking hell," he moaned out as I licked and sucked on him. He thrust his hips up to meet my mouth, hitting the back of my throat with each movement.

I gripped his thighs, letting him do what made him feel good, the whole time picturing Enzo being in my mouth. It made the entire thing bearable.

Ian wrapped his hand around my hair and pushed my head down faster. I opened wider for him, just wanting to get this over with. A burst of hot liquid splashed on my tongue moments later as he moaned loudly, his cock twitching.

I swallowed quickly and pulled away, watching as he flopped on his back, his breathing deep.

"Come here," he commanded in a raspy voice.

I crawled back up to him, and he pulled me down to his side.

"Lie with me."

We lay in silence.

"You did that on your own."

"I really want to be in the musical," I answered back, not

completely truthful with him. I wanted so much more than the musical. Not to being murdered was one of the things I really wanted.

"Fine. Just don't fuck up."

I knew there was a chance he'd lie, but I was over the moon at his response. For the most part, he'd been keeping his word to me. It didn't bring forth any warm, fuzzy feelings for the monster, but it gave me peace. It was the best I could ask for given my current circumstances.

He tightened his hold on me, his eyes closed.

"Can I get dressed?"

"No," he murmured.

I didn't argue. I lay against him in my bra and jeans, our skin touching.

"My dad gets out soon," he said softly.

"I know."

"I'm going to go meet him at the prison. We're going to dinner." He let out a dry laugh. I didn't say anything as he continued, "My mom is pissed I'm going, but he's my dad, you know?" *This* was the Ian I remembered. Just a guy talking and not beating the shit out of me.

Speaking to me like we were friends.

"You have to do what feels right for you, Ian. Doesn't really matter what anyone else thinks. Maybe seeing your dad will help." I had no idea why I was trying to counsel the lunatic, but there I was, being his damn friend when he only deserved my hatred.

"I don't need help with anything. I have everything I've ever wanted right now."

"But what about later? Don't you want more?"

"No." He didn't elaborate, and I didn't ask. It was probably the best conversation we'd had since all this shit started. It didn't make me love him or even like him, but at least I could see a shred of humanity in the monster.

Against my better judgement, I fell asleep beside him, all sorts of wild ideas racing through my head. Having Enzo buried inside me was a hard image to get out of my head. The thought of him doing the same with Juliet made nausea twist my guts, making bile burn my throat. Then seeing Ethan broken hurt even more. Every thought in my head circled around the horsemen and how I could break apart their circle to take what was mine. It would ruin their friendships. I'd fucked Enzo. If the guys found out, I was sure it would be a blow to their egos. *And Juliet.* I was going to bring that bitch to her knees.

There wasn't a downside to any of it.

And even if there was, I was still in because maybe I was a lot more like Cole than I cared to admit. Maybe I liked the torment too.

CHAPTER 14

When classes rolled around the following Monday, I followed my routine like always. Ian wasn't there, which made me ecstatic. He said he had something to do, but he didn't elaborate. And I didn't push because I simply didn't give a shit.

Jamie and I kept our distance, opting to text instead. Deciding to check out the backstage area to see if they'd started working on painting the set for the musical, I skipped lunch and made my way there. No one was in the auditorium, which didn't surprise me. I was looking down at a box of props when someone punched the wooden set wall next to my head. I let out a yelp and jumped away, worried Ian had come back.

But it wasn't him. It was Fox, and he looked pissed.

"What the *fuck* is this shit?" he spat at me, holding his phone out.

The blood rushed from my face as I took in the image of me shirtless, sleeping beside Ian in his bedroom. That bastard had taken the photo while I was out and sent it to Fox. But really, he'd done me a favor.

"You're seriously fucking this guy? I thought you were just teasing us, trying to torment me. I didn't know you were actually doing this shit!" Fox punched the wall again, his face red. I'd never seen him look so pissed. "What the *fuck*, Rosalie!"

I didn't back away from him. No, I approached him, our bodies so close they nearly touched, and glared up at him as his chest heaved in and out with his heavy, angry breathing.

"*You're* fucking Juliet. *I'm* free. I can do whatever the hell I want, Fox. How does it feel? It hurts, doesn't it?"

"Yes," he choked out. His body trembled. "How could you, Rosie? You know who he is. Who his family is." His voice cracked as he stared down at me. "He tried to hurt you. Did I push you into this? Do you really hate me *this* much?"

"I could ask you the same question," I murmured. "You cheated on me with my *enemy*. Juliet told me everything."

Fox snorted. "I doubt she told you everything."

"You lied to me. You tricked me. Used me for your own amusement, as a game. You broke my heart, Fox, when all I ever did was love you. I loved you even when you hated me. But you?" I shook my head sadly. "You took my heart and played a dangerous game with it. Everything I've done, you deserved. I'm not finished. Not by a long shot. By the time this is over, I'll have taken everything from you. I'll have ripped apart everything you ever loved because that's what you did to me."

"I'm begging you to stop before you destroy *everything*, Rosalie. Please, baby. *Please.* Come back to me. It's not too late." His voice was barely above a whisper. "I won't hurt you. I fucking swear it. *Please. Trust me.*"

"You already did. Besides, I don't want to *share* you, Fox, and I-I love—" The words were bitter on my tongue and a complete lie, but I said them with such ferocity, he paled.

"Don't you dare fucking say Ian Hall, Rosalie." His body quaked with fury as he glared down at me, a sheen of tears in his eyes. "Please let that bullshit go. Give me the chance to tell you everything. I just need you to listen, Rosie."

I stared up at him, my heart breaking. Before I could say another word, his lips crashed against mine, stealing the breath from my lungs. So many emotions fired off in my head, I couldn't think straight.

He wrapped his strong arms around me and held me tight as he kissed me.

"Fox, no," I managed to say around his fierce kiss.

"Yes," he growled back, kissing me again. "You're *my* girl. You always were. I'm not letting you go. You can't make me."

I pulled away, breathless, as he cradled my face. "Watch me."

"Don't do this," he whispered again, peppering my lips with kisses. "What does he have on you, Rosalie? Tell me so I can fix it. *This isn't you.*"

"I need to go."

"No." His bottom lip shook as he pulled away and looked down at me. "Please. *Stay.*"

I peered up at him, my resolve faltering. Ethan was in trouble. Enzo and I had fucked over the weekend. Cole had cornered me in the bathroom. They were each trying to steal back pieces of me. And I wanted to say yes, god help me, I did. It could end a lot of problems but would start a whole slew of new ones.

I opened my mouth, all my heartache bubbling to the surface. I was so tired of hurting. I was ready to declare a loss and let the chips fall where they may. If it meant letting go, so be it. Maybe the guys could help me with the Ian issue. Hope sprung up in my heart.

But could I forgive them?

Fox's breath caught as he stared down at me, like he knew I was ready to come back to whatever fucked up mess I'd go into. Maybe he'd leave Juliet. Maybe he'd be mine for good. I could have my guys back and be happy again. I could get rid of Ian and let whatever shit storm he had planned happen.

"Fox," I whispered. "I ..."

"Yes, baby?"

"I want y—"

"Fox?" Juliet called out.

He stiffened. His Adam's apple bobbed in his throat.

"What are you doing?" She sashayed closer, her eyes narrowed. He dropped his hands and took a step back.

"I hope your answer isn't what I think it is. You know what that could mean..."

He closed his eyes for a moment as I reached out for his hand. He took another step back.

My heart shattered at my feet as he shook his head at me, sadness morphing over him.

"There's nothing going on. We were talking."

And just like that, my hatred was back in full force.

"I want Ethan. Where is he?" Juliet twined her arm through Fox's as he tried to lock gazes with me.

I looked away, not falling for his shit.

"I don't know. Probably on the bleachers," Fox answered in a monotone.

"I miss him," she pouted. "He said he'd come over last time, but he didn't."

I ground my teeth.

Not Ethan, you raggedy bitch.

"Rosalie, were you going to say something?" Juliet asked, looking at me in surprise like she hadn't known I was there the entire time, a wicked glint in her eyes. She never told on me for the locker room, but I could see how heavy the makeup was around her eyes where the bruising was still healing.

"Uh, yeah, I was. I was going to tell Fox something." I gave him the best smile I could muster.

"Rosie," he murmured, giving a slight shake of his head. "No."

"I want you to go to hell."

"Fuck. Rosalie, wait!" Fox shouted as I spun on my heel and strode away as fast as I could.

"Fox! Don't you dare!" Juliet called out.

And for a moment I thought Fox might follow me and tell her to go to hell, but the second I made it to the hallway, I realized I was alone.

He hadn't come after me. But I'd expected nothing less. I had to find Ethan.

❦

ETHAN WAS HARDER to track down than I was. I still hadn't seen him by the following week. I even went to the cafeteria on lunch, hoping to catch a glimpse of him. When I'd tried to send him a text, it failed to send. When I'd called, I got a recording saying his number had been disconnected. Driving to his house seemed dangerous since Ian watched my every move. I couldn't just get a hold of the guys to ask about him, so I waited. Jamie was my next way in. As I sat in my first class of the day, I sent a text to her.

Rosalie: If you see Ethan, tell him to meet me in the nook at lunch. Tell him not to tell anyone.

Jamie: I saw him this morning. If he shows up for class, I'll tell him. Fingers crossed!

Lunch couldn't come quick enough. The moment the bell rang, I dashed away, making sure to avoid Ian. I'd told him I was going to use the time to learn my lines. He seemed fine with it considering he was still stuck on the blowjob I'd given him. Lucky for me, he hadn't asked me to do it again and hadn't really touched me since, other than his random fawning and kissing he did in front of people.

When I got to the library, I was thankful Mrs. Pierson, the librarian, wasn't there. She tended to leave the library for lunch, which was perfect. I went to the back, saying a silent prayer Ethan had shown up. Jamie had texted me and said she'd delivered the message. But apparently he'd only stared at her like he was confused.

When I entered the nook, I nearly jumped for joy. Ethan was sitting in one of the leather chairs. His hands shook as he raked his fingers through his hair. I frowned at him as he drew in a shaky breath, his hair now a wild mess on his head. I stepped forward, worry coursing through me.

"Ethan? What's wrong?"

"Rosalie..." His voice cracked as he rose to his feet to greet me. "I wasn't sure if you'd come."

He gave a slight tremor as I approached him.

"Of course I'd be here. I'm the one who asked you to meet me," I murmured, looking around to make sure we were alone.

"Right." He shook his head, his eyes finally locking on mine. "Right. I know that."

"Beats the bathroom, right?" I attempted a weak joke that didn't even make his lips twitch. He looked like hell. His clothes were rumpled. The dark circles around his eyes made his eye color more prominent. He looked thinner. Sicker.

I shifted awkwardly and backed away from him as he sat back in his seat. Maybe this was a bad idea.

"Don't go," he croaked, reaching for me. Desperation clouded his features, and my armor cracked.

I moved back to him.

"Do you want me to get Fox?"

He shook his head and stretched further to reach me. When he took my hand, I didn't tug it away.

"Do you love him?" he whispered, his voice cracking.

"Fox?"

He shook his head again. "No. *Him*. Ian. The one you're torturing us with. H-Have I really lost you?"

I didn't answer as he gave my hand a squeeze.

"Don't do it, Rosalie. *Sweetheart*. Please. I-It's killing me."

I kneeled in front of him. He immediately reached out and cradled my face, his brows crinkled.

"I miss you so fucking much. I can't live like this anymore. *I won't*."

Panic swept through me at his words.

"Ethan, don't do anything foolish."

"I'm not telling you I'm going to kill myself, but... if I take too much, I won't fight it."

"What are you talking about?" I didn't want him to know Enzo had told me.

His bottom lip quivered, and a river of tears flooded his pale cheeks. "There's so much you don't know about me. So fucking much. I have a past, Rosalie. It haunts me. You were my comfort. Without you, I'm going crazy. It's only a matter of time."

"Ethan—"

"Shh," he wept, his body trembling. "Hold me. Please. I need you." His Adam's apple bobbed in his throat as he stared back at me. "I'm losing it. I'm fucking losing it."

I moved forward and wrapped him in a tight hug. His body shook against mine as he wept, his face buried in my neck, his tears staining me with his torment.

"I fucked up, Rosalie. I fucked up." He repeated it over and over as I held him.

"It's OK. It'll be OK," I murmured as I held him.

"I don't love her. I *hate* her. I want her to die. I want to kill her." His words were broken and scattered as he continued to cry. "I'm going to do really bad things."

"Ethan." I pulled away amid his soft protests and stared him in his tear-soaked eyes.

"You're a beautiful person, and you're going to do beautiful things someday. None of those things will hurt anyone."

"But I already hurt you," he whispered, blinking. The tears clinging to his dark lashes fell down his cheeks.

I wiped them away and gave him a watery smile.

"And I'm still standing."

"But not beside me," he answered hoarsely. "How do I fix it? Tell me. I love you, Rosalie. I fucking love you so much. I always knew I would."

Before I could form a coherent thought, his lips crashed against mine, sending all remaining sense from my body. His kiss was rough, fierce, completely opposite of everything that was Ethan. He tangled his fingers in my hair, his strong arms holding me so tightly I had trouble breathing as he plundered my mouth.

I let out a whimper as he fisted my hair, sending delicious flickers of pain through my scalp. I allowed myself a moment of freedom with him, telling myself to stick to the plan of breaking the horsemen apart.

But I couldn't. Not right then. I didn't want to hurt him with ugly words. There wasn't anything within me that wanted to harm Ethan.

I wanted *him* though. I wanted him so badly it hurt. I needed my sweet, caring Ethan back. I wanted to kiss and touch him. I wanted to make promises to him that would make him smile.

But with Ethan's kiss, I found my reservations in ashes around my warded off heart. New ideas cropped up. Ugly ideas. Ideas which were borderline crazy and absolutely dangerous. But we both wanted something. Me, revenge. Him, my love. But I wouldn't hurt him. I'd keep him.

I focused on how Ethan's taut muscles felt as I ran my hands beneath his shirt. He shivered beneath my touch. Ethan Masters was all mine. *Always* mine.

"Seems you two are having a party I wasn't invited to."

I jerked out of Ethan's hold despite his grumblings and peered up to find Cole leaning against a bookshelf, his arms folded over his chest. His blue-eyed gaze flicked from Ethan to me, both of us wearing varying degrees of guilt. Cole dragged his fingers along his jaw and around to grip his neck as he shoved off the bookcase and stalked forward.

"I brought what you needed." He tossed a baggie of pills at Ethan. "You're welcome."

Ethan quickly fisted the bag before I could make out exactly what it was, but I didn't need them to tell me.

Drugs.

What kind, I wasn't sure, but Ethan's words from earlier took hold. *If I take too much...*

My heart raced in my chest.

"Ethan—"

"I'm sorry," he whispered. "I-I have to. It's the only thing that helps me."

"You don't have to, Ethan."

He glanced away from me, tightening his hand around the baggie, his eyes glassy.

I shook my head, got to my feet, and backed away.

He snapped his attention back to me. "Don't go."

"Ethan..." I shook my head, looking from his fist around the baggie to his face. Worry clouded his features. "I-I need to go."

I didn't wait to listen to his protests. I stormed out of the stacks, but I didn't make it far before a hand gripped my arm and pulled me to a stop.

"I know you're all about revenge and making us suffer, but if you're going to hurt us, don't fucking target Ethan."

"Don't tell me what the fuck to do, Cole," I snarled at him, trying to tug my arm out of his hold. I was already pissed about Ethan's drug issues and the way Fox had treated me. I sure as hell didn't want to deal with Cole's shit.

He tightened his hand, causing me to wince.

"Ethan is my friend, Rosalie. He's got shit going on in his head that isn't anything to do with you. And you just made it worse by sparking hope in him. If he dies, it'll be on your head. Fix whatever you just fucking started."

I swallowed the lump in my throat and glared up at Cole. "If Ethan dies, I'll share the blame with you, you fucking monster, because you gave him the means."

"I gave him relief. You gave him the fucking reason. *Fix. It. Rosalie.*" His words were clipped with venom as he glowered at me. "And when you're done, rethink your scheme to hurt us with your fuck boy. Ethan's not the only one who misses you. He's just the one who doesn't hide it as well."

"I'm never coming back, Cole."

He released my arm and smirked at me as he brushed his knuckles along my cheek. "Wrong, Rosebud. We're never letting you leave." He leaned in, his lips tickling my ear as whispered, "Only in death will we part, and even then, I'll search heaven and hell to find you."

He didn't need to elaborate further. Instead, he sauntered away, leaving me standing in the center of the aisle, my pulse roaring in my ears, his words on repeat in my head.

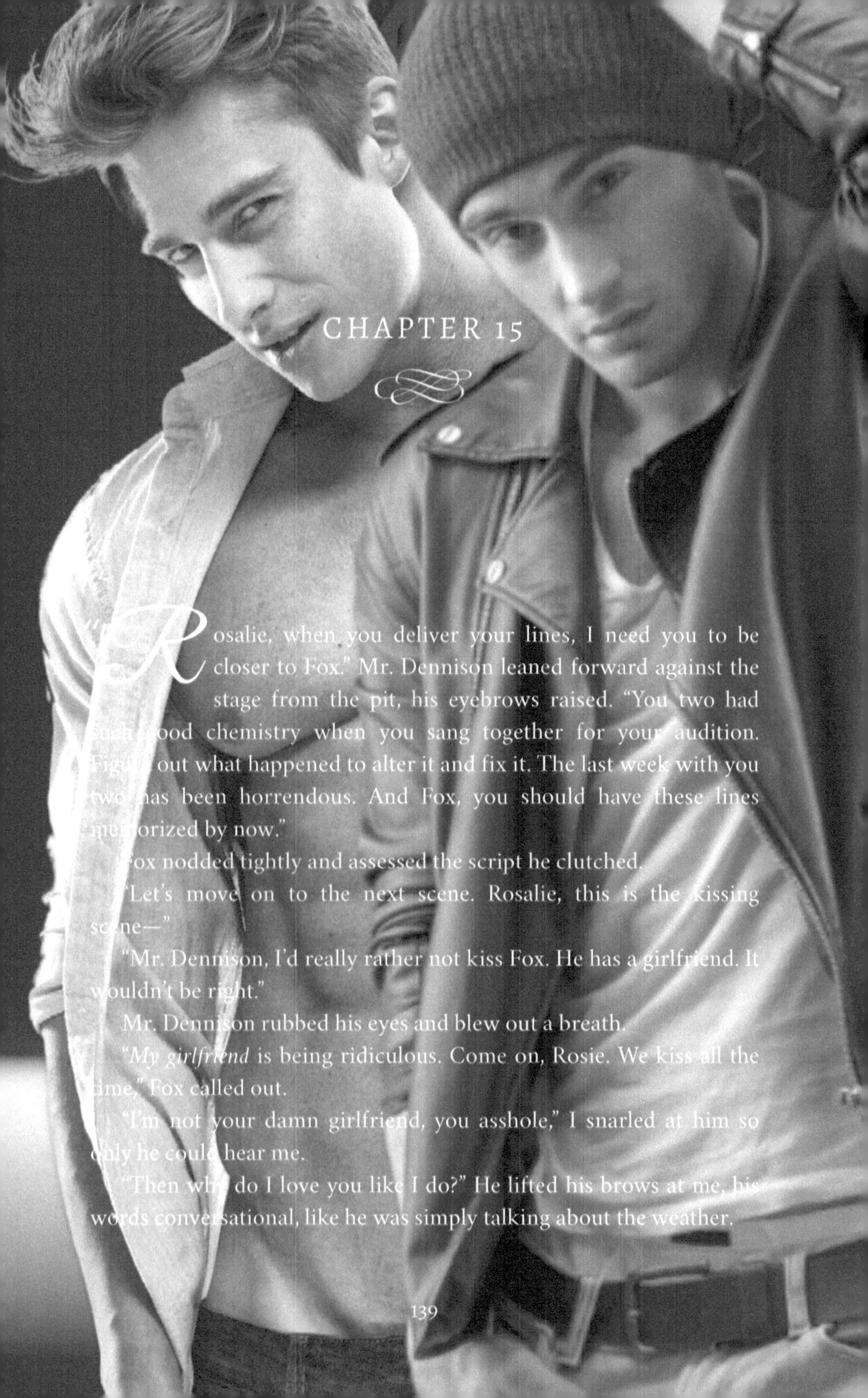

CHAPTER 15

*R*osalie, when you deliver your lines, I need you to be closer to Fox." Mr. Dennison leaned forward against the stage from the pit, his eyebrows raised. "You two had such good chemistry when you sang together for your audition. Figure out what happened to alter it and fix it. The last week with you two has been horrendous. And Fox, you should have these lines memorized by now."

Fox nodded tightly and assessed the script he clutched.

"Let's move on to the next scene. Rosalie, this is the kissing scene—"

"Mr. Dennison, I'd really rather not kiss Fox. He has a girlfriend. It wouldn't be right."

Mr. Dennison rubbed his eyes and blew out a breath.

"*My girlfriend* is being ridiculous. Come on, Rosie. We kiss all the time," Fox called out.

"I'm not your damn girlfriend, you asshole," I snarled at him so only he could hear me.

"Then why do I love you like I do?" He lifted his brows at me, his words conversational, like he was simply talking about the weather.

"Don't mix up love and obsession. They're two very different things, Evans."

He let out a soft chuckle.

"Let's just do the scene, please." Mr. Dennison waved his hand and backed away.

I glared at Fox. He fixed his face into an emotionless mask as Mr. Dennison called action. I delivered my lines without issue, having memorized most of them. Fox seemed to know this scene better than the others. I made sure to stand closer to Fox and really put my heart into the scene so we could get the hell out of there faster. The last thing I wanted to do was kiss him.

He reached for me and pulled me close before dipping his head down, his eyes locked on mine.

"I'm sorry about the other day, Rosie," he murmured.

"Kiss my ass," I whispered back.

"I'd love to, baby." He pressed his mouth to mine, his hands tightening on my waist.

I broke the kiss off quickly, my body betraying me as heat gathered between my legs.

"Not bad. Let's move on. That scene wasn't as atrocious as the others. Fox, I want you to go with Mrs. Adams and work on the vocals for your big solo number. Everyone else, listen up. The local paper will be here in the coming days to take photos and run our story in the paper. We want to sell out. The money from the musical funds the theater department. And trust me folks, we *need* it. That being said, I need all of you here at every rehearsal from here on out. That includes a certain quarterback." Mr. Dennison shot a look at Fox. "That's all. Rosalie, you can leave if you want. Tomorrow, we'll work on your solo."

"Thanks, Mr. Dennison." I sauntered off stage, eager to get the hell out of there. But worry coursed through me at the prospect of the paper running a story on the production. My dad was going to find out soon enough. Figuring out how to head him off needed to become my top priority.

"Rosalie. Wait!" Fox called out, trotting toward me.

I pretended like I didn't hear him and kept walking.

"Damnit, Rosie. Wait." He dashed in front of me, blocking my escape.

"You need to go meet with Mrs. Adams."

"She can wait. I want to talk to you."

"Email me." I shoved past him, but he got in front of me again.

"We both know you won't even look at it. Come on, Rosie. I'm sorry about the other day. I meant what I said though. I want *you.* Just...give me time, OK?"

"You want me to be your backburner bitch while you fuck my tormentor?" I snorted at him. "You're crazier than I thought. Get lost."

"It's not like that, Rosalie. Christ, how many times do I need to tell you—"

"That's the thing, Fox. You don't *need* to tell me at all because it doesn't matter. Go learn your lines so we don't look like a couple tools onstage when the musical opens."

"Does your dad know?" he asked softly.

I bristled. "No."

"Are you going to tell him? We're going to be in the paper, Rosie. He's going to see it."

"It doesn't matter." *Oh, but it did.* I needed to tell him before he was blindsided with it.

"I can be with you if you need someone—"

"I have someone," I snapped at him. "And so do you. So piss off, Evans."

"You're going to feel really fucking stupid when you realize why I'm doing what I'm doing, Rosie," Fox snapped back.

"No, because by that point, I'll have already moved on, and you'll just be a bad fucking memory." I shoved him aside and walked away. If he followed me, I vowed to plant my foot between his legs. Luckily, he didn't.

I had bigger things to be worried about. Namely, my father and Ethan.

I marched to the parking lot, my mind on Ethan since I couldn't do shit about my dad. Dusk had settled, casting an eerie glow around. Ian had told me we didn't need to meet after rehearsal because he was busy doing something for work, which I assumed meant selling drugs or something else equally illegal. I wanted to see Ethan. It had been eating at me since I walked away from him that day in the library. I knew choosing him was wrong, but I promised myself it wouldn't be like that. Maybe it would all work out in the end, and I'd at least get him somehow.

In that moment, wishes seemed to be coming true because there he was, standing beside my car.

"Ethan?"

He didn't say a word, his eyes wild. I paused, worry coursing through me. He rushed at me and wrapped his arms around my body after tugging my keys out of my hand.

"What are you doing?" I cried out.

He didn't answer. This wasn't like him. Ethan wasn't *this* guy. Fear gripped me as I realized I could be in danger if he'd completely lost his mind.

"Ethan!" I struggled against him, but his hold tightened.

He let out a snarl as I clawed at his arms. He lifted me off my feet like I was feather-light and carried me to my car. I kicked and thrashed against him, my pulse thundering in my ears. When we got to the passenger side, he set me back on my feet and shoved me against the door, his green eyes locked on mine, his body leveled against me. His chest heaved in and out as he breathed, a muscle popping along his jaw. If I had to guess, he was pissed, an emotion that didn't suit the sweetheart I'd come to know. Or at least *thought* I knew. Lord knew I'd been off the mark on all the guys.

"Shut up," he growled as I started to open my mouth again.

I snapped it closed, shocked by his harsh tone.

"What are we doing?" I asked softly as he grabbed my arm and opened the car door.

"Just get in the fucking car and keep your mouth closed."

"Ethan, this isn't like you—"

"Thing is, Rosalie, you never really got to know *me*. So maybe this is exactly like me." He didn't elaborate as he shoved me inside. "If you try to run, trust me, I'll catch you."

I swallowed the lump in my throat as he slammed my door closed. I watched as he walked around the front, his dark brows crinkled, his mouth turned down into a deep frown. Something was definitely wrong with him.

"Ethan," I started again as he slid behind the wheel and started the car.

"Don't fucking speak, Rosalie. I'm not joking," he murmured, putting the car into gear and peeling out of the parking lot.

"I'm not joking either, you asshole!" I shouted, grinding my teeth. "Pull the car over, Ethan. You're really scaring me. This isn't you. You're high or drunk or something!"

He clamped his jaws shut tightly as he sped up.

"I swear I'll jump out," I threatened, reaching for the handle.

He let out a dark laugh and shook his head. "Seems like a bad idea, sweetheart. Might hurt that pretty face of yours when it hits the pavement."

I stared at him, not sure who this man was. If I didn't know better, I'd think I was with Cole with how Ethan was behaving.

"Where are you taking me?" I whispered.

He remained quiet as we cruised along the highway.

"Ethan, answer me!"

"Just fucking ride, Rosalie!" he snarled, shooting me a glare that made my blood run cold.

His voice grew soft, "Just...Please. Just ride."

My heart thudded hard in my chest as he guided the car onto the freeway, heading away from the city. Scared, I pulled out my phone to call for help. Ethan reached over and tried to snatch it from my hands, but I jerked it away at the last moment, putting as much distance between us as I could. The car swerved. I gasped as Ethan growled, righting it.

"You call someone, and it'll be another mistake, sweetheart."

"The first being ever trusting you!" I snapped back as he tried to reach for the phone again. I let out squeak of pain as he latched onto my forearm and squeezed. The ache from his hold had me dropping the phone. It tumbled to the floorboards where I lost sight of it.

"You're hurting me," I whimpered when he didn't let go. "Ethan!"

His green eyes flashed at me as he whipped the car onto the offramp, his hold lessening just enough to stop me from crying out again. I gripped the arm rest as he jerked the car onto a side road. Then he whipped down an abandoned road far outside of town. The colors from the autumn forest whizzed past us in the headlights. Dust billowed up around the car as he slammed it into park inside a small clearing in the woods. Night had fallen. He locked the doors when they automatically disengaged.

"Ethan," I whispered, for the first time feeling afraid with him.

"I can't do this anymore, Rosalie," he answered back in a soft voice.

I swallowed as he twined his fingers through mine.

"Don't make me. It's making me crazy. I've been punished enough. We all have. If you only knew..." His voice cracked.

"This isn't just about *you*, Ethan. Or the guys. It's about me and what's been done to me. To all the girls."

"Nothing was ever done to them that they didn't want, Rosalie!" He stared at me with wide, green eyes. "No one was ever forced. Sure, we were dicks about them, but when it came down to it, we were just looking for you. I can't say we were just being guys. We were assholes. We all freely admit to it. And yeah, maybe we did a little blackmailing to get you, and even them, interested. But it boils down to us *never* forcing it. We would've never *made* you if you'd said no. *Never, Rosalie.* Know that."

"It doesn't matter—"

"It fucking does!" he shouted. He released my hand and punched the steering wheel before he unlocked the car and got out.

I watched as he came around to my side and pulled the door open.

"Get out," he said softly.

"Ethan, please. I'm scared. Like *really* scared."

He didn't offer me an explanation or comfort. He simply held out his hand.

With my body trembling, I took his hand and allowed him to pull me out into the dark night. He slammed the door behind me and pressed me against the car.

"I fucking miss you, sweetheart. I can't live like this." His hands traveled to my waist where he aligned our bodies against one another. "I don't know if I should put you back into the car and drive away with you, never looking back or just beg for you to fucking love me the way I love you. Instead, I'm just asking that you stop torturing me. I'm *begging* you."

I stood there, hands at my side as he gave me a desperate squeeze.

"Rosalie, please... *Say something*. End my torment." He rested his forehead against mine. I didn't know what I could say or do for him. I ached as much as he did.

"I'll do anything, babe. Anything. Name it. You want the stars? I'll fucking tear them from the night sky and drape them around you like diamonds. You want my heart? I'll rip it from my chest and lay it at your feet. Do you want your enemies to suffer? I'll kill them for you, Rosalie. I'd *die* for just a moment with you in my arms, telling me you care even a fraction as much as I do. Just tell me what you want from me."

A soft gasp worked its way out of my mouth at his words, my chest aching.

"Tell me," he commanded softly, slipping his hands beneath my skirt and cupping my ass. My breath stuttered in my chest as he used his body to pin me to the car. With his gaze focused on me, he explored beneath my skirt, his fingers brushing against my center.

"I'm sorry. I don't do this. I *never* do this, but I need you. Please don't tell me no, Rosalie."

I stared back at him as he paused beneath my skirt, his bottom lip quivering.

With his eyes locked on mine, he shoved my panties aside and ran his finger along my damp slit. I shivered beneath his desperate touch as he tentatively pushed through my folds and teased my clit.

"Mm," he breathed out. "*Sweetheart*."

"Ethan," I managed to choke out before his lips met mine, sending my heart spiraling into a place I wasn't so sure I could get it back from. The same place I'd lost it the first time. But I'd planned this. Well, maybe not *this* exactly, but he was here with me. This was fate. I could make it work.

His tongue delved into my mouth. He stole my breath, forcing it from my body. He devoured me with his red-hot kiss as he slid a finger inside me. I writhed against him, struggling to swallow the moan clawing its way up my throat as he thrust his finger into me before hooking it in place and pressing the hot spot inside me that made sanity fly out of my mind.

"Tell me," he repeated against my lips before kissing me again, his finger making quick work of bringing me high on the cliff of euphoria.

Unable to resist, I raked my fingers through his hair. His growl of approval filled my mouth as he rocked against me, his hard length making it deliciously obvious what he wanted as his finger continued its torture.

"Please stop torturing me. I'm sorry," he rasped breathlessly as he worked his finger faster. "I'm so sorry. Please, Rosalie. If you can't love me like I need you to, then kill me because I'm dying each day without you. Put me out of the misery of never having you." He kissed me again as I moaned softly against his lips. "I want you, Rosalie. Tell me you want me."

"Fuck," I whimpered as he slid another finger into me.

"Tell me, sweetheart."

He moved faster until my eyes rolled back, and I clenched around his fingers, the pleasure rolling through my body in waves. I shook against him, my knees buckling as he pulled his fingers from my body. He pulled me into his strong embrace. Instinctively, I wrapped my arms around his neck.

"Please, babe. I need hope or I'm a dead man."

My heart clenched at a world without Ethan's sweetness. His kindness. I pushed all the other ugly thoughts away, focusing on that moment with him. Perhaps a moment I'd regret never taking. He'd already given me so much in those few moments. If revenge was what I sought, I knew exactly how to get it from Ethan Masters.

I ran my hands down his hard chest, to the planes of muscle on his abdomen. He let out a hiss against my lips as I brushed my hand against the bulge in his pants.

"Tell me what to do to keep you mine." His lips brushed against mine. "You win. I don't want to play anymore."

He was never in charge. It was always me. That was just how Ethan was, even if he'd tried to play a different part. I owned everything about that boy, right down to his shaky breath and trembling hands. We both knew it.

"It's yours. Anything you want, sweetheart. I'll give it to you," he whispered breathlessly. "Just please make the hurting stop."

I couldn't guarantee the pain would leave. In fact, I knew my next move would only bring more, but this was a war where everyone was a casualty. Even my sweet Ethan.

"You're going to hate me," I choked out between his feverish kisses.

He pulled away from me and stared me in the eyes. "Never."

"Don't say I didn't warn you, Ethan Masters." I cradled his face and took in the tears glistening on his cheeks. "But if you want me. If you want *this*, then I have. . . demands." Now was my moment. Either he'd come to me or he'd run. My heart hammered unevenly in my chest as I stared up at him.

"Do your worst, Rosalie Bishop."

"I want you. *Only* you. You'll be mine, and I'll be yours. No one else."

He stilled as he stared down at me, his muscles tensing beneath my fingers.

"What about all of us?" He crinkled his brows. "We're a family, Rosalie—"

"Not anymore. If you want me, that's my price. I'll give you time to decide. I know it's a big decision. I trust you'll make the right one."

"Rosalie, no," he whispered, pain laced into his words. "Don't make me choose. They're all I have in the world—"

"You'll have me, Ethan. All of me." I brushed my lips along his jaw.

He let out a soft whimper as he angled his neck for me. I kissed down it as his hands tightened on my ass where he held me.

I let my lips brush against his ear as I murmured, "Just like you wanted."

I pulled away and observed him, feeling like a complete bitch. It didn't stop me as I pressed on, "But I want you to decide this on your own. Go home. Sleep on it. Get back to me when you're ready to decide. OK?" I waited, hoping he wouldn't snap and lose his shit again. If he did, I'd chuck the idea out the window, run like hell, and hope he couldn't catch me in the trees.

"Fine," he choked out. "But you promise, Rosalie? If I choose you, you'll be mine?"

"You'd have to leave Juliet too."

A muscle feathered along his jaw as he looked at a point over my shoulder. "That won't be an issue."

"Then yes. I'll be yours for as long as you want me."

His bottom lip quivered as he nodded. "And Ian?"

"Make your choice, and we'll talk. OK?"

"Fine." His answer was barely a whisper, but he still leaned down and pressed a kiss to my cheek like the sweet Ethan I knew. "I should get you home. For what it's worth, I'm sorry I scared you tonight. I just lose it sometimes. I-I really shouldn't have touched you like that—"

"I forgive you."

"Thank you, sweetheart. It's more than I deserve." He kissed my cheek once more and steered me to the driver's side of the car and handed me the keys. "I shouldn't have been behind the wheel. I could have hurt you. I'm so fucking sorry, Rosalie." His voice cracked. "I'm a fucking mess."

I cradled his cheek. "It's OK. We'll fix it. I promise."

A tear slipped down his cheek. "At what cost?"

"If it's worth it, then the cost doesn't matter, right?"

He blew out a breath and nodded. "Right. The cost doesn't matter."

God, I fucking hoped so. We were playing with fire.

CHAPTER 16

I barely slept. The anxiety of wondering if Ethan would tell me no had me curled up in a ball all night. Asking him to save the horsemen was a big deal. Hell, trying to go against Ian was a big deal. I still didn't have that issue worked out, but I figured I'd cross that bridge when I got there.

And hopefully set fire to it before he caught me.

When my alarm went off, I hauled my tired ass out of bed and got ready. Bidding my parents a quick goodbye without bothering to eat seemed like a good way to start the day. It beat listening to my dad bitch about whatever he felt like selecting to complain about. I still hadn't told him about the musical.

I got into my car and drove to school. When I got there, I parked in a space at the back of the lot and sat in my seat, staring out at the sea of students as they went about their mornings. Greeting friends, laughing, kissing their significant others.

My life was nothing like that. In a matter of a few months, everything had gone to shit. Sighing, I got out and wasn't surprised when Ian found me halfway through the lot and draped his arm around my waist.

"Morning," he said, giving my side a slight pinch that made me wince. "I feel like we hardly see one another anymore."

"Good," I muttered.

If my comment upset him, he made no mention of it, opting to continue the conversation. "My dad gets out this week."

I nodded tightly. "I know. And?"

"I want you to meet him."

"Ian, I really don't want to do that—"

"Doesn't matter, Rosalie. You need to meet him. Do you know how good we've been lately? Hardly any fighting? I've been cool with your lame ass play. I've been giving you some space. I haven't been pressuring you. I haven't even tried to fuck you. It could get better as long as you're doing what you're told. Wouldn't you like that?" He pulled me to stop and stared down at me. "And I want to meet your parents. I think our relationship here is really starting to blossom."

Just then, I saw Ethan crossing the lawn. His hair was a beautiful mess, and he didn't look so tired. I watched as he strolled past the guys without stopping to chat like normal. My heart jerked in my chest.

"Uh, yeah. Yeah. Sorry." I focused back to Ian, desperate to get away from him so I could find Ethan. "Sure. We can do that. Whatever you want."

"Mm, I like you like this." He pressed a kiss to my lips.

I kept my eyes open, watching Ethan enter the school. When Ian pulled away, we continued our trek.

"Looking good, Rosebud," Cole called out. "You'd look better over here though."

"Piece of shit," Ian growled, his arm tightening around me.

"Just keep going," I whispered. "Please? I don't want you to fight."

That wasn't entirely true. I'd like nothing more than for someone to beat his ass, I just didn't want it at that moment because I needed to talk to Ethan and stopping to break up a fight would slow me down in my quest.

Ian gave a grunt but didn't say anything as we passed by Fox, Cole, and Enzo. I could feel the weight of their gazes on my back until we entered the school. Either Ethan had snapped again, or he'd made his choice. Judging by how put together he looked, I was beside myself with the possibility that he'd made up his mind.

Giddy with excitement, I strode to my locker, Ian in tow.

"I can handle getting to class," I muttered, casting a quick glance around the hall to see if Ethan was nearby. I ground my teeth when I didn't see him.

"Suck my dick first." Ian's hot breath on my neck as he kissed along my jaw made me want to gag. "The nook. I'm stressed the fuck out and could use some relief."

Asshole. What happened to no pressure?

"Ian, no." I tried to play coy and timid. "If we get caught, I'd get in trouble and maybe lose everything. And you just got done bragging about how you've chilled out on this stuff."

"Think about it like this, Rosalie." He pressed a kissed to the pulse point on my neck. "If you don't, you could get into trouble too. I bet my punishment would be worse than anyone else's. That much I can promise you."

I swallowed my anger and raked my fingers through his hair. "I'd rather suck your dick when I can enjoy it too. I won't be able to if I'm worried about being caught."

"You mean that?" He breathed out.

All I wanted to do was roll my eyes, but I gave him a nod and my most innocent, wide- eyed look. "I do. I-I think I'm starting to like this arrangement between us."

"Fuck," he growled, hunger in his eyes. "Tonight. My place."

"OK." I leaned in and pressed my lips to his, wanting to make my show believable.

He bought it because he hauled me against his body and deepened the kiss. When he broke it off, he backed away and eyed me again before turning and leaving me there.

The moment he was gone, I swiveled around, wiped my mouth, and stuffed a piece of gum into it.

"Don't look so excited to get away from your fuck boy," Fox growled from beside me.

"Go away, Fox."

"We need to talk."

"You always think we need to talk. What we need to do is have you fuck off somewhere else and leave me alone." I made to shove past him, but he grabbed my arm and tugged me to a stop.

"We need to rehearse our lines."

I untangled myself from his hold. "No. *You* need to rehearse your lines. I actually know mine."

"What if I admit I don't give a fuck about the musical and am only doing it to be close to you?"

"Then I'd say that's the first piece of truth you've said to me since I've known you."

He let out a soft chuckle and twisted one of my red curls around his finger. "Trust me, Rosie. It's not the first truth. I want to tell you everything. You just don't want to hear it because then you'll realize what a fool you've been about this whole thing."

I glared at him. "If you want me, Fox, come and get me. Right now, all I see is a scared little boy, wondering what my next move is. How about *you* make the move this time? Or are you too afraid?"

He leaned in, his lips near my ear. "My next move involves you bent over the hood of my Jeep while I fuck you from behind."

I shivered at his words, trying to internally talk myself down from asking him when and where.

"Mm, that's what I thought. You do want me."

"I really don't." My words were hoarse and didn't sound a bit like the truth as they trembled on my lips.

"*You* come get *me*, Rosie. I'll be waiting. Just like I've always been." His lips brushed ever so slightly against my cheek, his blue eyes locking on mine as he backed away, no humor on his handsome face. He was serious. He knew how to play this game. He knew how much I still wanted him.

"It's you, Rosie. Always will be."

I swallowed the lump in my throat as he reversed and made his way down the deserted hallway.

I had to up the ante, or I was going to get eaten alive by the horse-men. I needed to find Ethan.

~

I HADN'T SEEN Ethan all day. When I texted Jamie and asked her, she said he hadn't gone to calculus. Texting him was out of the question since I didn't have his new number. Sighing in frustration, I went to rehearsals.

"Hi, I'm Winnie Doyle." A blonde with a mega-watt smile greeted me as I stepped backstage. She stuck her hand out for me to shake.

"She's with the paper," Jamie said as I took the young woman's hand.

"Oh. Hi."

"I heard you're the star of this show. You're playing Sadie Watts, the take no prisoners heroine," Winnie continued, pulling out a digital recorder. "It's Rose Bishop, right?"

"Uh, Rosalie Bishop."

"Right. I was wondering if we could grab a couple photos of you and your co-star really quick before we snap some of you guys on stage. Of course, we'll be back the night of the show to take more shots for our readers. Now, where's that handsome co-star of yours?" She craned her neck past me and gestured to a young guy with a camera. He came over and gave us a nod and a smile as he held out his hand.

"Gabe," he said. "I'll be doing some of the photos today."

"Hi. Rosalie," I said before nodding to Jamie. "This is Jamie. She's one of our producers."

"Nice to meet you." Gabe shook her hand after releasing mine. "Mind if I get some photos of you two?"

"Sure." I moved next to Jamie and smiled nervously. My brain swirled with the very real thought I was going to have to go home and break the news to my dad about this entire thing. Gabe snapped a couple photos before swiveling around to take candid shots of others milling around backstage.

"There he is!" Winnie called out as Fox approached. "We were looking for you."

"He must have introduced himself already," I grunted at Jamie who rolled her eyes at Winnie's excitement.

"Probably."

"Hey, Winnie," Fox greeted her. He shook her hand before moving to stand beside me. I stiffened as he rested his hand on my lower back.

Winnie's gaze flicked between us.

"Are you two a couple?" she asked.

"Yes," Fox answered the same time I said no.

"We've been best friends since we were in diapers. It's only natural for us to be together," Fox explained smoothly as he rubbed his thumb in small circles on my back. "She's my girl."

"Ugh, spare me," I snapped him. "I'm sorry, Winnie. Fox cheated on me with the school's mean queen. We broke up. He said he wanted to get back together yet he doesn't want to break it off with her. Can you imagine?"

"Oh." Winnie's eyes widened. "Uh, I'm sorry to hear that."

"Rosalie," Fox warned softly.

"Sorry, *babe*, just thought Winnie would like to report the truth."

Winnie cleared her throat as Jamie stepped away and let a giggle slip out.

"Gabe, uh, could you take our stars' photos?" Winnie called out, finally tearing her gaze away from us.

Gabe came back and snapped a couple pics before I shook Fox off and stomped away. "Can you believe him?" I snarled to Jamie as we moved to my dressing area. "What a douche."

"I'm not a douche, Rosalie. But you certainly were back there."

"Eat shit, Fox," I snarled at him, surprised he'd actually had the balls to follow me.

"I'm, uh, just going to go. I-I think I hear Mr. Dennison calling." Jamie scurried off, leaving me with Fox.

I raised a brow at him and folded my arms over my chest. "Don't do that shit again."

"The story about the musical is going to run in the paper, Rosie. You might want to tell your dad you're the star of the show."

"Thanks for the newsflash."

"I can be there with you if you need me. I know how much this means to you." He stared back at me solemnly, his blue eyes taking me in.

"I don't need you. We've been over this."

He nodded and looked away. "I know. You're moving on. I get it."

I sighed.

"Does he fuck you, Rosie? Is he as good as I was?" His voice was so broken.

"Fox, seriously, not here. Not now."

He closed the distance between us and stared down at me. "Are you in love with him? Will he protect you like I will? When he makes love to you, does he tell you he loves you? What is he willing to do just to make you smile?"

"What are you doing, Fox?" I whispered as I gazed up at him.

"Just trying to figure out what he has to offer that's better than what I have," he murmured.

I shook my head. "I'm not doing this with you." I pushed past him, but he caught my forearm. Our gazes locked.

"I want you to know that we can play dirty too. Just because we don't appear to be retaliating, doesn't mean we aren't."

"I know. You've shown me that in the past." My voice came out thick and shaky. "And I'm not afraid."

"Good. That's my girl. I'll still be here when this is over."

"We'll see." I pulled my arm away from his and left him standing there, my pulse thundering in my ears.

I knew they had to be up to something. I'd be stupid to think otherwise.

"ROSALIE, let's work on act two, scene two today," Mr. Dennison called out as he settled into his seat.

I nodded and blew out a breath. Winnie had left but Gabe was still there, clicking away. This scene didn't have Fox in it, thankfully. Glancing to the backstage area, I saw him lurking in the background, his arms folded over his leather jacket, his eyes narrowed in my direction.

Licking my lips, I launched into my lines. Jake Winston, one of the actors in the scene, did great. He didn't need help with his lines and performed nearly perfect with me.

"Nice work, Rosalie," he called out after we ran through the scene three times.

I smiled. "Thanks. You, too."

"Take a break. Evans! Let's get you out here for your solo," Mr. Dennison shouted out. Fox grumbled when he passed by me, his fingers running along my hand in a simple gesture to let me know we were still playing.

The intro to his song played, and I couldn't help but notice how everyone stopped what they were doing to listen to him. His deep voice boomed out in perfect pitch as he sang the song. He didn't falter once, causing Mr. Dennison to smile, a look of relief sweeping over his face.

"Nicely done, Mr. Evans! Nicely done!" Mr. Dennison nodded, grinning.

Mrs. Adams clapped loudly beside him, smiling widely at Fox who shot her a wink. I rolled my eyes at him. But it was the whooping in the auditorium that had me grinding my teeth.

Juliet.

She sat in the back with Cole and Enzo, clapping loudly. Neither of the guys looked interested in anything as they sat there surveying Fox. I hated that he'd brought *her* to watch.

"How was I?" Fox asked as he stepped backstage and stood beside me while the stagehands worked on changing props.

"Disgusting," I grunted. "Was your next move to bring your bitch to our rehearsal?"

Fox frowned, his brows crinkling. "I didn't invite her."

"Don't play stupid, Fox. She's out there with Enzo and Cole. This is fucked up, even for you. Haven't you hurt me enough? Is this how you're really going to play?" I didn't know why I was so bothered. It wasn't like I wasn't doing it back to him with Ian. Maybe Ethan's absence was getting to me. Maybe the impending blowjob I had to give Ian was weighing me down. Maybe the upcoming conversation with my dad had me on edge. Maybe seeing Juliet in the crowd supporting Fox with *my* guys beside her was the final straw that just weighed too heavily on my heart.

"You're literally fucking my enemy, Rosalie. You flaunt that piece of shit wherever you go. I'd say you're the one who's fucked up. All you have to do is come back to me and let me explain things. It could end right now."

I shrugged. "I-I almost did. Remember?" I gazed up at him.

A muscle popped along his jaw. His hands clenched. "That was bad fucking timing, Rosie."

I snorted. "Right. Because it's all just a game."

"The only game we're playing is the one to get you back. Say yes to me and end it."

I shook my head. "You're a liar. I can't believe anything you tell me. You *had* me, but *she* came in, and like always, you stuck your tail between your legs and let me go. And honestly, I don't know why I can't just say to hell with all of you and walk away."

"Because you love me. *You love us.*"

I shook my head, denying it. "I don't."

"You do, Rosie," Fox's voice was soft. His warm hand on the small of my back made a shiver rush through me.

"I-I can't anymore, Fox. You need to pay for what you've done. It wasn't just me. It was others. You need to be taken down."

"If you only knew how fucking low I already am," he whispered, his voice shaking. "You'd see what I've been willing to do for you. I'm protecting you."

"You're protecting yourself and using me as an excuse to do it," I snapped at him. "I'm so tired of having this conversation with you!"

"Rosalie, are you ready to work on your solo?" Jamie called out, her gaze darting between me and Fox. "Mrs. Adams is ready for you."

"I've gotta go." I backed away from Fox.

"You don't have to," he murmured.

"I do. If I stand here any longer, I might puke from being forced to witness your cheering section."

He sighed and shook his head at me. "So we're still playing this game? I thought maybe you'd come to your senses."

"Yep. Game on."

His gaze hardened. "Fine. Let's fucking do it. I wanted to give you a chance. Show me what you've got."

I didn't bother to answer him, opting to follow Jamie instead. I knew if I said anything, I'd probably cause a scene, and it was the last thing I needed.

CHAPTER 17

After completing my task at Ian's and earning a nasty slap on my ass, I went home. Not hearing from Ethan bummed me out more than I could put into words. That meant something, and I was well aware of what it was.

I'd fallen for the horsemen easily. Breaking off from them was the hardest thing I'd ever done in my life. They were easy to love, even Cor with his darkness and Fox with his secrets. Even Enzo's mafia ties didn't scare me. Ethan though. . . I worried for him most and longed to save him from whatever was going on in his life. For the most part, I assumed it was me, ego aside. If he hurt a fraction of how much I hurt, then I could seriously relate to him. The other three seemed content with their new girl. Ethan though? I hadn't seen him with her. That gave me hope even though Juliet claimed he'd been with her.

Pulling into the driveway, I sighed. My parents weren't home. That didn't surprise me. They'd been going out more often. I figured it was their way to prepare for an empty nest once I left for college. *If* I got to leave. With Ian with his videos, the future looked bleak.

I got out and went into the house. My stomach gave a grumble, but all I wanted to do was go to my bathroom and brush the taste of Ian from my mouth.

I stepped into my bedroom. Inside, I undressed and took a hot shower. Then I vigorously brushed my teeth. Takeout and a movie in bed seemed like a great way to spend my night.

When I'd pulled in, I'd noticed Fox wasn't home. No surprise there. He was probably out with Juliet. My guts clenched at the possibility, but I pushed it away. After I wrapped myself in a towel, I went back to my bedroom.

Once in my closet, I dug around for my sleep shorts and tank top. A scream ripped from my lips as I turned. Ethan's warm hand pressed against my mouth, his eyes bright.

"E-Ethan?" I choked out as he removed his hand from over my mouth. "What are you doing? H-How did you get in here?"

He smiled down at me and rested his hands on my toweled waist.

"I've been here since your parents left. They don't lock the window in your dad's study. I came in that way and waited for you."

"You could've called me instead of sneaking into my house like a damn criminal." My pulse slowed.

He cocked his head at me. "I wanted to surprise you."

"You nearly gave me a heart attack."

"Sorry," he murmured, brushing a damp curl away from my face. "I just figured we shouldn't let anyone know what we're doing here just yet."

"And what is that?" I asked as he took a step closer to me, closing the distance between our bodies.

"Isn't it obvious?" His voice was soft as he rested his forehead against mine.

"Maybe you should remind me."

He let out a soft chuckle. "I've made my decision. It's you, sweetheart. Whatever you're planning, I'm in."

"Yeah?" My heart jolted in my chest, warmth flowing through me. "You're mine?"

"You know you own me, Rosalie. Nothing in this world or the next will ever change that. It's the only fucking truth I know. You were made for me. Without you, I'm just Ethan Masters, drug addict and depressed horseman."

"And with me?"

"I'm yours. It's the only thing that matters in my world." His words were simple and to the point. He angled my head up, his eyes searching mine, asking for permission.

"So we're doing this?" I asked, my voice soft and shaky.

"We're doing this." He pressed his lips to mine so gently I all but melted against him.

I didn't know what to expect with him since the last time we were alone, he'd scared me.

He tugged me out of the closet, keeping his lips fused with mine. We stumbled to my bed where he laid me down on it and balanced over me. The adoration on his face made my heart clench. All I knew was I didn't want to hurt him.

"I've missed you," he murmured against my lips.

"I've missed you too." I ran my fingers through his silky hair, enjoying the way it tickled.

He beamed down at me. "I have so much to tell you, Rosalie." He kissed me again.

I arched myself against his body. His hand gripped my waist and helped to keep me against him.

"So tell me." I nipped his bottom lip.

A beautiful grin spilled over his face.

"I'm having a hard time concentrating knowing I could have you naked in one tug." He worked his hand along my thigh and skimmed the edge of my towel.

"Then why don't you?" I challenged breathlessly.

His pretty eyes darkened as he peered down at me.

"Don't tempt me, sweetheart. I'm walking a fine line between being a gentleman and a monster."

"My world could use a monster like you, Ethan."

What little control he seemed to have slipped. He let out a growl and pushed his hand beneath my towel and up my thigh.

A gasp left my lips as he ran a warm finger up my slit.

"Fuck, you have no idea how long I've wanted to touch you for. Being able to…" He surveyed me in awe as he explored me with his fingers. "You're so wet, sweetheart." His thumb pressed gently against the tight bundle of nerves.

I closed my eyes as he circled it slowly.

"I'm sorry about the other night. I was so fucking wasted, Rosalie. Everything is a blur. But your words brought me out. Your kiss. Your touch." He let out a soft sigh against my lips.

"It's OK, Ethan. I'm not mad."

"What you do to me. . . I want to taste you, sweetheart." He groaned softly as he shifted off me so he could lie beside me, his fingers still working beneath my towel. He kissed along my jaw.

"You can," I whispered in a choked voice.

His fingers stilled, and he stared at me, his brows crinkled. "Are you sure? I don't want to push you so soon. I feel guilty as hell about the other night. I don't do things like that, Rosalie. Even this is probably too much—"

"You were always so sweet, Ethan." I kissed him tenderly. "But there are some really ugly memories in my head that I want to disappear. So please, help me. Make them go away."

"Oh, Rosalie," he murmured, running his nose along mine. "I'm so sorry. I'll make it better. I promise."

My breath hitched in my chest as he moved south, his gaze never breaking from mine. When he reached the bottom of my towel, he pushed it up.

"Damn," he breathed out, his lips parting. "So beautiful."

My face heated from his words. But this was Ethan being Ethan.

He leaned in and pressed his warm lips to my damp, aching center. I closed my eyes and swallowed as he ran his tongue up my slit before he pushed forward through my folds.

"Oh god," I gasped as his warm tongue swirled around my clit in smooth, gentle motions. He sucked and licked it as I twisted my fingers in his hair, pulling him as close to my center as I could get.

"More," I pleaded softly, whimpering beneath his hot mouth.

He growled his approval and upped his speed. He pushed a finger into me and hooked it to the spot which made my eyes roll back in my head.

"Ethan. Please," I groaned as the flurry of hot tingles surfaced, making my breath stutter. He kept up his quick, steady pace, building my euphoria until it hit the surface, sending me spiraling through the glorious waves, his name on my lips.

When I finally came down, my body shook. Ethan licked up my folds one final time before planting a gentle kiss to my trembling center. He sat up and ran his tongue over his lips, his green eyes shining brightly. He smoothed my towel back into position, not once tugging it apart to look at the rest of my body.

"Was that OK?" he asked as I reached for him. He came to me eagerly and wrapped me in his arms on my bed, his fingers in my hair as he pushed it gently away from my face.

"It was so amazing." I kissed him, tasting myself on his lips.

"Promise?" he murmured.

"Yes." I kissed his soft lips again. "I swear it."

He smiled against my lips as his kisses continued. "I've missed you so fucking much."

"I've missed you too." I paused. "Ethan?"

"Yes?" he purred.

I reached out tentatively and rubbed my hand against his groin. He hissed out a soft breath at my touch.

"I-I can return the favor."

"As much as I'd love to have your lips wrapped around me, no, sweetheart. I-I want to take care of you."

"You have—"

"Shh," he chuckled softly. "In time, OK? You don't have to suck my dick to make me happy, Rosalie. Just holding you right now has made me the happiest man alive. We'll get there, OK?"

I nodded and rested against him, breathing in the way he smelled, like soap and fresh air. He grew quiet for a moment before he cleared his throat. "Are you breaking up with Ian?"

The words were ugly on my tongue even before I said them. "I can't."

Ethan sat up on his elbow, his brows crinkled, as he took me in. "What? Why?"

I bit my bottom lip, trying to get the words to come out right, but nothing sounded good.

"Do you love him? You can tell me if you do." His voice cracked as he said the words.

I cradled his face.

"I don't love him, Ethan. Not even close. He-he has the videos that Fox had. Ian has them all and some he took himself. He's holding them over me like you guys were. Plus he threatened to hurt Jamie. I wanted to save her from him. And I wanted to hurt all of you for hurting me. I-I really screwed up. Now I'm trapped and can't get away." The words tumbled out of my mouth in a rush, tears gripping my eyelids. "I don't know what to do. He'll hurt me if I try to leave. In more ways than one."

"Babe," Ethan murmured, wrapping his arms around me again. "Why didn't you tell us?"

"You're not my friends, Ethan. I mean, *you* are now, but the others... they aren't—"

"*They are.* Let me tell you everything—"

"I don't want to hear it, Ethan. It's all just bullshit to me. I have more important things to worry about than what games they're playing."

"There aren't—"

"Are you in this with me or not?" My voice shook as he wiped a tear from my eye.

"I'm with you wherever you take me, sweetheart," he said gently. "But I can't have some piece of shit touching my girl. We need to fix that."

"How?" I whispered, assessing him, desperate for him to tell me he had a plan.

He shrugged. "I'll kill him."

CHAPTER 18

"What? No, Ethan. You're not going to *kill* him." He'd said it like someone would speak of the weather. Just hearing Ethan say such ugly words made me shudder. They belonged nowhere near his lips.

"I already told you I'd do anything for you. That includes taking out the trash who's hurting you. I'm in this for life, Rosalie. You're my girl. I'm not going to allow that piece of shit to hurt what's mine." A muscle feathered along his jaw.

"There has to be another way."

"He's garbage, Rosalie. He hurts good people. He's hurting you. I know he is, and I won't allow it."

"Then help me find a safe way out where I won't lose you in the process. I'm already scared for you because of—"

"The drugs?" He chuckled softly. Sadly. "I'm trying to quit. I am. It's just really fucking hard once I'm hooked."

"But you have me now," I said, resting my head against his chest, hoping I was enough. "I'm here, Ethan. I want you."

"*Fuck.* These past few weeks without you have been pure hell, Rosalie. Hearing you say you want me makes me want things no one else has ever been able to make me want."

"What's that?" I murmured.

"Want to live." His laugh was soft.

I twisted my fingers in his t-shirt, desperate to cling to him so he wouldn't let go. Like if I held on tightly enough, I could keep him safely beside me.

"I'm afraid I'll lose you, Ethan."

"Never, sweetheart. I'm never leaving you. You're the fucking light at the end of a really long, dark tunnel. A little slice of heaven made just for my personal hell."

"What happened to you?" I asked, my voice cracking as I noted the pain in his voice.

His Adam's apple bobbed in his throat like he was thinking hard and whatever was swimming around in his mind caused him great pain. He seemed to finally come to a decision.

"Touch me." He took my hand in his and brought it beneath his shirt.

I let him guide my hand over his body until he paused it over a strange spot on his skin which felt rippled. It was just over his left ribs. I crinkled my brows as he moved my hand over his heart. More ridges. More bumps of hard flesh.

I pulled away and looked up at him. "What happened to you?"

He gave me a sweet, sad smile. "It's an ugly story." He paused for a moment, seeming to collect himself before he continued, "My dad didn't always like me, Rosalie. Neither did my mom. When I was ten, I was taken from my mother's custody. Until that time, they hurt me. But not just them. Dad's friends. Mom's friends. Whenever they needed drugs, th-they'd use m-me a- as- as p-payment." He stumbled on his words, wincing as they fell off his lips. Tears filled his eyes as the horror of his words took hold.

"Ethan, they-they—"

"Touched me. *Forced* me. Fucking hurt me, Rosalie. It's an ugly truth I don't tell people. Only you. And Fox, Enzo, and Cole."

"Enzo said your parents made you learn piano." I recalled the conversation I'd had with Enzo weeks ago in his basement.

Ethan shook his head. "Not my real parents. The ones who adopted me."

"You're adopted?" I guessed I should've known that since he wasn't with his real parents anymore.

He nodded. "Yeah. They're good people. Mom's a music teacher. She works at the elementary school on Rucker Street by the library. Dad's a plumber. I-I don't live with them anymore though."

"What?" I went up on my elbow and looked down at him. "The house—"

"I rent it from my parents. Dad bought it for extra income. The price was good. When I started to spiral the first time, they let me move in if I promised to get my shit together. I have a younger brother and sister who didn't need to see me sick. Jase and Emma. They're my adoptive parents' real kids. Mom didn't want me to go. But Dad trusted I could do it. The guys helped me get my life sorted. I sell my photos to pay my bills every month. When my grandpa passed away last year, he left me some money, so that's helping too."

"Why didn't you go live with your grandpa when they took you from your birth mother?" I asked, giving his hand a squeeze.

He shrugged. "He didn't have time to deal with me. He was still working and wouldn't have had anyone there to give me the care I needed. Taking some fucked up kid with night terrors and emotional issues to therapy five days a week was too much for a lot of people. Gramps still visited me until his stroke last year. Janie and Robert, my adoptive parents, took on the role I needed and kept me sane. I owe them everything, which is why I had to be on my own. I didn't want them to see me the way I am."

"The way you are? Ethan, you're so beautiful and strong." I kissed him gently. "I'm so proud of you."

He gave me a sad smile. "I'm a million shades of fucked up, Rosalie. But with you, I feel like I can be myself."

"You can." I kissed him again, my heart aching for him. "Always."

He swallowed, his sad, moss green eyes meeting mine. "I have a darker secret."

I crinkled my brows as I looked at him, waiting for him to tell me.

"What is it?"

He licked his lips, his hand trembling as he twined his fingers through mine. His face twisted into something heart-wrenching. His beautiful features knotted like he was in pain before he spoke, his words so soft I could barely hear them.

"I killed my real father."

CHAPTER 19

"What?" I frowned at him, not sure if I'd heard him right.

"I killed him," he whispered. "H-He was hurting me. One night his friend had me pinned to the bed. Th-they hurt me so much, Rosalie." Tears clung to his eyelashes.

Pain raced through my heart as I watched him sniffle. He drew in a shaky breath before he continued.

"I knew he'd come for me again the next night. So, I took a knife from the kitchen. When he came into my room drunk, I stabbed him. I didn't stop until he wasn't moving." His words tumbled out fast and soft, his entire body trembling as he recalled those last moments. When his gaze met mine, it was like a hundred storms had gathered in his eyes. "I don't regret doing it. If my mom had been home, I'd have killed her too. She never made him stop hurting me. Moms are supposed to protect their children." He let out a soft sob.

I wrapped my arms around him as he shook, his tears warm on my skin.

"She never protected me, Rosalie. Why didn't she protect me? Why did they do that to me?"

"It's OK," I murmured, holding him as he clung to me. Nausea twisted my insides. I had no clue this was Ethan's past. Anger bubbled inside me, making me want to find his mother and kick her ass.

"They tried to make me be like them." He sobbed softly against my neck, his large body shaking with each breath.

"You're nothing like them, Ethan." I held him tighter.

"I am. *I fucking am.* I'm a user just like they were. I didn't kill the demons, Rosalie. I just made them my own." His hold tightened around me. "I hurt myself so I can feel something. Anything is better than the pain I'm in. All the scars and cuts. The drugs. I'm a fucked-up mess, Rosalie."

A tear slid down my cheek at his words. "I'll keep you safe. I'll save you. We'll get through this together, Ethan. You're mine."

"Promise?" he whispered in a shaking voice.

"I swear."

"I don't want to be this person, but it's who I am. I-I didn't want to go into this with you without you knowing the real me." He pulled away and scrutinized me, so much agony on his face it made my heart clench in my chest and my stomach twist.

"I don't care, Ethan. I want you. Scars and nightmares."

"Really?" he whispered, hope springing to his pretty eyes.

"Yes," I breathed out, kissing his lips tenderly.

"Oh, sweetheart. Where have you been my whole life?"

"Right here. Where I'll always be. I'll save you, Ethan."

"I believe that." He kissed me slowly, sending heat pooling between my legs again. "And I'll save you." His soft words against my lips sent a ripple of warmth through my body.

"Then we need a plan."

"We'll get it, OK? Even if I do have to kill him."

"No killing—"

He pressed his lips to mine once more before whispering, "Fox doesn't have to protect you from the monsters. Not anymore. You have me now."

And I believed him. But I wouldn't let Ethan become another ugly monster. Even if I had to kill Ian myself.

CHAPTER 20

We arranged to have a secret romance. It was pure shit, but that was what we had to do until we figured out a way around Ian. Ethan insisted on staying away from the guys as a means to prove his loyalty to me. I caved and told him to talk to them because I did know how much they meant to him, especially after he divulged his secret to me.

But he refused my offer to let him be near the guys.

When I arrived at school the next day, my stomach was in knots. Hauling in a deep breath, I got out of my car and made my way through the parking lot. The guys, minus Ethan, stood on the sidewalk. I ducked my head as I walked, hoping they'd ignore me.

"You look beautiful today," Enzo called out to me.

I picked up my pace. Hearing his voice made my stomach twist harder. The image of him buried inside me kept replaying in my head. It drove me wild for far too many reasons, but one stood out above the rest. *I liked it.*

The day was miserable. It only got worse when Ian made me sit with him at lunch. He kissed on me and acted like he wasn't the biggest snake in the world. Trying out for the musical should've been on his list of things to do because he was one hell of an actor. Behind closed doors, he was the devil. No one would ever know it but me, and that pissed me off.

"Where are you going?" Ian demanded as I rose from my seat.

I was desperate to see Ethan. I had no clue where he was, but if I had to take a guess, it would be the library or the bleachers.

"I need to do some quick studying. Matthews is supposedly dropping a pop quiz on us." I reached out and gave his hand a squeeze as a way to defuse what I knew could be a bad situation. He was always on edge. Jamie had mentioned Mr. Matthews giving a pop quiz in her class.

I didn't need to study for it, but it was the perfect excuse to get away and look for Ethan.

Ian narrowed his eyes at me before he glanced across the cafeteria, taking in the horsemen at their table, still without Ethan. Juliet sat perched on Fox's lap, her head resting against his shoulder. Disgust washed over me as she giggled and pressed her lips to Cole's.

Seemingly satisfied by seeing the guys within his view, he squeezed my hand back and nodded. "I'll see you later." He didn't pay attention to me beyond that as he returned to the conversation with his friends.

Breathing out a sigh of relief, I strode toward the cafeteria doors, but not before I caught Fox's eye. A pained expression adorned his face, but it only made me scowl as Juliet turned to him and kissed his cheek.

Bitch. Her beating in the locker room needed a part two.

The cafeteria doors slammed shut behind me as I hurried to get away before I lost my shit. I marched quickly outside, eager to see if Ethan was on the bleachers. When I got there, my heart fell. He wasn't there. Sighing, I slipped back inside and decided to check the nook. Again, nothing.

"What the hell," I grumbled, feeling let down as I made my way to my locker. I only had about ten minutes left before classes would start. I was just passing by the janitor's closet when a hand reached out and snagged my arm.

"Hey—" I started as I was tugged into the small, dimly lit closet, the door slamming closed behind me.

Ethan's warm lips met mine. Immediately, I melted against him and wrapped my arms around his neck.

"Miss me?" he murmured against my lips.

"I was looking for you." I kissed him again. I raked my fingers through his hair, enjoying the way the silky strands felt against my skin. "I don't have your new number."

"We'll fix that after I'm done with you. I'll text you," he answered as he brushed his knuckles against my cheek. "Have I told you lately how beautiful I think you are?"

"No." Heat rose to my cheeks as I ducked my head.

He chuckled softly. "Well, you're fucking beautiful, sweetheart. I can't stand not being able to touch you whenever I see you."

"You saw me today?" I stared up at him. I hadn't seen him at all.

He smiled down at me. "Yes. It's pure hell to not be able to kiss your lips or feel your touch. I'm my worst without you."

"And with me?"

"I'm a fucking god, capable of anything, Rosalie." He pressed his lips to mine as his fingers glided beneath my shirt to hold me at my ribs. "I'm unstoppable."

"Tell me more," I whispered against his mouth between hot kisses.

"Unbeatable." Another kiss. "Un-fucking-touchable."

"More." I angled my neck as he trailed his lips along my jaw and down my throat.

"And so fucking yours."

"I like the way that sounds."

"Yeah?" he murmured, pressing a kiss to my pulse point. "I wanted to tell you something."

"What?"

He pulled away and looked down at me. "I haven't used today. Or yesterday. I-I'm trying, sweetheart."

"I'm so proud of you." My heart soared as I wrapped him in a hug.

He held me tight, his chin resting atop my head.

"It's hard, Rosalie. It's so fucking hard. That shit's the devil, calling me home. I don't want to fail you. Then I see that prick touching you. Kissing you. I want to get fucked up just so I don't have to deal with it."

"I'm sorry, Ethan—"

"Shh." He pressed a finger to my lips as he pulled away and assessed me. "I have a plan."

"You do?" My eyes widened, and my heart lodged in my throat.

"I do. But you're going to have to really trust me and be brave."

"I trust you."

It seemed that was all he needed to hear because he kissed me again.

"Meet me tonight. My place. Can you do that?"

"If Ian sees—"

"He won't. You can park in the garage. No one will know you're there. OK?"

I nodded, my stomach churning. "OK."

"Good." He thumbed my bottom lip, his eyes heavy with want. "I'll make the risk worth it. Now go before the bell rings." He gave me one final kiss before releasing me.

With as much willpower as I possessed, I left the tiny closet, my heart hammering a mad rhythm in my chest.

He was intense. More than I ever imagined.

I grinned, eager to see just what other surprises my sweet Ethan had in store for me and hoping beyond anything, I could really save him. It would destroy me if I couldn't.

CHAPTER 21

Later that day, I yawned and rubbed my eyes, desperate to get the hell out of rehearsal. Fox had been late because of football practice, which had sent Mr. Dennison into an angry tirade about the importance of dedication.

When Jen, one of Fox's fan girls, piped up and told Dennison that Fox was dedicated to his priorities, he'd let out a huff and grunt before calling the chorus line onto the stage.

"Miss Bishop, fantastic job. You can leave," Dennison called out. "The rest of you, I need more heart in this."

His words faded as I gathered my bag and started to leave. Dread filled my belly as I knew where I'd be going in just a few short minutes. Ian's house to make good on another promise.

"Rosie, hey, wait up," Fox called out, trotting to catch up to me.

Sighing, I turned to face him. "I'm tired, Fox. I'm having a really shitty evening. If you aren't going to improve it, then leave me alone."

"Are you talking to Ethan?"

I frowned and stared up at him. "No. I'm talking to you. Are you drunk? High?"

He rolled his brilliant blue eyes. "You know what I mean. I saw him leaving your place in the middle of the night."

"Are you spying on me now?"

"To be fair, Rosie, I'm always watching. But Ethan? What's going on? You forgive him but not us?"

"*To be fair,* Fox, Ethan isn't an asshole like you and the other two are. I've seen the notebook. Remember?"

"I told you to not try to break us apart."

"And I'm not." I crossed my arms over my chest.

"So you and Ethan aren't talking again? Why was he at your house in the dead of night?"

"Why the fuck do you care?"

"Because. Ethan is my friend, and we do this together or not at all. He's been avoiding us. He's really fucking up what I'm trying to fix, Rosalie. Juliet—"

"Oh, fuck her and fuck you, Fox," I snapped at him. "If I want to fuck Ethan, I will."

"So you're cheating on Ian with Ethan?" He let out a bitter laugh.

Anger took up residence in my body, and I spoke without thinking. "No, I'm cheating on Ian with Enzo. I fucked him days ago. *Alone.* Or didn't he tell you?"

Fox's face paled. "What?"

"That's right. I bet if it comes down to it, *your* boys are really *my* boys. Loyalty runs pussy deep, Fox. You should know that since you let it decide your loyalty."

A squeak of air left me as Fox lunged, his hand around my throat. His eyes were filled with hurricanes, as he shoved me against the wall in a dark corner.

"Don't fucking play this game with me, Rosie. I'm fucking *sick* of playing. Do you have any idea what it's like to watch Ian touch you? Kiss you? To know that he's controlling you? Fucking *hurting* you? And then you take that pain and turn it back on me? *Me,* Rosalie? After all I've done for you—" He lessened his hold on me, his eyes shining.

"Bullied me. Cheated on me. Broke my heart?" I rasped softly. "Those things you've done for me? And yeah I have some idea what it's like to watch all those things. I have to watch you with *her.*"

His eyes wavered as his bottom lip trembled. "I hate this musical. I'm here for you. I hate Juliet. I'm buried inside her at night for you. I fucking hate that you're hurting, but I'm here, Rosalie, even if I am a fuck up. I'm. Still. Here. Don't fuck with what's mine. Don't tear apart everything that makes me who I am." He dropped his hand from my throat.

I approached him and rested my hand on his chest. His heart beat hard and fast beneath my touch. I went up on my tip toes. He immediately inclined his head for me as I whispered in his ear.

"Maybe we should end this now. I get Ethan. You get Juliet. And Enzo and Cole can decide for themselves who they really want to fuck. Me... or you." I trailed my lips down his jaw as he shook against me before I pressed a tender kiss to the edge of his lips and pulled completely away.

He didn't move. He didn't speak. He only stared at me.

"I'll see you around. Tell Enzo I said hi." I backed away, my heart hammering so hard it was all I could hear. I wasn't sure if he'd lunge again, so when I spun around to leave, it took all I had to keep my head high.

I knew my words hurt him. Enzo had betrayed him. Ethan was betraying him. And he was losing me. Or maybe I was already gone because as I walked away, my heart was with Ethan, not Fox. I had to save Ethan. Fox could save himself.

The damage was done, and maybe we couldn't come back from it. After all, war often laid claim to those we loved the most.

And I loved Fox.

CHAPTER 22

"You're late." Ian shoved me into his room, his mouth turned into a deep frown.

I didn't deny it. After leaving rehearsals, I'd driven around, feeling sick to my stomach. Truth of the matter, I was tired of playing these games. Even though Ethan and I had just become an *us*, I knew I'd pick him over Ian any day, and continuing this bullshit was only making me feel crazier.

"Sorry. Rehearsal ran late," I muttered, rubbing my eyes.

He grunted and motioned for me to sit on his bed. "That's all?"

"What else would there be?"

"Evans or any number of the guys you were fucking."

I closed my eyes for a moment to collect myself before I answered. "I'm not a slut, Ian, and even if I was, that's not bad news for you."

He cocked his head at me and smirked.

What the hell. He hardly ever smiles.

"It is bad news for me because if you're a slut like everyone says, you're holding out on me, Rosalie. What's up with that?"

"I'm not holding out, Ian." I chewed my bottom lip, not sure how to navigate my lie. "I just was hurt. I don't want it to happen again."

"I get it, but this entire thing is a little on the side of suck for me. You give incredible head, sure, but I'd like to experience your pussy."

I needed to change the subject. "Ian, what's going to happen when we graduate? Are we going to go our separate ways? Do you just let me go?"

He frowned. "I want you to be with me."

"Forever?"

He nodded, his eyes locked on mine. "That's the plan."

"But Ian..." I licked my lips. "Once I'm out of high school and in college on my own, I won't give a shit about any of this. You could send autographed copies to my parents, and I wouldn't care. We're on borrowed time. *This* is temporary." The moment the words were out of my mouth, I regretted them, worried he'd lose his shit on me again.

I was surprised when he let out a sigh and took my hand in his.

"I was really hoping you'd like me enough to stick around."

"You hurt me," I whispered. "It would be like Stockholm. When I love someone, it's because we care about one another and I have free will. I'm a prisoner in this relationship."

"Then don't be, Rosalie. Fucking let go of all the shit and be with me. Really *be* with me. Stop focusing on using me for revenge. Let me in a little." He got to his feet and went to his desk. He pulled out a small thumb drive and held it up to me. My name was on a sticker on the front.

"This is everything I have on you. Right here. No backup. Just this one piece of fucking plastic. Try with me and it's yours. I'll drop everything if you try. I'll give this to you. It's your freedom. Do you want it?"

"Yes," I whispered, eyeing the small black drive in his hand.

"Then kiss me. Fuck me. Date me. I won't hurt you."

"You already have." I chanced a glance at him.

He closed his eyes and let out a slow breath before he stared back at me. "I fucked up. The truth of the matter is, I really fucking like you. These feelings I have for you make me insane. I can't even think about another girl when I have you in front of me. I'd like to be normal and fall in love the way it's meant to be, but it looks like that's not in the cards for me. Or you, it would seem. So why not just fucking do this and try to make the best of it? Maybe if we try and you still hate me by graduation, we call it good. At least I won't wonder."

"OK." The only thing I could think of was getting that damn device in his drawer then graduation wouldn't matter if he was telling the truth about it being the only thing he had on me. I decided to try my luck. "You swear that's the only spot you have my stuff?"

"Yes."

"And if at the end of this I don't feel anything, you give it to me and let me go?"

He moved to me and eyed me, hunger burning in the depths of his eyes. "Yes. I promise."

"Fine. I agree." Disgust washed over me, but a girl had to do what a girl had to do.

"Good," he murmured, leaning in and pressing his lips to mine. "Now, I want to meet your parents."

"Right now?" I lifted a brow at him as he pulled away.

"No time like the present. Besides, my dad gets out tomorrow, and I want you to come with me. I need you on this."

The last thing I wanted to do was meet the guy who'd killed Fox's mom, but I gave Ian the smile he sought and nodded. "Fine. I'll call my parents and let them know you're coming."

Ian smiled and backed away from me. Blowing out a breath, I dialed home and waited until Mom came on the line.

"Honey? Are you going to be late? I just made pot roast—" She didn't even bother saying *hi*, since I'd been late coming home the last few nights with my lies of studying and working on the yearbook, which I wasn't even a part of.

"Uh, no. Not really. I was wondering if I could bring a friend to dinner." I fiddled with a string on my shirt.

"Jamie? You know we love Jamie—"

"No, it's not her. Uh, we still aren't talking. It's someone else. H-his name is Ian. He's my boyfriend."

"Boyfriend?" Surprise colored Mom's tone. "I had no idea you were seeing someone. Of course. Bring him. We'd love to meet him."

"Thanks, Mom. See you soon." I hung up the phone and looked to Ian. "She said OK."

"Great," Ian muttered. "Let's go."

"What about your brother? No one will be here—"

"Andy is fine. He's nine. He knows how to handle his shit. His friend lives down the street if he needs anything." Ian held his hand out to me, and I took it, allowing him to pull me to my feet. We left his room and went to the front door.

"Andy, I'm leaving. Don't burn this shit hole down while I'm gone," Ian called out.

"Whatever. Bye, Rosalie." Andy waved to me.

I'd never know he was related to Ian. He was his polar opposite, or so it seemed.

"Bye, Andy. Be good, OK?"

"You know it." Andy turned away and went back to this video game as we left the house.

"Little asshole likes you more than me," Ian muttered, turning to plant a kiss on my lips at my car. "I'll follow you there."

"Great." I pulled away and peeked up at him.

He lifted a dark brow at me. "What?

"My parents don't know I'm in the musical. Can you not say anything?"

"Of course." He backed away and offered me a smile. "You can trust me." He turned and went to his car as I slid into mine.

The last thing I could do was trust him. But it was really all I could do at this point. I said a little prayer, just in case, though.

CHAPTER 23

"Ian, would you like more roast?" Mom asked as she lifted her tongs.

"No, thank you Mrs. Bishop. I've had plenty," Ian said. "It's delicious by the way. My mom doesn't cook, so this has been a real treat."

"Aw, I'm glad you like it. I'll send some leftovers home for you." Mom beamed at Ian who grinned back.

I wanted to roll my eyes at the exchange. He played nice but was a real snake.

"So, Ian. What are you planning on doing after high school?" Dad placed his glass on the table and lifted his fork. "Any colleges you're looking at?"

"Not really. The rising cost of colleges is ridiculous, and I can't afford a lot. I figure I can grab a two-year degree at a local college and work my way up the ladder somewhere. Maybe something in business."

"A decent plan." Dad nodded. "At least you're not too much of a daydreamer. Rosalie had it in her head she was going to go into music. Can you believe that?" Dad laughed like he'd told the joke of the year.

Ian glanced at me and smiled. I widened my eyes at him, hoping he wouldn't say anything about the musical.

"Rosalie is a really good singer. She sings for me sometimes." Ian took a bite of his dinner and winked at me. "She sounds like an angel."

"Singing won't get her anywhere in life. What she needs to do is buckle down on her academics," Dad answered gruffly. "You're a good kid, Ian. Talk some sense into her. Get that foolishness out of her head."

"I'll see what I can do." Ian chuckled, offering me another wink.

I let out a breath of relief at him not spilling the beans. The rest of dinner was an easy affair. I offered to help my mom clean up, but she laughed and nudged me toward Ian, telling me to show him my room. I thought it was an odd request, but I really didn't want Ian to have any more opportunities to interact with them, so I led him upstairs.

"So this is it, huh? The chastity queen's bedroom," he commented, surveying my stuff.

I grunted a response and sank down onto my bed. He went to my window and pulled my curtains open.

"Ah, and of course, the boy next door. How cute."

"Ian, don't." I sighed. "Close the curtains."

"Why?" He glanced back at me. "Looks like Fox is home."

I cast a quick peek at Fox's window and saw him and Cole inside, looking at a notebook. *Probably adding more names to it. Assholes.*

"Stop." I got up and reached for the curtains, but Ian grabbed me and pressed his lips to mine, his hands sweeping over my waist and up my back.

"What are you doing?" I gasped, breaking away from his kiss.

"Kissing you," he grunted, going back in for more.

The last thing I felt like doing was kissing him in my bedroom, but he moved me to my bed. He pushed me down on it, his hand working its way beneath my shirt to squeeze my breast.

"Suck my dick, Rosalie," Ian breathed out, grinding his erection against the apex of my thighs.

"No," I choked out.

He stopped kissing me and stared down at me. "You don't fucking tell me *no*."

"Please, what if my parents come in? What if—"

"*They* see?" He snarled. "You're worried about your fuck boys seeing you sucking cock? I thought you guys were into that sort of thing."

"Ian, it's not like that. Please. Just stop. I'll do it but not here. Not now."

He rolled off me and got to his feet. "Whatever. He closed the curtain anyway."

I chanced a glance to Fox's window to see that he had closed his curtains.

"I need to use your bathroom," Ian said gruffly.

I pointed toward my adjoining bathroom and watched Ian disappear inside. I sat up and rubbed my eyes as my phone buzzed on the dresser. I snatched it up and looked at the screen.

Fox: No one fucks you like I fuck you. Remember that.

I sighed and darkened the screen. All I wanted to do was go to Ethan.

"You're on the pill?" Ian called out, coming back into my room, holding my birth control in his hand.

"Hey." I got up and tried to grab my stuff from him, but he held it high over my head.

"You're on the pill and won't fuck me?" He glared down at me.

"It's not about that," I snapped, reaching out again.

He scoffed and shoved the pills to my chest.

"Whatever. If we're going to make an effort at this, then you need to put it forward too."

"I just wanted time, Ian," I murmured. "I don't want to just lie down and spread my legs, OK? I want to make sure this is right. I got hurt so much before. I don't want to ever feel that again." I was milking it, sure, but whatever worked.

He sighed when I thought he'd slap me. I clutched the pill packet in my hand and stared up at him, waiting for the hammer to fall.

"Fine. I accept it." He leaned in and pressed a kiss to my lips. "I will. For now. But if shit doesn't start changing, I'll just take it. I don't think you want me to do that." He nodded to the pill packet in my hands. His dark smirk sent chills down my spine. "Besides, these don't matter anyway. I want you forever and will do what I need to just to get it. Do you understand?"

"Yes," my voice was hoarse as he kissed along my jaw.

"It's hard not to do what I *need* to do. Sometimes I fail at it and do really bad things. You need to know that I don't know how long I can control myself. You're so fucking sexy, especially when you tell me no." He twined his fingers through my hair and tugged my head back. "But I'll give you the chance to tell me yes."

"Thank you," I rasped before he kissed me again.

"I need to go. I have to meet with some of my associates. I'll see you later." He pulled away, and I nodded. "Remember, we're seeing my dad tomorrow." He kissed me again and backed to my door, giving me a wink. "I look forward to all of this, Rosalie. I'm not as bad as you think I am. Just give me a chance."

I offered him a tight smile before he departed.

IT WAS WELL after nine before I made it to Ethan's. He met me outside and directed me into the garage where he closed the door. The moment I was out of my seat, his arms were around me, his lips on mine.

"I missed you," he murmured between kisses.

"Mm, show me how much," I answered as he kissed me once more then led me inside. He chuckled, giving my hand a squeeze. When we got inside, he urged me to the couch where we sank down, our lips molding to one another's again.

"I got you flowers and chocolate," he whispered against my lips. "They're on the counter."

I giggled and tugged him closer. "Let me show you my appreciation then."

"You haven't seen them yet." He chuckled back.

"I don't need to. They're from you, so I already love them." My fingers were already in the waistband of his pajama bottoms.

"Easy." He laughed, pressing his hands against mine to stop me.

"Why?" I pouted, pulling away from him.

He cleared his throat and glanced away from me, his Adam's apple bobbing.

"Ethan, what's wrong?" Worry coursed through me. I'd ground against his dick before, so I knew he was packing in that area, so he had nothing to be shy about. "Did I do something wrong?"

"No, sweetheart." He turned back to me, his pretty eyes shimmering with tears as he cradled my face. "Of course you didn't. It's just, I-I..." The words faltered on his lips, and he grimaced.

"Tell me." I squeezed his hand.

"I'm a fucking mess."

"Ethan, I already told you I don't care. I want you. Whatever *you* comes with it, I'm in."

"I'm scared that once you see me, you'll be disgusted by me." His words were soft.

"You could *never* disgust me. I think you're beautiful." I leaned in and kissed his lips. "Perfect. Mine."

He let out a soft moan as I kissed down his neck, my fingers back in his waistband. When he didn't stop me, I reached inside and grasped his thick hard-on.

"Fuck," he groaned as I pumped him in my hand for a moment.

"I want to see you, Ethan." I kissed his neck. "I want to taste you. I want to feel you inside me."

"Shit," he hissed out, shoving his pajama bottoms off and exposing himself. I moved south and looked down at him in my hand and gasped.

"Don't hate me," he whispered.

"Why are you hurt?" I asked, staring at the deep tears to his thighs. It looked like he'd fought a razor and barely won. There were wounds in various stages of healing. Some of them were fading, and some were angry, red cuts.

"I-I cut myself to make the other pain go away," he whispered. "I'm sorry, Rosalie. I'm fucked up."

"No. Shh." I straddled his lap and peppered his lips and face with kisses as he cupped my ass. "I don't care. I want you."

"Still?" He stared up at me with wide eyes.

"Always, Ethan."

"Babe," he murmured, pressing his lips to mine.

I ground against his dick, both of us breathing hard.

"Will you come to my bedroom?"

"Yes," I answered breathlessly.

He kicked his pajamas off the rest of the way and lifted me into his arms. Ethan carried me to his room where he laid me on his bed and hovered over me.

"You're beautiful, Rosalie. I'm a lucky man." His hands worked beneath my shirt so he could tug it off. He tossed it aside and went for my pants next. In moments, he had me bared before him. His remaining clothes joined mine on the floor.

I took great delight in running my hands over his hard muscles, enjoying the way he trembled beneath my touch as he kissed along my breasts before pulling a hardened peak into his mouth and sucking.

"Do you want me to keep going?" he asked. "I don't want to push you."

"Keep going. All the way," I managed to rasp as he slid a finger through my folds and teased my clit.

He let out a soft chuckle before pulling away and opening his bedside drawer. I heard the rattle of a condom wrapper before he rolled the condom over his dick.

He positioned himself between my legs and gazed down at me, so much adoration on his face it made my heart race.

Slowly, he pushed inside me, his thickness stretching me until I gasped. His eyes never left mine as he slid deeper. When he was fully seated inside me, he kissed along my jaw before whispering in my ear, "I love you so much, Rosalie. You're my entire world."

"I love you too, Ethan," I answered back. And I did. Right down to my bones, I loved this incredible man. The most beautiful smile graced his lips before they met mine.

He thrust in and out slowly, tormenting my body with his movements, his dick buried so deeply inside me I was sure I could feel it in my navel. All my guys could take care of my needs.

But were they still my *guys?*

"Where did you go?" Ethan breathed out as he moved in and out of me.

"Right here," I answered, kissing him.

"I thought I lost you."

"Never."

He moved faster, thrusting harder as our kisses grew more passionate and more frantic. The tingles grew, building quickly, before I came undone on his dick. He followed a moment later. He lay breathless over me, our bodies covered in a sheen of sweat.

"Amazing," he whispered, resting his head against mine. "I always wondered, but now I know."

I chuckled softly. "Good?"

"The best, sweetheart." He placed a kiss to my lips before pulling out of me and disposing of the condom. The bed creaked as he settled back beside me and pulled me into his arms.

"Stay with me tonight?"

"Yes." I nuzzled against him. "I already told my parents I was going to stay at Jamie's so we could talk about things."

"On a school night. Such a rebel," he teased, kissing my temple.

"You're one to talk." I giggled. "You're here seducing me on a school night."

"I think you seduced me, sweetheart." He gave me a squeeze.

"Mm, maybe."

He chuckled again and pulled the blanket around us.

"Ethan?"

"Hmm?" He twined our fingers together.

"What's your plan for Ian? How am I going to get free?"

He tensed for a moment before speaking. "You might have to do things you don't like."

"Fucking him?"

He let out a low growl in his throat. "I don't want him to *ever* fucking touch you, Rosalie, but we may have to get creative."

"He has one copy of the videos." Quickly, I told Ethan everything I knew and waited for his answer.

"Then maybe you need to get into his room and steal it."

"He watches me like a hawk."

"Then maybe turn the tables on him," he murmured. "Drug *his* ass."

"What?" I sat up and gawked down at Ethan.

He shrugged. "It's not like you're going to steal his virtue. Plus, he'd do it, and *has* done it, to you. Sometimes you gotta do what you gotta do. This is probably one of those times ... unless you just want me to kill him."

"I don't want anyone to die," I mumbled, only half-lying. I hated Ian.

"I can get something that'll knock him out. You can take it with you and try to slip it to him. You'll have to plan it just right. If it doesn't work, I'll do what I have to do. OK?"

"It'll work. I don't want you to kill anyone, Ethan."

He chuckled softly. "I'd take down the entire world for you, Rosalie. I'd die for you. Know that." He pressed a fierce kiss to the top of my head as I settled in beside him.

I knew he would, but I didn't want him to. I could do this. I could take Ian down without him dying for it.

Hopefully.

CHAPTER 24

Ian blew out a breath and ran his fingers through his hair. I knew he was nervous about seeing his dad. Hell, I was too, but for different reasons. The fact I had to look the monster in the eyes made me sick to my stomach. He'd taken Amy away from us. He'd changed the course of my whole life. Of Fox's.

My guts clenched as a muscular man came into view dressed in sweatpants and a t-shirt. He looked so much like Ian I cringed. Having two of them in the world was far too much.

"Dad," Ian called out, tensing beside me.

A wide grin spilled onto the man's face, the skin around his eyes crinkling.

"Ian. How are you, boy?" He reached out and gave Ian a quick, one-armed hug.

"Good. Great."

"Your mom and brother didn't come?" Daniel looked over Ian's shoulder to the parking lot behind us. The smile slowly slid from his face.

"No," Ian answered with a tight smile. "She had to work and said to remind you to stay away."

"Of course she did." Daniel's dark-eyed gaze swept over to me.

I shifted closer to Ian like his ass would save me. He'd probably throw me to the wolves if he thought he could have a scrap of me when I was done being eaten.

"Looks like you brought me something else instead. What a beauty." Daniel reached out for me, but Ian shifted so he was in front of me.

"No. This is Rosalie. She's my girlfriend."

Daniel lifted a brow. "Is that a fact? Well, at least you did something right." He let out a soft laugh. "So you're fucking this girl?"

I ground my teeth. "He's definitely not fucking me."

"Rosalie," Ian warned, gripping my wrist tightly.

I winced beneath the pressure.

Daniel laughed louder and shook his head. "Son, don't you know you need to keep your woman in line? Pretty girl like her should only be opening her mouth for your cock. If she's opening for anything else, get rid of her."

"Is that what you did to Cindy?" I asked, mentioning Ian's mom.

Daniel narrowed his eyes at me. "You're a smart mouthed, little bitch, aren't you? Ian would do well to show you some manners."

"Rosalie, come," Ian snarled, tugging me toward the car. He shoved me hard when we reached his vehicle, and I stumbled, banging my hip on the mirror.

"Get the fuck in, and if you say another word, I won't hesitate to shut you up. Got it?" Ian hissed in my ear.

I nodded tightly and got into the back seat as Ian went around to the driver's side and slid behind the wheel. Daniel moved into the passenger's seat. Once we were on the highway and Ian and Daniel were engaged in conversation—bullshit catch up stories and talk of all the chicks Daniel planned on fucking—I pulled out my phone and sent a quick text to Ethan.

Rosalie: I hate this.

Ethan's answer came immediately.

Ethan: I do too, babe. It's tearing me up to know you're stuck with those two fuckers. I'll make it up to you tonight. Promise.

A picture message of Ethan smiling at me came through, making my heart thrum happily. I darkened the screen and stared out the window at the passing scenery, wondering how exactly I was going to get to Ian and his flash drive.

"What are we doing here?" Daniel demanded as Ian pulled into the parking lot of a hotel.

"Mom said you can't stay at the house."

Daniel let out a snort. "Just because she decided to get a divorce doesn't mean *I* wanted it. I didn't plan on killing that dumb bitch—"

I'd had enough. I pushed open my door and got out.

"Rosalie, what the fuck are you doing?" Ian shouted, following me.

"I'm leaving. I will not sit another minute in the car with that man. In the few moments I've known him, he's managed to not only insult me, but Amy, the woman he murdered. Beat me if you need to, Ian, but I'm out." I glared up at him, my chest heaving.

He surveyed me with cool eyes before glancing back to his car. His dad hadn't gotten out.

"Fine. Go. You'll have to walk though. I'd like to spend some time with him alone anyway. He's been locked up for five years. He could use a decent meal." He reached out and tilted my chin up. "I'll call you later or something."

"Fine."

He didn't bother kissing me, which I wasn't even upset about. He simply turned and stalked back to his car, got in, and drove away.

When he was out of sight, I pulled my phone out and dialed Ethan.

"Are you OK?" Ethan asked the moment he answered.

"Yeah. Can you come get me? I'll be at Wanda's Ice Cream Palace," I said, noting the ice cream parlor across the street.

"I'll be there in a minute. I love you."

"I love you too," I said before clicking the phone off and making my way across the street to Wanda's.

The sooner I was out of Ian's grasp, the better. I couldn't live like this.

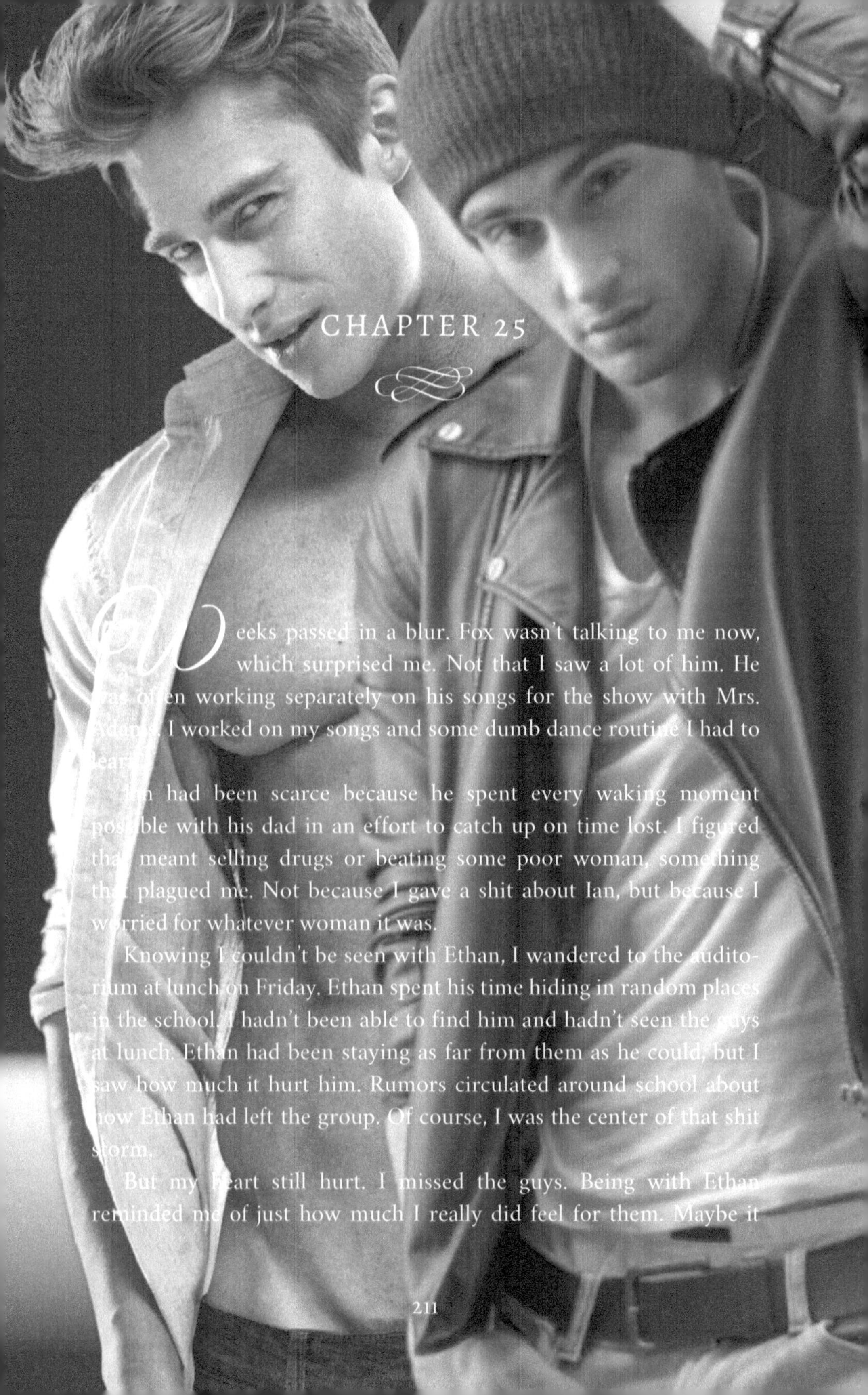

CHAPTER 25

Weeks passed in a blur. Fox wasn't talking to me now, which surprised me. Not that I saw a lot of him. He was often working separately on his songs for the show with Mrs. Adams. I worked on my songs and some dumb dance routine I had to learn.

Ian had been scarce because he spent every waking moment possible with his dad in an effort to catch up on time lost. I figured that meant selling drugs or beating some poor woman, something that plagued me. Not because I gave a shit about Ian, but because I worried for whatever woman it was.

Knowing I couldn't be seen with Ethan, I wandered to the auditorium at lunch on Friday. Ethan spent his time hiding in random places in the school. I hadn't been able to find him and hadn't seen the guys at lunch. Ethan had been staying as far from them as he could, but I saw how much it hurt him. Rumors circulated around school about how Ethan had left the group. Of course, I was the center of that shit storm.

But my heart still hurt. I missed the guys. Being with Ethan reminded me of just how much I really did feel for them. Maybe it was history with Fox which made me feel closer to them, like they were simply an extension of my former best friend. Dwelling on the past was taking away from just enjoying Ethan, and despite him saying he wanted me, I knew he wanted them too. They were his life. His family. I was a piece of shit for even thinking I could break up their friendship in the petty game I was playing.

I wanted my guys back more than anything. My steam for playing had run out the moment Ethan had kissed me.

I ran my hand over the fresh paint on the backdrop, marveling at how pretty the clouds were. I allowed myself to think about how I could *maybe* talk to the guys once I got the flash drive from Ian and was free. Maybe if I went all in with them, they'd drop Juliet and reveal their secrets. Imagining it brought hope to my heart. I dug in my bag for my phone as I walked toward the stairs behind the stage so I could text Fox to see if he'd meet me at the treehouse. Before I could, a hand shot out and pulled me back onstage. My backpack fell to the floor with a thud, my books spilling out.

"Cole?" I gasped as I swung around to face my captor. "W-wha—"

His hair was a mess, and his blue eyes were filled with that darkness he typically kept so well hidden.

Before I could finish my question, he spoke, "Shh," he hissed, shoving me roughly against the backdrop, his hand covering my mouth. "I have something to say to you, and you need to fucking listen, Rosebud."

His body moved along mine as I gazed back at him, my heart thudding in my ears. The thickness of his erection had me wide-eyed as one of his hands moved lower, finding its way between my legs. This was a sudden turn of events. My heart leaped in my chest at his nearness, hope blossoming. But something was wrong. Cole was upset.

"I've been waiting for you to wear a skirt," he growled, his hand still over my mouth. "Because it makes this so much easier for me."

"Cole—" The moan I emitted was muffled against his warm hand over my mouth as he shifted my panties aside and slid a finger into my tight channel, moving it slowly as his thumb swirled around my clit.

I tried to squirm from him because I wanted to tell him I was giving up, that I wanted him, but he pressed against me harder, his lips brushing along my ear, sending a torrent of goosebumps across my skin.

"You're pissed off. I get it. I'm pissed too. I think a little hate sex is just what we both need, so this is what's going to happen. I'm going to take my hand from your mouth. You're going to spread your legs and let me fuck you on this stage. When I'm done filling your pussy, I'm going to walk away. No one has to know. Do you understand?"

He inserted another finger into me as I whimpered beneath his hand.

"I know you're fucking Ethan. And I know about Enzo. You already fucked Fox. Now, it's my turn. I want you so much, Rosebud. You don't even fucking know. I lie awake at night thinking of you. Wanting you. Fucking *needing* you. You've done something to me I just can't get over. I've *never* felt this way about anyone before."

He pressed a shaky kiss against my temple as his warm breath blew against my skin. I remained frozen beneath his confession, my heart dancing with promise.

"*I want my cock buried in your pussy*. Tell me you want it too. That you want my mark deep inside you, claiming you, owning you. You belong to me. *To us*". He hooked his fingers inside me, hitting the perfect spot, making my eyes roll back. "You being pissed and fucking around with Ian doesn't change a damn thing. I know what you're going through, Rosebud. I ache for your pain alone. I know you're saving Ethan. If it's for real, I want in. I want *you*. You win, babe. I'm done playing." He pulled out, his blue eyes locked on mine as he sucked my wetness from his fingers.

Holy baby Jesus.

I knew I could stop this, and he wouldn't push me any farther. But I knew what I wanted, though. What I'd always wanted. Cole showing up in my moment of clarity was a sign. Originally, I'd wanted revenge. But now, I just wanted my life back. No more lies. No more games. Just my guys back.

I'd never been with Cole. We'd been so close, but then the shit with Juliet went down.

"Don't say a fucking word. If you scream or try to run, best bet I'll bury my cock in your ass instead. I'm not playing. Got it?"

I stared back at him, my heart racing so fast I was sure he could hear it. His hand fell away from my mouth, his eyes locked on mine. I didn't say a word as he lifted me up like I weighed nothing and shoved my panties aside. I'd give Cole Scott anything he wanted. Just like Ethan. Fox. Enzo. All of them had me. In that moment, I realized they'd never lost me. *Did I hate that about myself?* A little because I knew Juliet was still a problem. But in the words of Ethan, *Fuck Juliet.*

A moment later, the sound of his zipper was the only warning before he thrust into me with his bare cock in one fluid motion. Whimpering, I winced beneath the ache of his intrusion. The heat from his erection mingled with my own fire.

"Fuck," he hissed, breathing hard as he thrust viciously into me, both hands cradling my ass. The noise of slapping skin and heavy breathing filled the darkened auditorium as he ravaged me.

When his lips crashed on mine, I parted them to allow him entrance. His tongue danced in my mouth, hot and wanting, the kiss so deep and frantic I could barely breathe. I twisted my fingers in his blond hair, earning a growl of approval from him as he thrust faster.

"Come on my cock, Rosebud," he commanded against my lips as the flurry of tingles intensified through the heat of our connected bodies. "You're so fucking wet for me. Show me how much you like me fucking you against the wall."

His words were my undoing. I exploded in waves of euphoria, soaking his dick and moaning his name.

"Shh," he murmured breathlessly against my lips. "Not a sound from you, Rosebud."

My body trembled as he continued his fierce thrusts. I choked down my moans as I wrapped my arms around him, his mouth hot on the tender flesh of my neck, kissing and sucking with breathless fervor.

His hands tightened on my ass before he released a cheek. A

moment later, I buried my face in his neck, breathing in his cologne, as he clapped my ass cheek hard. Again. And again.

"Such a bad girl. Flaunting that fuck boy. Breaking my fucking heart," Cole snarled as he smacked my ass again. "You're playing a dangerous game." Another smack. "I'm not the one you want to fuck with."

"Cole," I choked out, tears prickling my eyes. I had to tell him what I'd decided.

"I told you no talking," he growled, smacking my ass again. It wasn't the smacking that made me swallow down tears. It was his raw admittance at me breaking his heart. Cole wasn't the type to display his feelings.

He smacked my other ass cheek. I sobbed into his neck, clinging to him, as he smacked again and again. He thrust deep. He wasn't gentle with his love. I bit his neck, sucking against it as tears dampened his skin.

"Look at me," he commanded roughly, fisting my hair and tugging my head back.

I stared into his blue eyes. So much turmoil clouded them. So much anger. Pain. Desire.

Love?

He released my hair so his fingers could wrap around my neck as he pressed me against the wall. His hold was firm, but not so tight that I couldn't breathe.

"Fuck," he hissed, his dick twitching inside me as he groaned out his release, my name on his lips on repeat.

He stilled, his eyes locked on mine, before pulling out of me and setting me back on my unsteady feet, both of us breathing hard.

His eyes bored into mine as he tucked himself into his pants. I stood, staring back at him, my body trembling from his onslaught, floored by what had just transpired.

He leaned into me and whispered in my ear, making my heart clench. "I want to drip down your leg all day. I want you to fucking remember who cares about you. Come back to us, Rosebud."

And then he walked away without bothering to sweet talk me into it. But he didn't have to. I knew what I was missing.

I'd made my decision.

It was time for a new game.

CHAPTER 26

"I'm sick," I whispered, my voice shaking as Ian escorted me to my car a couple of weeks later. It wasn't a lie. The guilt over being with Cole was eating me up inside. I wasn't sleeping. I couldn't eat. "I think I just want to go home and sleep."

He let out a sigh and rolled his eyes. "That sucks because my dick isn't going to suck itself."

"Ian, please. I need to rest. I-I don't feel well." I'd let Cole fuck me against a wall weeks before. The guilt at having done it and not telling Ethan was eating at my soul. It was a bitch move to fuck Cole and then have Ethan cutting off his friends for me. The disgust over it had me nearly vomiting.

Every day since, Cole shot me looks of longing in the halls. It made everything that much worse. All I could think about was fixing this mess. The stress of everything was tearing me apart.

"Fine. Go fucking home. I don't feel like listening to you bitch tonight." Ian rolled his eyes before stepping away from me. "I don't want to get sick anyway."

I let out a breath of relief as he turned and strode away. Wasting no time, I got into my car and started the engine. Moments later, Ian roared out of the parking lot, leaving me alone.

"Hey, sweetheart." Ethan slid onto my front seat.

"Ethan," I breathed out, surprised he'd gotten into the car. I hadn't seen him, but he must have been watching.

"Are you OK?" He reached out for me and cradled my face. "You've been so quiet lately. Do you want to talk?"

"No," I whispered, not even sure how I'd come out and tell him what I'd done. I didn't want to lose him once he found out that I was basically a lying, cheating bitch.

Ethan frowned and released me. He pulled a pill out of his pocket. "For you. Or rather, for that shit stain. It'll knock his ass out so you can grab the flash drive."

"You got it?" I stared down at his palm in wonder. Not that I'd doubted him, considering his history with drugs.

He nodded. "I don't dabble in Molly, Rosalie, so it took me a bit to get it. Just drop this in his drink. Make sure you don't drink it." Worry clouded his features.

"I-I won't." I took the pill from him and stared down at it. *Freedom.* I held it in the palm of my hand.

"You really don't think he has copies?"

"At this point, I don't think I give a shit." I locked eyes on his. "But no, I don't. Ian is a narcissist. He thinks he's got this on lockdown. I really do think his ego only allowed him one copy."

"OK, sweetheart." Ethan closed his hand over mine, covering the pill. "Then I think we both know what you need to do now." He pressed his warm lips to my hand. "It's time to end this and be my girl for everyone to see."

"Your eyes are glassy," I whispered as I stared at him, my heart fluttering at his words.

He offered me an ashamed smile. "I smoked weed behind the school to take the edge off. I-I took a few pills. I swear that's all it was. I, uh, actually want to talk to you if you have some time."

I sighed at his confession. At least he had the balls to be honest with me. I, on the other, lacked them. "I do because I want to talk to you too."

"My place then?" His voice shook.

I nodded wordlessly.

"I'll see you there in a few, OK?" He left a kiss on my cheek and opened the passenger side door. "Don't worry. Everything will be fine."

"Promise?" My voice cracked. I had to tell him about Cole.

"Swear it, Rosalie. There's nothing in this world or the next that could make me believe otherwise." The way he said that and the tiny, sad smile on his face made me think he already knew about Cole.

I offered another wordless nod as he got out of the car. "I love you," he said.

"I-I love you too."

And with that, he closed the door and walked to his car across the parking lot, his head down. I figured I'd just follow him in case he wrecked. I said a silent prayer he wouldn't though.

He had to know something. Or maybe it was just my anxiety. Either way, the truth would come out. It always did in the end.

WHEN I ARRIVED at Ethan's, he was already out of his car and waiting for me in the garage. I pulled in and cut the engine as he closed the door behind us.

"Come here, sweetheart," he murmured, pulling me into his arms as I closed my door. His warm embrace made me sniffle. "Talk to me."

"Inside," I whispered, pulling away and offering him a shaky smile.

He took my hand and led me into his house where we collapsed on the couch together. "Do you want a drink?"

I shook my head. "No, thanks."

He smiled and squeezed my hand. "Do you want to go first?"

"No." My voice was hoarse.

"OK. I'll go." He licked his lips. "I'm leaving Monday evening to check into a facility to help me get sober. Or at least so I'm not clawing at my flesh to use."

"What?" I stared at him in shock. "Really?"

He brought our joined hands to his lips where he kissed my

knuckles. "Yes. I need this. You're what the doctor ordered. I don't want to lose you because I'm fucked up. I-I don't want to die."

"Oh, Ethan." I wrapped my arms around him, and he immediately returned the embrace, his warm hands rubbing up and down my back.

"You're my inspiration and motivation, Rosalie. I want to make sure you know you've made the right choice in me. I don't ever want to disappoint you. This will help me. It gives my family peace knowing I'll be safe. It's for two weeks. I leave Monday night. I just don't know if I should go right now—"

"I won't let you stay behind just for me. Go. I'll be fine." I kissed him. "I'm so proud of you, Ethan. Know that." I brushed my lips against his again.

He deepened the kiss, pulling me onto his lap. We hadn't had sex since our first time, opting to simply enjoy one another's company. It was more his choice than mine because god knew I'd ravish his bones if he'd let me. Ethan liked taking things slow. He said he enjoyed savoring them.

"I won't leave you behind in this. Help will always be there. I-I'll tell Fox to look out for you while I'm gone. I know he will. He still cares, Rosalie."

"I know," I answered back, my heart clenching at the mention of Fox, hopeful that Ethan's words were true, and I hadn't lost him, or any of the guys, for good.

"I love you so fucking much," he murmured as his lips trailed across my jaw and down my neck.

I allowed my head to fall back, giving him better access to the sensitive skin. He took it, leaving his white-hot heat across my skin as he peppered kisses along it.

"I love you too," I moaned softly as he cradled my breast in his hand.

He let out a contented rumble as I tugged his shirt over his head. It landed behind me with mine since he had the same idea I did.

Tell him what you did. Do it, Rosalie, before this goes any further.

"Ethan, I—"

"Whatever it is, it's OK. I forgive you." He unclasped my bra, letting my breasts spill out against his chest. "I'll always forgive you."

"I-I did something bad with—"

"Shh." He silenced me with a deep kiss, his hands all over me. "No more, Rosalie. Trust that whatever it is, I'm OK. I promise."

I nodded, swallowing the lump in my throat.

"You're so fucking beautiful," he appraised as he stared down at my bare breasts.

I reached down and unbuttoned his jeans. When I slid off his lap, he shifted his hips up so I could tug his pants down. Going to my knees, I tugged his boxers down, his cock springing free.

He had so many scars on his legs and groin. I winced as I took them in. At least no fresh cuts had been made. That offered me some relief.

I wrapped my fingers around his thick length and pumped him up and down, staring up at him from my knees.

"W-Will you suck my cock, babe?" He purred softly. The fact he asked made heat gather between my legs. I'd yet to taste Ethan, and god knew I wanted to. I owed him this pleasure because I was such a bitch.

I answered by licking the pearl of liquid off the tip of his bulging head. He responded with a hiss, his eyes heavy with his lust.

When I sucked him into my mouth, he let out the sexiest moan. His fingers tangled in my hair as he thrust his hips up to meet my suck.

He hit the back of my throat with each frantic lift of his pelvis, his breathing growing more ragged as I sucked his long, thick length.

"Fuck," he groaned, his fingers tugging at my hair, sending delicious torrents of pain through my scalp. His hips kept their movement steady, his breaths panting until his cock twitched against my mouth and he filled it with his release.

I swallowed him down before pulling away from him and licking my lips.

"I-I've never done that before. Came from head," he said softly as he drifted down from his high. "If I was too rough or hurt you—"

I got to my feet and shimmied out of my pants. "Shut up and kiss me," I retorted, reaching for him.

He gave me his sweet smile and dragged me onto his lap, so I was straddling him, his mouth on mine as his fingers slid through my folds and into my aching center. I was breathless when he broke our kiss off to suck my hardened nipple in his mouth, the left then the right. With no effort, he shifted me to my back where he loomed over me before kissing down my chest. When the heat of his mouth met my pussy, I let out a soft moan.

He nipped and sucked at my swollen bud as I jutted my hips up to meet his mouth, my fingers in his hair.

And when I came, it was a blinding whirlwind of emotion.

He ate everything I gave him, a smile on his face as he came up for air. I was so done for.

CHAPTER 27

"How are you? We hardly get to see each other outside musical rehearsals." Jamie lurked down the hall by her locker and pretended like she was looking for something inside it.

"I'm good. Great," I said, talking into my own locker.

"I heard Ethan is leaving for a few days."

"Where did you hear that from?" Ethan wasn't exactly forthcoming on his personal life to people.

"I overheard Enzo and Fox talking about it."

It seemed unusual, but at the same time, Ethan did say he was going to tell Fox to look out for me while he was gone. And of course, Fox would let the other guys know. On the other hand, that meant they knew I was at least talking to Ethan. *Maybe.* I did have that fight with Fox about all of it weeks ago. Maybe they were still in the dark about my secret relationship with Ethan, and he'd just told them he was concerned for me.

I shook my head. It didn't matter. Everything would be out in the open soon. I planned on drugging Ian at my next opportunity and ending this shit.

My cell buzzed in my bag. I pulled it out and smiled down at the screen.

Ethan: I leave tonight. Closet?

"I gotta go." I stuffed the phone into my bag and grinned at Jamie.

She smiled knowingly. I hadn't told her, but I suspected she was aware of me sneaking around with someone. Lord knew she had lots of experience on my behaviors in the subject.

I rushed off to the janitor's closet near the auditorium. The door was cracked, so I pulled it open and stepped inside to find Ethan waiting for me.

"Sweetheart," he breathed out, tugging me into his arms and wrapping me in a tight hug. "I've been missing you."

"Same." I pressed my lips to his as his hands traversed my body. "I'll miss you even more when you're gone."

He smiled against my lips. "I'll be right back, sweetheart. Then I'll never leave again. Things will be better."

"Mm." I grinned as he rested his forehead against mine.

"But I'm worried about you, Rosalie. I-I don't know if my leaving right now is a good thing. What if you can't get the flash drive, and Ian—"

"Shh." I silenced him with a kiss. "I'll be fine, Ethan. I promise. I can do this."

"I just worry. If anything happens to you, it'll kill me. I-I can't lose you again."

"*You won't.* I want this with you."

"It's just, I haven't been completely honest with you, Rosalie. I want to come clean about what's going on with the guys and why things are the way they are with Juliet—"

"It doesn't matter. I've made my choice." My brain screamed at me to just tell him about that choice, but I didn't want to give him false hope. I wanted him better, and if things didn't work out with the guys, it would crush him.

Get the flash drive. End this.

That was the next step in this damn mess and the only thing I should be concerned with. After that everything would be better. Hopefully.

"OK," he whispered, giving my waist a squeeze. His smartwatch beeped, and he pulled away, grimacing. "Warning bell, sweetheart. I won't see you for two weeks. This is it. My parents are picking me up after school to take me."

I nodded, my throat tight. Reaching up, I cradled his face in my palms. "I believe in you. And I'll be here waiting when you get back."

He gave me a watery smile. "I love you so fucking much, Rosalie." His lips met mine, his kiss frantic and desperate as his large, warm hands moved to cup my ass through my jeans. We were both breathless when we broke apart.

"Come on. We need to go before the bell rings. You first. I'll give you a few seconds' head start."

I gave him another quick kiss and turned away, but he captured my hand. "Please be safe." His eyes glittered, worry on his face.

"I swear it."

He released me, and I left the closet only to find myself face to face with Juliet.

"Well, well, what do we have here?" She raised an eyebrow at me, her arms folded over her chest. "Does a little *Rosebud* have some secrets?"

Fuck.

CHAPTER 28

"What are you doing? Stalking me?" I demanded, glaring at her.

She examined a long, pink fingernail and shrugged. "No. Not really. More like looking for someone. But you wouldn't know anything about that, would you?" She cocked her head at me.

"If you're looking for Fox, he's not with me."

"I know that because he was just with me." She shifted closer to me. "Now, I know you weren't in that closet with Ian because Ian bailed after second period when his dad turned up in the office. So, if you weren't with Ian, who were you with? Because if Rosalie is doing bad, bad things with someone in a closet, I might have to save her boyfriend from the heartache of discovering it on his own. It's the nice thing to do, after all."

We were toast. And if she told Ian, *I* was toast.

"How about you save yourself the heartache and walk away," I said, clenching my teeth as we stared one another down.

She let out a laugh and shook her head, her blonde hair tumbling around her, before she pushed past me. I stared in horror as she yanked the door open. Ethan stepped out, his gaze roving from her to me.

When I caught the look on his face, I took a step back. There was only anger and pure hatred marring his handsome features. Juliet must have sensed it too because she stumbled away as he closed the door behind him.

"What *the fuck* are you doing here, Juliet?" he snarled, glaring down at her.

"I-I was looking for you. You never come around anymore—"

He advanced on her until she was against the wall. "And *why* do you think that is? You didn't take the hint the first fucking time I told you? *I don't want you.* You disgust me."

"But we—"

"*Have nothing*, Juliet. *We have nothing. You* have something with Fox, and if he wants to play your pathetic games, that's on him. Same for Cole and Enzo. But me?" He snorted. "Go fuck yourself because you won't be getting it from me. *Ever.* And if you so much as think about hurting *my girl,* I'll kill you and bury your body in your mother's fucking flower garden. Got it?"

Juliet parted her lips and reached for Ethan as he backed away. He swatted at her hands, disgust on his face.

"Never again will a person touch me that I don't want. You got that?"

She visibly swallowed and nodded, her eyes glistening with tears.

"Fucking monster," he growled, backing away further. "*Disgusting, fucking monster.* Stay away from me and Rosalie. I mean it, Juliet. If you start shit, best believe I'll finish it. You've already fucked everything up enough."

And with that, Ethan turned his back on her and took my hand, leading me away. I cast one last glance over my shoulder at her to see tears snaking down her cheeks, her chest heaving.

Whether she was actually sad or pissed, I had no idea. Nor did I want to stick around and find out.

~

"It'll be OK," Ethan soothed, pushing my hair away from my face. "Don't worry."

"We can't be seen together," I croaked as I cast a hasty look up and down the empty hallways.

Ethan frowned and backed away from me. "I'm going to stay. You need me here—"

"No!" I surged to him and grasped his hands. "No, Ethan. You have to go. If you want to do anything for me, then leave. I-I need you to go. I need you well."

"Oh, Rosalie," he sighed, resting his forehead against mine. "I'll call you when I can. I can't take my phone with me, but I can use a community phone. When I get back, we need to talk. I can't do this shit anymore."

"What shit?" My pulse thundered in my ears. *Was he done with me? Leaving? Did all of this push him over the edge? But he promised...Oh, god, maybe he does know about Cole...*

"Where'd you go?" Ethan cradled my face in his hands.

"Is it bad? Whatever we need to talk about?" I swallowed the lump in my throat and peered into his eyes.

A small, sad smile graced his lips. "Not unless you want it to be. You and me? We're good. I promised no matter what, we would be. I meant that."

I nodded, my throat tight. The bell jangled, and the voices of students surrounded us as the cafeteria doors opened around the corner.

Ethan pressed his lips to mine in a deep kiss, breaking it off before I could collapse into his arms. When he moved away from me, the coolness of his departure left me feeling empty inside.

"I'll see you soon, sweetheart. Promise." And with those words, he turned and walked away from me as the halls began filling with students.

CHAPTER 29

Cautiously, I made my way to my car a week later. Worry over Juliet ratting me out to Ian had long since settled into my bones, so I was wary all the time. Ian didn't act like anything had changed. If he knew, I definitely wouldn't be crossing that parking lot that evening after rehearsals. Once again, Fox hadn't bothered talking to me. But he'd stared at me. It wasn't just a look, though. There was so much turmoil in his baby blues that I nearly went to him.

But I knew I had to wait until I was free of Ian to do that. I still hadn't had a chance to get the damn flash drive. Tonight, Mr. Dennison informed us the paper would be running the story about the musical in next week's edition. Ethan had called me once since he'd left. He'd sounded tired but happy. It was the only saving grace I had since I'd also started feeling ill earlier today. I'd even dashed out of fourth hour to kneel in front of a toilet, hoping my nausea would pass. Luckily, it did, but that awful churning and exhaustion still plagued me.

"Hey, there, Sunshine," Enzo called out to me as I crossed the parking lot.

"Enzo?" I stopped at my car and spun around. None of the guys had spoken to me in so long, so for him to be following me to my car had me curious. And nervous. Really nervous.

"How are you?" He stuffed his hands into his dark, ripped jeans and cocked his head at me. His black hair was in its perfect faux hawk, and he seemed cheerful.

"I'm OK," I answered, frowning up at him.

"Yeah?"

I nodded. "What's going on?"

He shrugged and stared at the setting sun and squinted his dark eyes before he focused back on me. "Do you want to talk?"

I sighed. "Enzo, I'm really not feeling well. I have a lot going on and really just want to sleep."

It was his turn to nod. "Yeah, I get it. I'm sick and tired too. That's why I wanted to talk."

I bit my bottom lip for a moment, recalling the last time he and I talked.

As if reading my mind, he winked at me. "I won't fuck you unless you want me to."

The heat of embarrassment flooded my face, and I ducked my head. Enzo reached out and tilted my chin up and stared down at me.

"I think about that day all the fucking time, Sunshine." His voice took on a deep, sexy growl. "Even now, my cock is hard knowing you're thinking of it too." He stepped so close the heat from his body warmed me. "I'm very good at keeping secrets, Rosalie." He leaned in and brushed his lips across mine. "I won't tell."

"I-I can't," I breathed out, squeezing my eyelids shut tight.

Enzo's hands landed on my waist as he leaned in and ran his nose across my jaw. When he got to my ear, he whispered, "Because you love him, and betrayal isn't part of who you are. Right?"

"I-I don't love Ian," I choked out, trembling and wanting beneath Enzo's hold.

He let out a soft chuckle that sent a flurry of goosebumps rushing across my skin. "I'm not talking about Ian." He kissed my pulse point. "I'm talking about Ethan."

I said nothing, my heart racing, as he tightened his hold on my waist, his whispers continuing. "It's OK. I can feel your want, Rosalie. If I touched you right now, you'd be wet for me. You'd be wet *for us*. Tell me, Sunshine. I'll keep it a secret."

"Yes," I answered in a soft, shaky voice, not wanting to fight the truth. "I want you."

"Care to show me?" His hand moved from my waist to between my legs. He snaked his fingers beneath the hem of my skirt and into my panties. Enzo gently brushed against my aching center. "Tell me yes and I'll pick up where Ethan left off. Tell me no and I'll walk away."

"I-I can't. It'll hurt Ethan. I-I already—"

"Our world isn't what you think it is," he cut me off softly. "Fox. Me. Ethan. Cole. We've all been here." His fingers slid lightly over my gash, making me shiver.

"Y-you know about Cole?" I rasped.

Enzo let out another dark chuckle. "I know *everything*, Rosalie. It's part of what makes me so damn special."

I swallowed thickly, my legs trembling as Enzo continued to brush against my wetness. "Enzo?"

"Yes?"

"I...can we just... talk?" I held my breath, waiting for his answer. I'd changed my mind. I needed to talk.

"Of course, Sunshine," he murmured, withdrawing his fingers and gazing down at me with crinkled eyebrows. "What's wrong?" He'd completely shifted gears.

I cast a furtive look around.

"He's not here. It's OK." Enzo thumbed my bottom lip. "I'd never put you in danger by risking him knowing, Rosalie."

I nodded. I knew that, and despite everything that had transpired, I also knew Enzo was trustworthy, even if he could be cryptic. "Did you tell anyone a-about me a-and Cole? Ethan?"

"No." The answer was simple. "I didn't say a word." He gave me a small smile.

I winced and rubbed my stomach, the nausea churning a storm. "What's wrong?"

"I don't know. I think I'm getting sick or something." I frowned as bile rose in my throat.

The words had barely left my lips when I was shoving past Enzo and rushing behind my car to empty my stomach. Enzo was by my side immediately, holding my hair back as I threw up. When I was done, I leaned against the trunk of my car and squeezed my eyelids closed.

Enzo reached out for my forehead and frowned. "You don't have a fever." He was silent for a moment before he spoke again, "Do you and Ethan use condoms, Rosalie?"

"What?" *What a weird question.* "We've only done it once, and yes, we used a condom."

"I used one," he continued softly, moving a lock of hair away from my face. "And you haven't been with Fox in a while. Ian?"

"No," I snapped at him, wondering what the hell he was getting at.

Enzo nodded, his Adam's apple bobbing. "And Cole?"

I froze, remembering that day over a month ago when Cole and I had been together backstage.

No condom.

"Y-you don't think I-I'm p-pregnant, do you? I'm on the pill."

Enzo scratched his face for a moment as he surveyed me. "Ian was in your room. Fox and Cole were pissed about it."

I winced at the memory but nodded.

"Did he have access to your pills?"

I nodded wordlessly again, the ugly memory of his hands on my pills.

These don't matter anyway.

I hadn't thought anything of it at the time, but if that bastard did something...my body shook. All Ian's words from that day in my bedroom came rushing back.

"Did you miss your period this month, Rosalie?" Enzo's voice snapped me back to the moment.

"I-I did. It happens sometimes. It's been late before, but not like this. I should've had it already. I-I thought it was stress. I shouldn't even tell you this stuff. No guy wants to hear—"

"Rosalie." Enzo reached out for me and pulled me into a tight hug. "It could be nothing, but I think you should get a test if you don't start feeling better in a few days. And don't ever think I don't want to hear about anything going on with you. This is important. Everything to do with you is."

I twisted my fingers around his shirt and clung to him, a painful possible reality settling in. "Enzo, I'm scared."

"Shh," he soothed softly. "It's probably nothing. Try not to worry—"

"How the hell do I not worry?" I asked desperately. "What do I do if-if I am?"

"Then I'll be there for you. So will Ethan and Fox. And Cole."

"Oh god. What's Cole going to say?" My breath came in short, sharp gasps.

"Stop, Rosalie." Enzo gripped my shoulders and stared down at me. "Stop. Get the test. Don't fly off the handle until you know. OK? One step at a time."

I swallowed and nodded, feeling numb and frantic all at once.

"Do you want me to get you a test?" he asked softly, his dark eyes wavering as our gazes locked. "I'll be there with you if you need me."

"No. No. I-I'll call Jamie." I started to back away, but Enzo reached for me and took my hand.

"Rosalie. Nothing has changed. Don't think it has. We still want you. We just wanted to give you some space. Whatever happens, we'll be here for you." He thumbed the tear on my cheek away.

"And Juliet? Will she be gone?" I asked the question I desperately needed the answer to.

"Yes. Soon, Sunshine. I'm working on a way to make her... go away."

"I-I thought you guys wanted her over me—"

I was silenced as Enzo's lips met mine in the softest, gentlest kiss. His hand cradled my face as his other rested on my waist.

When we broke apart, he whispered, "No one would *ever* choose her over you. In all of this, you're the one we've chosen. I know it doesn't look that way, but I swear to you it's the truth. Once she's gone for good, you'll be ours. We aren't ever letting you go, Rosalie. We never did. We never will. Do you understand?"

"Yes," I whispered, my heart thudding hard.

"Tell me, Rosalie, will you come back?" His voice shook as he continued to hold me. "Even if you know the truth about everything and it scares or hurts you, will you come back?"

"I-I want to, but I'm scared—"

"You don't need to be afraid, babe. Not when I'm here. Not when I hold you. Anything that happens, we'll get through it together, OK? Promise me."

"I promise. But Ethan—"

"Ethan will be happy, Rosalie. You know he will. Me kissing you. Cole and you. He won't be mad. He wants this just as much as any of us do."

I knew his friends were his family. I knew how much this all meant to him. But I'd gone behind his back with Cole. I'd kissed Enzo. I'd basically made Ethan choose. It all made me a monster. Maybe I'd stressed myself out to the point of sickness, but Cole didn't wear a condom. And I was sick in so many other ways.

The nausea churned again.

"And if I'm pregnant, you won't leave?"

"Not a fucking chance." He pressed a fierce kiss to my forehead before his breath ruffled my hair. "For what it's worth, I'm sorry for coming on to you earlier. I only wanted to talk, but damn, Sunshine, you do something to me when you open your mouth and look at me with those big, beautiful eyes. You're my enchantress and fuck if you don't have me under your spell."

I gave a soft laugh and hugged him. I wasn't feeling great, but I wasn't freaking out as much inside. Not really. Enzo was right. I needed to take a test. One step at a time. I now had two birds to knock out: Pregnancy test and Ian. I wasn't sure which one made me more nervous.

"You should go call Jamie. I'll follow you home. I'm stopping at Fox's anyway." Enzo steered me back to my car door and opened it for me. I got behind the wheel, and he closed me in.

"Are you going to tell Fox and Cole?"

"No. You know I keep secrets, baby girl. Besides, there's nothing to tell other than I was lucky and got to kiss you and hold you again. You don't know how much I've missed that."

"Maybe once we get this sorted, we-we can try again. I-I just need to get my stuff figured out right now. I have so much going on, and I really want to know what Ethan wants. If he says no—"

"Ethan won't say no."

"If he does a-and if I'm pregnant..." my voice cracked.

"Cole won't walk out, Rosalie. Trust me on that."

I nodded, my throat tight. "OK. No sense in worrying yet, right?"

"Right." He offered me a sweet smile that made my heart tumble in my chest.

"You know, if I wasn't supposed to be just with Ethan, and my life wasn't falling apart right now, I'd have taken you up on your offer." My words came out barely above a whisper.

"I know, Sunshine. I know." He winked at me and backed away. "Raincheck?"

I gave him a shaky smile. "Yeah. I hope so."

The smile on his face widened. "Let's plan for the first Saturday of next month. My place. You in?"

"We'll see."

"That's not a no. I accept it."

A lot of factors were in play. Factors that could change my life or end it.

CHAPTER 30

I stared down at the pack of birth control pills in my hand.

"They look like birth control," Jamie offered as she stood at my side. "I mean, they're the right color at least and look to be about the right size. Some are still unopened in the packaging."

I chewed the inside of my cheek as I surveyed them. They really did look like my birth control. Jamie took them from me. I went into one of my other drawers and pulled out an unopened pack. With shaky hands, I popped a tiny pill out of the tin. Jamie took one from the pack she held, and we compared the two pills like I'd suddenly become the Sherlock Holmes of the pharmaceutical world.

"Whoa," Jamie choked out. "They're different."

Horror raced through me. I knew Ian was sneaky. He had to have switched out the packs with one of his own. I was sure he had the means, considering his side hustle. Bile burned my throat, this time not from being sick, but from disgust at what that monster did to me.

"He said he'd put a baby in my belly, and we'd be together forever," I managed to say in a trembling voice. "Do you think he did this so that if I did do it with him, I'd be trapped?"

"Rosalie, we both know he's a snake. I think your gut instinct is right. But you didn't, right? You swear, you and Ian never had sex?"

"I *never* had sex with Ian." I leaned against the sink, my head down as I drew in a shaky breath. "And I never will."

"I got a test. I think you should take it." Jamie reached into her purse still on her arm and pulled out three packages. "I got three different brands, just in case."

"Fuck," I groaned, rubbing my eyes. "Jamie, I'm scared—"

"It's OK, Rosalie. I am too, but we can do this together, OK? I'll be right here with you."

I nodded, taking the boxes from her. I wiped at my damp eyes and drew in a calming breath. "OK. I need to know."

"I'll be in your room. We'll wait together." She backed out of the bathroom and offered me a comforting smile that didn't quite reach her eyes. She was just as worried as I was.

It took everything I had just to get through peeing on all the sticks. When I was done, I placed them on the bathroom counter and stepped back into my room to wait the agonizing ninety seconds for the results.

It had taken me four long days to decide to even look at the pills or tell anyone other than Enzo. I'd hope it was just a stomach bug. Worry had made sleeping impossible, which led to me and Jamie having a long phone conversation last night.

"If you are pregnant, you think it's Cole's?" Jamie asked as she sat beside me.

"Yes. Without a doubt," I answered, my heart racing faster as the seconds slipped by. Questions and fears kept throwing down in my head, making all the nausea worse.

What if I was pregnant? What would I say to Cole? To any of the guys? And, oh my god, Ethan. Not only did I make him choose between me and the guys, but then I'd gone and gotten pregnant after that choice. I was sick. Despicable. Disgusting. My parents would disown me. Would I be able to finish school? College? What if I had to do this on my own?

The beeping of Jamie's phone pulled me out of my thoughts. "It's time," she said, giving my hand a squeeze.

I shook my head, not wanting to know yet desperate to know. "Together, Rosalie. OK?"

I nodded, and she got up and went to the bathroom. When she returned, she was holding the tests in her hands.

"I didn't look." She kneeled in front of me. "It's going to be OK even if it means we move far from this shit hole just the two of us and take care of a baby together. I won't leave you alone in this. We're best friends, Rosalie."

I nodded, my throat tight, as she handed me the first test. Drawing in a deep breath, I stared down at it, my lips parting.

"Look at the next one," she urged, her voice shaking, as she handed me the next test. The same result greeted me.

"Last one," her voice cracked this time, and I took the final test with trembling fingers.

Same.

Two pink lines, a plus, and a *"pregnant"*.

"I'm pregnant," I whispered.

Life never went according to plan. I should've learned that long ago. I mean, I had a best friend I thought would be by my side forever until tragedy tore him from me.

If I'd learned anything in my life, it was that the status quo was never meant to last.

"We need to talk," Ian's voice broke into my daydream. Or rather, nightmare, as I sat in the cafeteria at lunch alone.

Jamie had been a rock the last week. She'd been there for me as much as our secret friendship could allow. Whenever I saw Enzo, he cast worried looks at me. He'd even texted me, which I hadn't answered.

What could I say?

Nothing. The person I needed to talk to was Cole. And then Ethan. Or maybe Ethan then Cole. It was a screwed-up situation I was dreading partaking in.

"About what?" I asked listlessly.

"My place. Tonight."

"Ian, I have rehearsal—"

"Then after. Long story short, I'm moving in with my dad until college starts for you. Then I'm getting a place near your college so we can be together. I just want to know if you plan on rooming on campus or with me." He gave me a smile as I stared at him in disbelief. "I guess I should rephrase that. You're going to live with me, so I want to at least include you in on the planning."

"Ian—"

"Save it for tonight. I might be late getting there. Just wait for me in the living room with Andy. My mom won't be there, and the kid could use the company."

Alone. In Ian's house. Where the flash drive was.

"OK. I'll be there."

"Maybe you can spend the night," he added, leaning down to whisper in my ear. "We can finally get down to business."

I swallowed the lump in my throat. "Maybe. Want me to make you dinner?"

Ian straightened and stared down at me. "You want to make me dinner?"

I shrugged and fixed a fake smile on my face. "I want you to be happy. We're going to move in together. What if you don't like my cooking? We should probably practice some domestic duties."

"The only domestic duty I want to practice is fucking your tight, little pussy," he growled, his eyes glittering with darkness. "Don't worry about food. You already have what I want to eat." With those parting words, he turned and left me sitting at the table, more than ready to feed him his just desserts.

"ROSALIE, I NEED YOU MORE DESPERATE," Mr. Dennison called out during rehearsals later that day as I stood facing Fox.

Not one word past his lines had left his lips.

How much more desperate could I get?

I squared my shoulders and nodded. I had not one ounce of desire to do this stupid musical at the moment. All I wanted to do was call Ethan, fall into Fox's arms, whisper my secrets to Enzo, and tell Cole what the hell was going on. I felt defeated. I was ready to be done.

"Again. From the top!" Dennison shouted, backing away from the stage.

"Nothing is as it seems," Fox declared, his deep voice booming out around us as he delivered his line. "Not the sun. The moon. The stars. We only think we know, but it's but a little piece of the truth."

The truth in those lies doesn't matter when we want to conquer the world. Say the line, Rosalie! Come on!

My throat tightened as I stared back at Fox. He cocked his head slightly as he surveyed me. *I love you. I need you. God, please hold me again. I'm drowning in this mess.*

"Rosie, you can do it," Fox murmured so only I could hear him. They were the first words he'd spoken to me in weeks.

I'd missed the sound of his voice. The way his touch was tender yet demanding. His fierceness. The way he reached for me when I needed him.

I shook my head, my bottom lip trembling. I backed away. He stepped forward. I backed up again.

He reached for me, his brows crinkled, and drew me into his arms. Without a word, he tilted my chin up and studied me for a moment. Torment blanketed his face. It was the same thing which was eating me up inside.

And then he kissed me. His tongue slid over mine. I didn't fight him. I fell into the kiss, letting my fingers twine through the silkiness of his hair, letting him hold me tight as he worked his mouth against mine.

There were catcalls in the theater. Mr. Dennison cleared his throat. In the distance, I was sure I heard Juliet, who was in the seats with Cole and Enzo, swear.

I broke the kiss off, my heart aching.

"Don't," Fox whispered frantically, clinging to me. *"Don't run, Rosie."*

"I-I have to. I'm sorry."

And I did exactly what he told me not to do. I ran off the stage and didn't stop until I was in my car. Then, I drove to the one place I hated. Ian's.

<h1 style="text-align:center">CHAPTER 32</h1>

"Ian's not here," Andy said, holding open the door for me.

I stepped past him and went into the living room. "I know. He said to wait for him here."

Andy shrugged and went back to his Xbox. "You can wait in his room if you want. Just don't touch anything. He gets really mad about that."

"Does he do that a lot? Get mad?" I asked, shifting my weight nervously.

Andy frowned. "Yeah. He's not nice."

"Tell me about it," I muttered, looking around at the small, tidy space. I barely ever had any interaction with Ian's mom. She was always working.

"Is he mean to you too?" Andy asked, placing his controller on the coffee table.

I nodded, swallowing hard. "Sometimes."

"He's mean to me and Mom. Sometimes he pushes her. He hits me when he's angry. He's like Dad."

"I'm so sorry, Andy." I moved and kneeled in front of him. "You should tell someone."

Andy stared back at me with his big, brown eyes. "Why don't you tell someone?"

I gave him a watery smile. "Guess I'm scared."

"Me too," he whispered. "I wish he'd leave. He hurts a lot of people. If he can't leave, Rosalie, maybe you should. You're pretty like my mom. I think she wants to leave sometimes like she did with Dad."

"Promise you'll tell someone the next time he hurts you, Andy."

"I will if you promise to tell on him too."

I nodded. "Promise."

He gave me a relieved smile as I moved away. He picked up his headset and put it on. I got to my feet and backed away, ready to do what I had to, hoping like hell the flash drive was where I'd seen him put it. If everything went to plan, I wouldn't need the tiny pill nestled in my pocket.

When I got to his room, I entered and headed straight to his desk. Hauling in a deep breath, I said a silent prayer as I pulled open his drawer.

And there it was. The same drive he'd held in his hands. I quickly brought my laptop out of my bag and stuck the flash drive into the port. In a few seconds, I was able to open the files to find all the videos. Everything he said was there and more.

He'd taken a video of me, Cole, and Fox. Ian must have been behind a building off to the side of the corner we'd been. He had the video of me, Enzo, and Cole from Enzo's basement. Ian had videos of me at my locker, talking to the guys. Everything was there.

I erased every damn file on it and shoved it back into his desk. Quickly, I snapped my laptop closed and stowed it back in my bag. Then I went back to the living room and called out goodbye to Andy who offered me a smile and wave.

My hand was on the doorknob when the door burst open and Ian came in.

"Going somewhere?" he demanded. He looked pissed.

"I-I need to get home. My parents want me there for dinner—"

"No. My room. Now."

"Ian—"

"Now, Rosalie!" he bellowed.

Andy looked over at us, fear on his face. I gave him a smile, not wanting him frightened, and followed Ian into his bedroom.

"Andy. Leave. Go see if Ben is busy," Ian snapped over his shoulder, mentioning Andy's friend, Ben, who lived a few houses down.

Andy cast me a terrified look before rushing out of the house.

The moment we were inside Ian's bedroom, he shoved me down onto the bed.

"Guess where I was?" he seethed.

"Your dad's?"

"I was until I got a very bad text. You want to know what that text said?" He glared down at me.

"No," I squeaked out.

His wicked laugh sent chills down my spine. He tugged his phone out of his pocket and shoved it in my face. There was a picture of Fox kissing me onstage only hours before.

"Imagine getting this and then being asked to meet someone. Guess who I met?"

"I-I don't know, Ian—" My words came to an abrupt halt as his hand connected with my face, the sting of the hit making my eyes water. But I knew who he'd met. *Juliet.* She was the only one with this information.

"Don't fucking lie to me, you little bitch," he snarled. "You've been lying to me."

"I-I haven't—"

He let out another laugh. "I want to hear you say it, Rosalie. Tell me the fucking truth. You're *fucking* Masters, aren't you?"

"Ian, I—"

"Fucking tell me the truth!" Spit flew from his mouth as he shouted, his face red, his hands clenched into fists.

"You can't hold me prisoner, Ian," I whispered. "I don't want this life. This isn't a relationship! This isn't how you love someone!" I rose to my feet and glared at him, knowing I was done. "Why do you want to ruin my life? What the hell is the matter with you? Don't you want to fall in love and be happy? You can't force someone to love you. *Just fucking stop!* You're a psychotic asshole! No one will *ever* love you like this." I balled my hands into fists, my body trembling from anger.

He stared at me for a moment before slowly approaching to tower over me.

Without a word, he gripped my face painfully. "Fucking tell me the truth," he repeated. "Are. You. Fucking. Masters?"

"Yes," I whispered.

His hands shook for a moment before he released me. Like a flash of lightning, he struck me again, snapping my head to the side. The pain reverberated through my skull, making my ears ring. Immediately, my hand cradled my aching cheek as I backed away.

"When did it start?" he snarled, his chest heaving as he raked in breaths. "Do you love him instead?"

"I don't owe you an explanation, and yes, I love him," I whimpered, taking another unsteady step away from him.

"You fucking slut! I'm your fucking boyfriend—"

"You're my nightmare, Ian. Nothing more. I don't love you. I *hate* you. I made a mistake ever being anything to you. You don't deserve my friendship let alone my love."

He let out an angry snarl and shoved me hard. I hit the wall and bounced off. His hands came at me again, this time twisting through my mess of hair and yanking. I let out a cry as he hauled me across the room by my tangles straight to his adjoining bathroom.

My mind immediately raced to the baby snuggled in my belly. I couldn't let him hurt the baby.

"Stop!" I slapped at him, my eyes burning from the pain of his fingers tugging on my hair. Horror filled my chest as he pulled out a pair of scissors from his drawer, a look of pure hatred on his face.

"No. No!" I shrieked as he shoved me hard. I lost my footing and fell sideways. Without wasting a moment, I crawled as fast from him as I could with one goal in mind: *Protect the baby.*

His foot met my back in a ferocious stomp, sending me to my stomach in a painful slam. Wasting no time, he straddled my back and gripped my hair in his fist, tugging my head back.

"You won't be so fucking hot without any hair," he snarled. "No one wants a bald whore."

"Ian, no! Please!" I struggled against him, but it only fueled his fire.

When the first ribbon of red fell, the damn broke inside me. I gripped my hair, trying to protect it. I bucked and kicked beneath him as every chunk of hair fell in ugly, broken strands beside me.

And all I could think about was what Fox would say when he saw me. How he would react if he didn't have my hair to run his fingers through. What he would say. What he would do. He'd always loved my hair.

I needed him. He'd save me from Ian. He promised he'd protect me from the monsters all those years ago.

And Ethan. What would Ethan do? Would he kill Ian? Would I let him? Would I risk losing one of the ones I loved just to be free?

And the baby. I had to tell Cole, but if Ian killed me, I'd never get the chance.

Ian let out a snarl and slammed my face to the floor. A sob ripped from my chest as I struggled to break free from him. It was no use. He was too strong.

I lay sobbing on the floor as the final strand fell. Ian stopped moving, and I stopped struggling.

"Why did you make me do this?" he whispered in a choked voice. "Why can't you just fucking love me, Rosalie?"

I said nothing, sniffling softly.

A cry left my lips as he rolled me onto my back and stared down at me.

"Fuck. Fuck!" He shouted, his eyes wild as he took in the damage his rage had caused. "Rosalie—"

"I want to go home. Please, let me go home," I whispered in a choked voice.

He moved off me without a fight and held his hand out to me. I took it, and he pulled me to my feet, wrapping his arms around me.

"I'm sorry, Rosalie. I fucked up. Please forgive me. I forgive you. I only wanted—"

"Let me go," I said softly. "Please. I need to go."

He released me, and I stumbled away, taking in the look on his face. It was something between anger and sadness.

"Rosalie," he called out when I got to his bedroom door.

I paused and stared back at him as he stood in the center of his room.

His Adam's apple bobbed in his throat. "This doesn't change our deal. You're still mine."

"I'm really not, Ian. Not anymore." I stumbled out of his room amid his silence, praying he wouldn't follow.

When I managed to make it to my car, I locked the doors and peeled out of his driveway, tears snaking down my cheeks and my body aching. I was free.

CHAPTER 33

**Ethan: Where are you, sweetheart? Are you OK? I'm home.
I want to see you.**

My hand shook as I dimmed the screen and lay in bed with my blanket pulled up to my cheeks. I couldn't face Ethan in the state I was in. He was back a day early.

I didn't respond. Hell, I couldn't even think straight. Instead, I turned and faced my bedroom window. The curtain was open, and so was Fox's. His room was dark, meaning he was probably buried inside Juliet somewhere, even after our kiss.

I was crazy wanting him when all this shit was going on. *What the hell is the matter with me?*

A fresh wave of tears overtook me, and I shook, sobbing softly, curled into a ball. *When had my life gotten to this point?* I was pregnant. My hair was a mess. I'd been beaten. I hadn't bothered to survey the damages. I just knew I hurt, and my hair barely brushed past my shoulders in uneven, choppy strands.

My heart gave a jolt when Fox's bedroom light flicked on. I watched as he tossed his jacket onto his desk chair and ran his fingers through his hair. As if sensing my eyes on him, he stopped and slowly glanced to my room.

In moments, he'd crossed the room and stood at his window, staring at me. The tears continued to slide down my cheeks as our eyes locked. His brows crinkled before he pulled his phone out and dialed a number. A moment later, my phone buzzed. I made no effort to answer it as we continued to stare at one another.

He rested his hand against the glass, his mouth turned into a deep frown. Not able to handle seeing him, I closed my eyes, my body shaking from my soft sobs. I must have lay there forever before the creak of my door opening barely registered in my ears. Quiet footsteps padded across my floor. A rattle signaled my curtains being closed. My parents were out for the night, so I knew it wasn't them.

"Sweetheart," Ethan called out softly, my bed shifting beneath his weight. "What's wrong? I texted you. I'm home."

My heart clenched as Ethan shifted beside me and curled up against my body, his arms around me.

"Talk to me, Rosalie."

"How did you get in here?" I asked, my voice barely above a choked whisper.

"Your dad's study."

Of course. The window.

"You didn't come to me tonight when I messaged. I was worried." He adjusted the blanket so only the top of my head was poking out. "Are you sick?"

"No. I just want to be alone."

He grew quiet for a moment then he cleared his throat. "Sorry, sweetheart, I can't do that." He ran his fingers through my hair and froze when my hair stopped short.

"What happened?" His voice shook, and he stiffened against me.

I sniffled again.

"Rosalie, what happened?" He turned me onto my back and tugged the blankets down. His eyes widened as he took in the disaster I'd become.

"What the fuck happened?" he demanded, his eyes darkening. "Who the fuck did this to you?"

I couldn't even choke out the words. Instead, a fresh wave of tears overtook me, and I sobbed like a baby. Ethan went up on his knees and grasped my shoulders before giving me a slight shake.

"Tell me, Rosalie."

"Ian," I managed to say, my voice cracking.

"Mother fucker," he snarled, getting to his feet and pacing, his fingers yanking his hair.

"I'm sorry, Ethan. Don't be mad—"

"Mad? Rosalie, I'm fucking *pissed*! I'll kill him. I'll fucking kill him." He stopped and came back to my side. He reached out and cradled my face in his hands, a look of torment washing over his features. "Your face. He hit you. Your cheek is swollen."

My bottom lip trembled. "I'm sorry," I repeated.

"You don't have a reason to be sorry. But he fucking does." He pulled away, but I reached for him.

"Don't go. Please, Ethan. Don't." I knew exactly what he was planning to do, and I couldn't allow it to happen. "I need you. I've missed you so much. Please stay with me."

He chewed on his fingernail for a moment before he came back to me and gently shifted me into his arms as he moved to lie beside me. I closed my eyes as he thumbed my tears away.

"I'll fix it, sweetheart. I'll make it better."

"There's nothing left to do," I whispered.

"There is. Let me take care of you. OK?" He pressed a gentle kiss to my lips. "Let me see it."

I shook my head, swallowing hard.

"Rosalie, please."

I opened my eyes and stared into his.

"It's OK," he murmured.

I nodded and shifted beside him so I could sit up. His eyes drank in how I looked. He reached out and tugged on a short lock.

"You're beautiful. Believe me?" There wasn't a doubt written on his face.

I nodded sadly, wanting to believe him. "Is it bad?"

"No, sweetheart." His Adam's apple bobbed. "It's fixable." He thumbed away another tear before he leaned in and placed a kiss on my bruised cheek. "Ian, however, won't be when I'm done with him."

I grasped his wrists as he cradled my cheeks and shook my head. "No. I don't want you to get involved."

"I got involved the moment he drugged you all those months ago, Rosalie. I should've ended him then. This is my fault. I won't fail you again."

"Ethan, I'm *begging* you not to do something stupid. If something happened to you, I don't know what I'd do. I-I need you. *I love you so much.*"

His eyes widened at my proclamation then his lips met mine in a deep, passionate kiss, his fingers tangling in what was left of my hair. I pulled him down onto the bed with me, relishing in how it felt to have him positioned over me, in control.

We said nothing as we made quick work of disposing of our clothes. Before long, we were both naked, Ethan's hands gliding gently over my body, his lips still molded to mine. My body ached. I tried not to wince under his tender touch because I wanted him so much. If he knew I was in pain, he'd stop.

He slid his hard erection against my damp center, making me mewl with want, his warm breath mingling with mine as we touched one another.

"I want you," he whispered against my lips.

"Take me," I answered back, my fingers working their way through his thick hair.

He gazed down at me sheepishly. "Would you believe me if I said I don't have a condom? I don't want to put you at risk of getting..."

I had to tell him.

"What's wrong?" He breathed out, not finishing his previous sentence. "You haven't been yourself lately. Tell me, sweetheart. Is it because I was gone? Are you upset—"

"I'm pregnant."

He froze over me, his eyes wide. "What?"

I pushed him off me and sat up. He reached out, captured my arm, and pulled me to him. "What did you say?"

"I-I'm pregnant."

"Is it Ian's?" His voice cracked as pain flickered through his eyes.

"No. I've been trying to tell you something the last few weeks, Ethan. I cheated on you. I'm so sorry." A tear slipped out of my eye as Ethan gaped back at me, wordless. I quickly grabbed my shirt and panties and pulled them back on as Ethan sat in stunned silence.

"Y-You cheated on me? *With who?*"

"Cole. I-I had sex with him right after you and I got together. I'm so sorry. It's been eating me up inside, Ethan. And I kissed Enzo. I kissed Fox tonight. I know I'm a horrible person. I know I lied. I'm so sorry." Tears ran in rivers down my face.

"You thought I'd be mad?" he asked. All emotion had left his voice and face.

"I know I made you choose. I'm horrible. I wanted to get back at the guys. All of you. You all hurt me so much when I cared about you all. I-I screwed up, Ethan. I thought I could break you guys apart." I let out a choked sob at my confession. "I knew you were the weakest link because of your feelings for me. Selfishly, I hoped you'd be willing to love me. Just me. Even though my intentions might not have been totally pure, but I promise that I wanted you, still want you. My heart is yours. I hoped I'd get to keep you in the end."

He didn't move. He didn't speak. My heart sank.

"If you want to leave, I'll understand," I whispered, wrapping my arms around my middle, trying to hold my broken pieces inside. "I'm pregnant. I'm a liar. I'm a piece of shit at this point —"

The words faltered as they left my mouth because Ethan's warm lips met mine. His fingers clutched my short tresses.

"I'd never fucking walk away from you for following your heart. And I'd *never* leave you because you're pregnant. Don't you dare ever think that. Do you understand me?" He cradled my face between his hands.

I nodded as he brushed my tears away.

"I'm here at your side. Always. I made you a promise, Rosalie, and I won't walk away now. I love you."

"I love you too, Ethan."

He let out a soft chuckle. "And you thought I was the weakest link?"

"I'm sorry—"

"Shh," he laughed softly again. "You silly girl. You just haven't realized I'm the strongest of the group yet. You'll see."

"I already know how strong you are, Ethan. You've been through so much. I'm proud of you."

He smiled at me, got to his feet, and put his clothes back on.

"Where are you going?" I reached out for him, the fear of him leaving coursing through me.

"I'm going to get some ice for your cheek. Then I'm going to come back here and help you finish dressing. After that, I'm taking you to my place where I can properly take care of you without having to worry about your dad busting in and beating my ass for being in your bed. OK?"

I nodded, my laugh breaking through my worries. "I'll let them know I'm leaving."

"Good girl. I'll be right back."

I watched as he backed out of my doorway, his footfalls fading away as he descended the stairs.

Wasting no time, I dialed my mom's cell. She answered on the third ring, the sound of laughter and tinkling glasses in the background.

"Hey, sweetie," she greeted me.

"Hey, Mom. I'm, uh, going to spend the night at a friend's."

"It's not Ian, is it? Because we don't want you staying at your boyfriend's—"

"Ian and I broke up, Mom. It-it's not him."

"Oh, honey, I'm sorry to hear that. Are you OK?"

I fiddled with a strand on my blanket. "Yes. I guess. I just didn't want you to worry."

"We can come home, honey, if you need someone to talk to—"

"I'm fine. You guys have fun. I'm just going to go mope somewhere else."

"Call me if you need me, Rosalie. I worry you need me, and I'm not there."

"Mom, it's fine, really. I promise."

"OK. I love you."

"I love you too." I hung up before I burst into tears again. I'd never cried so much in my life. I knew I had to break the news about the baby to them eventually. They'd be devastated. If my dad thought music was bad. . . I shuddered just considering his response to this. I'd managed to hide the paper with the musical in it so he couldn't see it. Luckily, he'd been running late the morning it arrived and didn't ask about missing it.

"Here, sweetheart." Ethan came back in the room and handed me an ice pack.

I took it and thanked him. With the ice pressed to my sore cheek, I watched as he rummaged through my closet, pulling out various clothes and stuffing them into my overnight bag.

"Am I leaving for a long time?" I asked, watching him.

"I'd keep you with me forever if I could, sweetheart," he called over his shoulder, offering me his sweet smile. "But I'm thinking we can start with an early weekend."

I nodded, eager to be away from my house and school. The looming threat of having to tell my dad not only about the musical, but about my pregnancy was enough to drive me mad.

Once Ethan was done packing, he helped me to my feet. I winced as my muscles screamed at me. Ian had really screwed me up. Again.

Fury passed over Ethan's handsome features, but he quickly righted his face when he noticed me looking.

"Rosalie, should I take you to the hospital to get checked?" Worry replaced his anger.

"I'm OK. I'm just sore. But I have to tell you something else."

"What." He set my bag on the bed and waited for me to speak.

"I erased the flash drive. I'm free."

His eyes lit up at the news, and he swept me into his arms, fusing his lips with mine. "Fuck yeah, babe. I knew you could do it."

"I still have that pill."

"Flush it. We don't need it anymore." He released me and grinned. "We can be officially together now."

I nodded, excitement coursing through me before I frowned.

"What's wrong?"

"I need to tell Cole."

Ethan gave me a gentle smile. "You do. When you're ready. Right now, let's get you rested. We can make you a prenatal appointment in the morning and get your hair fixed if you'd like."

"Why are you being so nice about this?"

"Why wouldn't I be, Rosalie?"

"I'm having someone else's baby, Ethan." I stared up at him, trying to read his expression.

He gave nothing away, as he kneeled at my feet and urged my legs into a pair of leggings he'd snatched from my drawer.

"You're having my best friend's baby. Someone who loves you like I do. You know he does. You know we all do. Why on earth would I ever not be nice? I'm so in love with you, Rosalie. You just don't get how much. Let me show you, OK?" When he stood, he brushed a short lock of hair away from my face. "And maybe we can all be together again someday." His bottom lip trembled as he studied me. "Right?"

God, I wanted that. To be with my guys again. *Us against the world.* But there was just so much we had to fix before it could be a possibility.

"Maybe," I answered. "I need to tell Cole first."

"One step at a time. We'll get there. I have faith in that, my love."

My heart fluttered as he placed a gentle kiss on my lips. "Come on. Let's get you smiling tonight."

The smile he spoke of graced my lips as he led me out of the room a few minutes later. If there was one thing Ethan Masters was good at, it was making me happy.

CHAPTER 34

"You look beautiful," Ethan praised, his eyes shining with adoration as I rose from my chair at the salon the following morning.

I spent the night in his arms as he whispered his promises to me, assuring me that everything would be OK. I'd never felt so loved in my life.

But I couldn't ignore the guilt as he rubbed my stomach with his hand and commented on how much he already loved the baby. Excitedly, he told me he couldn't wait to teach it to ride a bike and play piano. It made my heart both soar and sink as I tried to focus on his words, all while ignoring the doubts in my mind about how Cole might walk away once he knew.

Ethan reached out and ran his fingers through my much shorter hair, pulling me back to the moment.

"Do you really like it?" I asked as I went to the counter to pay.

He kissed my cheek and handed the girl at the register some money before I could dig into my wallet.

"I love it, sweetheart."

"You don't need to pay—"

"Shh." He gave my lips a quick peck. "I do what I want."

I laughed and shook my head at him. He grinned back and took my hand to lead me out of the salon and onto the sidewalk.

My hair brushed just past my shoulders in a longer, shaggy cut. At least the asshole hadn't ruined my hair to the point I'd have had to shave it. But I would have to straighten it because I'd look ridiculous when it curled.

I accepted the compromise. It beat looking like a clown.

"What do you want to do now?" Ethan asked as we walked to his car.

"Would you be upset if I said I wanted to rest?"

"God, you're perfect because that's what I want to do too." He chuckled, opening my door for me.

I slid onto the seat and snapped my seatbelt into place just as my phone buzzed. I pulled it out and stared down at the screen to see Ian's name.

Ethan got into the car and glanced at me for a fraction of a second before his eyes caught my phone. A storm cloud passed over his features. Before I could put my phone away, he grabbed it and answered.

"Listen, Hall, you fucking piece of shit, stop calling my girl," he growled into the phone. He grew silent for a moment before laughing softly. "Try me, bitch. I know what you did to her... You think so... Why don't you go see if you even have your evidence? Pretty sure it won't be there."

Ian must have gone to check because a moment later, Ethan let out a bark of laughter.

"That's what I thought. Go fuck yourself. If you ever come near her again, I'll fucking kill you... If you hate me as much as you say, then don't do me any favors." He hung up and stared down at my phone for a moment before he blocked Ian's number.

"You don't need to deal with that shit, Rosalie. It's not good for you or the baby. He knows the flash drive has been erased. He's pissed, in case you were wondering."

"He's going to do something stupid."

Ethan nodded. "Probably. But I'll keep you safe, OK? I won't let him hurt you again. I should've ended this shit a long time ago. If I'd have known. . ." His voice trailed off.

"It's OK. We'll be OK." I reached for his hand.

He gripped mine tightly and pressed his lips to my knuckles. "We will. Things are working out. I'm better than ever, and you're going to see your doctor next week. Now I just have to convince you to love the others as much as you love me."

"I already do, Ethan. You know that. It's just—"

"I know. You have a lot going on."

"I do. I need to talk to Cole. I'm just so scared."

"You don't need to be, Rosalie. Cole isn't such a monster."

"I know," I murmured, taking my phone from him and opening it to Cole's number.

"I can leave you at my place so you can talk to him in private. Would that be OK?"

I nodded, my throat tight as I hit SEND on Cole's number. He answered on the second ring.

"Rosebud?"

"Hey, Cole." I swallowed hard and hauled in a deep breath.

"Are you OK? Where are you?"

"I-I'm going to Ethan's. I was wondering if you could meet me there."

He was quiet for a moment. "Yeah. Yeah. Are you sure you're OK?"

"Yes," my voice cracked. I could hear Fox and Enzo in the background. No Juliet, though.

Thank god. I may have hung up and tucked tail if I'd heard her.

"Rosalie, what's wrong?" Cole called out gently.

"J-Just meet me, OK? Only you."

"I'll be there in a few minutes."

"Thank you," I whispered. I pulled the phone away from my ear and hit END.

Ethan pulled onto the street, and we made our way to his house, neither of us saying a word. I knew Ethan was trying to give me time to think.

When we pulled into his driveway, Cole was already there, sitting on the hood of his new car. Ethan didn't bother cutting the engine, opting to simply pull me to him and press his lips to mine.

"It'll be OK. I'll go pick up some dinner. Call me if you need me."

"OK." I kissed him again. "Thank you."

"No worries, sweetheart."

I pulled away from him as Cole opened my door. He had his hands on me, gently tugging me out within seconds. His eyes went wide as he took in my hair and face.

"What the fuck, Rosalie?" he choked out. "What happened to you?"

"We should talk inside," I said.

He nodded tightly and turned to give Ethan a quick wave.

Moments later, we were settled on the couch, Cole staring expectedly at me.

"What happened to you hair and face, Rosalie?" Cole reached out and thumbed a small bruise on my chin, his blue eyes filled with storm clouds.

It was now or never. I launched into the story, divulging everything to him from the night I keyed his car to last night when Ethan held me after Ian attacked me. He listened, not saying a word.

"He's dead," Cole growled when I finished the story. "I'll fucking kill him." He got to his feet and rubbed the back of his neck,, his body trembling with rage.

"Cole, no. I-I need to tell you something else."

"What else is there, Rosalie? This guy has been abusing you for months now. And for what? So you could try to get back at us? What the fuck were you thinking?"

I shook my head, tears gathering in my eyes.

"You could've sat and listened to what the hell was really going on, but you wanted to run. *Why, Rosalie?* I get being pissed at Fox, but the rest of us have been through hell watching that fucker touch you and kiss you and now *this?*" He let out a snort and shook his head. "Why did you call me here? To see this? You had to know how pissed I'd be! What I'd do!" He let out an angry snarl and tugged at his blond hair.

"Cole, it's more than Ian. It's about us."

"Us?" He let out a loud laugh. "There is no us, remember? You want nothing to do with *us.*"

"That's not true," I whispered.

"Then what, Rosalie? Are you here telling me you want me to be with you and Ethan now? Make me choose like you did him?"

"Why are you being an asshole?" I demanded, glaring up at him. "I genuinely need to talk to you."

He let out a groan and rubbed his eyes. "I'm just pissed, Rosalie. I hate that you're hurt. I hate that he's done this to you. I fucking hate all of this shit."

"I know."

"Fox tells me to relax. Enzo says I need to just wait for you. You know I'm not good at waiting. And in case you don't remember, I fucked you only weeks ago without even asking you what you wanted. I couldn't fucking *wait* any longer."

"Cole, please."

"What do you want, Rosalie? To inflict more fucking agony on my heart? Are you here to tell me you're knocked up?"

"Yes," I whispered, staring up at him through bleary eyes.

He froze. "What?"

"I-I'm pregnant."

"Is this another g-game?" he choked out, his eyes wide as he turned to face me. "Don't fuck with me, Rosebud."

I shook my head. "It's no game. I have to go to the doctor next week."

Cole's bottom lip trembled as he stared at me. "Who's the father?"

"You," I whispered, my voice shaking.

"Me?" He strode over to me and fell to his knees. *"Me?"*

I nodded, taking in his face. I couldn't read his expression though. His eyes were dark, his lips parted. He reached out for me, his hands going for my abdomen. He rested a large hard on it, his Adam's apple bobbing.

A sheen of tears gathered in his baby blues as his hand continued to rest on my stomach. I watched as he blinked, a tear slipping down his cheek.

"Cole?" I called out softly, worry coursing through me. "Say something. Please?"

He blinked rapidly for a moment before shaking his head. "I-I've gotta go." He stumbled to his feet and backed away. "I'm sorry. I can't. I-I need to think."

"Cole!" I got to my feet and reached for him, but he pushed my hands away and marched to the door. He jerked it open and left, not casting me a second glance.

I wasn't sure which hurt more: His words or his absence. Either way, they both spoke volumes.

CHAPTER 35

"Rosalie, he's just in shock," Ethan soothed as we lay on his couch later that evening. "He'll come around."

"He left," I whispered, burying my face in Ethan's chest. "He walked out. I saw the look on his face. He doesn't want this."

"Sweetheart, trust me. It's just a shock, OK?"

Before Ethan could elaborate any more on it, there was a knock on his door. He quickly pressed a kiss to my temple and got up to answer it. A moment later, I heard the deep voices of Fox and Enzo.

Quickly, I sat up and wiped my eyes. The guys came into the room, Ethan walking in first.

"They just wanted to make sure you're all right," he assured me as he sat next to me and rubbed his warm hand on my back.

"Hey, Rosie," Fox said, kneeling in front of me as Enzo took the spot beside me.

"Hey," I swallowed thickly but maintained eye contact with Fox.

He immediately reached for my hair, a sad smile on his face. "You look beautiful."

"I look like hell," I countered, self-consciously raking my fingers through my shorter tresses.

"Not possible." His fingers brushed against the shorter strands before his fingertips traced along the bruise on my cheek. His eyes darkened, but he said nothing.

"I like it," Enzo said, taking his turn with my hair. "I really liked it before, but now..." He clicked his tongue. "Now, it can really be wild. It's perfect."

I knew they were trying to make me feel better, but it wasn't helping when all I could think about was where Cole was. I peeked around Fox, hoping to see Cole standing in the doorway.

"He didn't come, Rosie," Fox said softly. "He got busy."

"I get it." I nodded, my throat tightening for what felt like the millionth time that day.

"You really don't," Enzo murmured taking my hand in his and giving it a squeeze. "He'll come around. He just needs some time to process it."

"So you guys know?"

Fox exchanged looks with Enzo before nodding. "Yeah. He told us."

"For what it's worth, I'm sorry," I said softly. "For all of it. The games and whatever."

Enzo scoffed. "You have no reason to be sorry, Sunshine. *We* fucked up. We know we did. And we're working on righting the wrongs."

"We're all idiots," Ethan broke in, taking my other hand in his. "But we do all love you, Rosalie."

I nodded, trying to hold off the flood of tears.

"Hormones," I managed to say through a tight smile.

Fox returned my smile with his own, but it was his eyes that said what he was really thinking. *Adoration. Pain. Love.*

"We want you back," he said, shifting forward and resting his forehead on my thighs.

I froze beneath the gesture, watching his body shake with his silent tears. "*I* want you back, Rosalie." His hands rested on my waist as he continued to lay his head on my lap.

I untangled my hands from Ethan and Enzo and ran my fingers gently through Fox's hair, my heart hurting.

"Come back to me, Rosalie," Fox whispered in a shaky voice. "I'll do anything." He sat up and stared at me, his cheeks damp with tears. "I'll keep the monsters away." He reached out and brushed his fingers along the bruise on my cheek again, his bottom lip quivering.

"I never left," I said, my voice barely above a whisper.

Hope lit Fox's eyes as I reached out for him and cradled his cheek. He immediately nestled into my palm, a contented sigh leaving his plump lips.

"But I have a lot I need to think about now. It-it's not just me anymore. There's a baby involved. My entire future. . ."

"We'll be at your side through all of it," Enzo vowed softly, resting his warm hand on my thigh.

"There's a lot I need to come to terms with. You guys leaving me for Juliet—"

"I *never* left you for her, Rosalie." Fox reached out quickly and pulled me to the edge of my seat. "I was protecting you."

I scoffed, my eye roll imminent. I opened my mouth to tell him I was ready to forgive him, but the lies needed to stop, when he moved forward and pressed his lips to mine, silencing me.

"One week. Give us one week, Rosalie." He rested his forehead against mine. "Please."

"You want me to give you a week with your *girlfriend*?" The idea was absurd and only made anger and frustration unfurl in my guts. "Is that where Cole is? With Juliet?"

"Cole is at the bottom of a fucking bottle right now," Enzo broke in. "And the week isn't so we can get one last fuck in with Juliet. It's so we can ensure we have shit on lockdown with her."

"We can all be together right now." Ethan cleared his throat. "Fuck Juliet."

A tiny, bitter smile moved across Fox's face. "It's Rosie's call."

I looked from Enzo's sad face to Fox's hopeful one to Ethan's small smile.

Could I just say to hell with it and be theirs again? I wanted my guys back. But they'd still be with Juliet.

Could I share? What if they were lying?

My guts churned at the thought of being another game to them. There was still the issue of Cole to deal with. *Would he bow out?* The painful reality that he might made the sickness grow.

"I-I can't. I want you. All of you in more ways than you know, but I won't play second to Juliet. I think we got to this place because of the lies. As much as I desperately want us all to be together, my answer has to be no right now." The words hurt to say, but I knew I had to say them. Until they decided to walk from Juliet, no would be my answer. I hated making anyone choose, but that was what it had to be.

"Me or her," I finished. "When you choose, I'll choose."

"I understand," Fox said, giving me a slight nod. "But you need to understand something. I already made my choice the moment I kissed you all those months ago, Rosalie. This thing with Juliet isn't what you think it is."

"You're fucking her."

He winced at my words. "To protect—"

"I really don't want to hear about any of it. You have no idea the shit I've been through. I chose to take the hurt over screwing Ian. It was survival." I held my hand up. "If you want me, prove it. Leave her. If you don't, I'll move on."

"With me," Ethan said. He'd been quiet through most of it. "I'll never choose Juliet. I'm yours, Rosalie. If it's just me and you, then that's what it'll be. We'll be a family and take care of the baby together. I'll even marry you right now if it'll prove my devotion to you."

"Rosalie will be with all of us," Fox said, his voice a low growl. "We don't need to make plans beyond that. Give me the week, Rosie. That's all I'm asking for. One week to prove everything to you."

I glanced at each of them. I knew it was stupid to have to wait a week, but I wanted what I wanted. If Fox couldn't make it happen in a week, I'd walk away with just Ethan. I'd still be winning because Ethan was a hell of a catch. Besides I might only get three of them since Cole had already made his feelings known. It hurt.

"And you'll listen to the why behind all of this," Enzo said. "You have to know the truth, so you'll never doubt us again. Swear to it if you say yes. You haven't let us speak on the matter this entire time. We want you to know everything."

"I'll listen once you make your choice—"

"There was never a fucking choice. It was always you. It'll always *be* you," Fox cut in, his blue eyes glittering with passion. "Get that through your head, and you'll almost be up to speed."

"Fine," I answered hoarsely. "One week."

"You won't regret it." Fox's lips met mine again in a deep kiss before he pulled away, both of us breathless, only for Enzo to move in and kiss me just as deeply. When the kiss ended, both of them got to their feet.

"We need to go get Cole," Enzo said, eyes locked on mine. "Soon, Sunshine. You promised."

I only nodded at him. Fox said nothing, but he didn't need to. I could see the determination on his face as he eyed me hungrily before spinning on his heel and striding to the door, Enzo in tow.

"We'll see you soon, Sunshine," Enzo called out before he closed the door behind him.

When they were gone, I turned to find Ethan grinning at me.

"About time shit started looking up," was all he said before pulling me into his arms and holding me.

He was right about that.

CHAPTER 36

"I'll see you tomorrow," Ethan said, pressing a kiss to my lips as we sat in my driveway the following evening. "I'll pick up some special snacks for us. We'll cuddle and watch movies."

I smiled at him. "You're the best."

"You are." He kissed me again.

"Are you really OK, Ethan? We haven't really talked about you and rehab—"

"And we don't need too, sweetheart. I swear on everything I am that I'm better. It's a long road, but with you at my side, nothing is impossible. So don't worry. I don't even have an urge for any of it. The only drug I want is you, babe."

He peppered kisses along my jaw until his lips brushed against my ear. "You have no idea how much I want to feel you from the inside."

My cheeks heated at his words as he let out a soft laugh.

"When you're ready, of course."

"Maybe tomorrow?" I murmured back, zings of excitement coursing through me.

"Mm, I like the way that sounds." He kissed my lips once more then pulled away. "See you tomorrow?"

"Yes." I opened the door and stepped out. I'd already told him he didn't need to walk me to my door before we got there. My parents didn't need to see I was already with someone new after just breaking up with Ian. Ethan had been disappointed over me shutting down the gentleman in him, but he'd agreed as long as I promised to kiss him. Seemed like an easy deal, so I made it.

I glanced over at Fox's yard. He wasn't home. I prayed he was simply trying to talk to Cole and not with Juliet. I looked over my shoulder when I got to my front door and waved to Ethan who blew me a kiss then backed out of my driveway.

It was still early. My parents had wanted to have dinner together, so I'd agreed.

"Rosalie," Mom called out, popping her head out of the kitchen. "I'm glad you're here. Lord, your hair! You cut it!"

"I'm good," I said, stepping into the kitchen. "Yeah. I cut my hair. Do you like it?"

"It's different. You look so mature! Wow." She beamed at me. "My little girl, all grown up."

"Guess so," I said softly.

"Are you OK?"

"Mostly. I mean, yeah. I will be."

"Really? I know you and Ian were close."

I snorted. "Trust me, Mom. I'm fine when it comes to Ian."

She surveyed me for a moment then nodded. "I'm here if you want to talk."

I stared at her as she turned back to chopping vegetables. At some point, I'd have to tell her about my pregnancy. My heart twisted in my chest at the prospect of having *that* conversation with my parents. It was made worse knowing I might have to tell them the father wanted nothing to do with me.

If I thought Dad would be pissed about the musical, it would be nothing compared to how'd he'd feel about me getting pregnant by a guy who walked out on me.

The thought did little to comfort me.

"Hey, pumpkin," Dad greeted me, coming into the kitchen and pouring himself a drink from the fridge. "I feel like we hardly see you anymore. And wow. Your hair!"

I gave him a forced smile. "Yeah. Just been super busy. Thought I could use a change." I fluffed the ends self-consciously.

"You look good. Mom told me you and Ian broke up. I'm sorry to hear that. He seemed like a nice kid."

"He wasn't."

Dad and Mom exchanged looks. I'd caked on foundation before leaving Ethan's. With any luck, they'd never notice the bruises.

"Well, if you need to talk," Dad said awkwardly.

"I'm fine, guys. Really."

That seemed good enough for him because he patted me on the shoulder and left the room.

"Need help?" I asked Mom.

She smiled and handed me some vegetables to chop. I took the knife and began working.

We were five minutes into chopping when the doorbell rang. A moment later, Dad called me into the living room, his voice gruff.

I exchanged a quick look with Mom who followed me to the living room. I stopped in my tracks as Ian stood there.

"What the hell are you doing here?" I demanded.

He offered me that smile I hated so much. "I figured you've been lying to your parents long enough, and they deserved to know what you've been up to."

"Ian," I snarled, taking a step forward. "Don't you fucking dare start your shit in my house."

"Rosalie," Dad snapped at me.

I didn't bother looking at him as I continued to glare at Ian. He pulled a newspaper out of his back pocket and handed it to my dad.

"She's in the musical. She's the lead," Ian said, his eyes locked on mine, his lip turned up into an angry grimace.

Dad took the paper, and Mom peered over his shoulder.

"I thought I said no theater." Dad swiveled and glared at me. "What the hell is this? You've been lying to us?"

"It's not just that. Rosalie is a cheater. She's been screwing Fox

Evans and his friends. They pass her around, and she lets them record it."

I froze, my mouth falling open. My parents didn't move.

"Ian," I choked out.

"Sorry, Rosalie. Figured if you wanted to screw me over, I'd return the favor. Seemed fair."

"Is this true?" Dad growled, his eyes dark.

I swallowed thickly. "It's not like that."

"Then what is it like?" He took a step toward me, but Mom rested her hand on his arm. "Is my daughter a lying, cheating whore? A fucking porn star?" His face reddened as a vein bulged in his forehead.

"Stop," Mom called out as Dad stalked toward me.

"I never cheated. I'm not a porn star. I-I like Fox. And his friends," I whispered.

"She's dating Ethan Masters. He's a drug addict," Ian piped up, fueling the fire.

"You've lied to us. You're making sex videos. You're ruining your future!" Spit flew from my dad's mouth as he raised his voice. "What the hell is the matter with you?"

"Nothing! It's not like that—"

My words were cut short as my dad's hand connected with my face.

I grabbed at the sting on my cheek from his slap, my mother staring wide-eyed at us.

"No. No!" she shouted, springing into action and grabbing Dad as his chest heaved.

"No whore or liar is allowed in my home."

"How about your pregnant daughter?" I breathed out, glaring at him as I clutched my face. "I suppose she's not either."

"Get the fuck out of my house," he snarled in a dangerous whisper. "I want you gone."

"No," Mom called out, reaching for me as I backed away.

Ian smirked in the background.

"Rosalie. No. Stay."

I jerked out of my mom's reached and shook my head as I glared at my angry father.

"No. He's right. I don't belong here." I didn't bother waiting for Dad's rebuttal.

My mother's sobs were all I heard as I raced up the stairs and started stuffing my items into a bag. I grabbed everything I could shove into my suitcase in five minutes. From my desk, I scooped up my sparkly purple notebook. The last thing I grabbed were the earrings from Amy. I tucked them inside the front pocket and didn't bother looking around at the room that held so many memories. I raced down the stairs, my guts churning.

Thankfully, Ian was gone, but my parents were still in the living room.

"Rosalie. Please. Don't go. If you're pregnant, you need help," Mom cried, her eyes bloodshot from her tears.

"She's not welcome here. I want her out of my house. She's disgusting. I can't even look at her right now."

"Don't do this—" Mom pleaded.

Dad approached me as I opened the door and plucked my keys from my hand. "Walk."

I shook my head at him then glanced at my weeping mother.

"I'm sorry, Mom," I whispered before I stepped outside.

"Rosalie," she choked out as I closed the door on her.

There was no way I could go back there now. Not after what my dad had said to me.

Instead, I pulled my suitcase down the driveway and shouldered my bag. When I'd made it to the corner of our street, I pulled my phone out and dialed Ethan.

"Hey, sweetheart," he greeted me.

"Ethan," I choked out.

"What's wrong?"

"C-Can I stay with you? My parents know everything. Ian. I-I got kicked out." My words were broken as the realization hit.

"I'm coming, sweetheart. Where are you?"

I heard Ethan's keys jingling and other voices before a door closed.

"I'm at the corner of my street. Please hurry."

"I'll be there in a minute. Just stay there, OK?"

I nodded even though he couldn't see me.

"Rosalie, sweetheart. I love you. It's going to be OK. I promise."

The sound of Ethan's car starting helped calm me.

He was coming.

CHAPTER 37

I lay on Ethan's couch, sobbing, later that night, my head in his lap. He didn't say anything. He just held me and ran his fingers through my hair.

After I'd cried myself to sleep, I woke up later to find myself in his bed, his body curled around mine. I cuddled into him, my heart aching.

Then the tears started again. *When had I become such a blubbering baby?* Maybe it was the hormones. Whatever it was, I felt annoying and disgusting as Ethan's arms tightened around me.

"Shh," he soothed. "It's OK, sweetheart. It's OK. I'm here. I promise it'll be all right."

And that was how we stayed the rest of the night. I'd fall asleep only to wake up crying, and Ethan would be there to brush the tears away and hold me.

In fact, the entire weekend was spent that way. I didn't bother getting out of Ethan's bed unless it was to use the bathroom. I barely ate, much to Ethan's displeasure, and when I heard Fox and Enzo in the living room, I didn't get up.

I never heard from Cole, which broke me even more. The one

person I needed to hear from wanted nothing to do with me or the baby.

So I stayed in bed, wallowing in everything I'd become and hating myself for it.

～

By Tuesday morning, my tears were less frequent.

"I'll stay home with you again if you need me to," Ethan said, leaning against the bathroom doorframe as I brushed my teeth.

"I need to go to school. I already emailed Mr. Dennison and let him know I was having issues at home and won't be able to go to rehearsals."

"He was OK with it?" Ethan asked.

I shrugged. "He emailed back this morning and said I was doing well, and we'd figure something out, so I think it'll be fine."

"Good." Ethan stepped into the bathroom and wrapped me in a tight hug from behind. His eyes locked on mine in the mirror. "I love you."

I turned in his arms and rested my head on his chest. "I love you too."

He kissed the top of my head.

"Have you heard from Cole?" I whispered.

"I haven't. I asked Fox and Enzo, and they said he took off a few days ago to see Colt. He'll come back. He loves you too."

"Doesn't seem that way."

Ethan pulled away and cradled my face. "He does, Rosalie. Don't doubt it. He'll be back and stronger than ever."

I nodded sadly before breaking away from him and grabbing my bag from the foot of the bed.

"We're doing this?"

"Yep," I said, breathing in deeply. "I'm winging it."

Ethan smirked. "Don't worry. I've got your back. You won't be doing it alone."

I gave him a grateful smile as he took my hand in his and led me out the door.

"Wow," Jamie murmured after I told her everything that had transpired over the weekend.

"I can't believe your dad is such a prick. I already knew Ian was."

I nodded morosely and poked at my salad. Ethan rubbed his hand down my back reassuringly. Word was out that Ian and I had broken up and I was with Ethan now. Ian wasted no time telling everyone I'd cheated on him and Ethan got me knocked up. I guess he assumed it was him since we were together. Ethan took it in stride and smiled, not bothering to correct anyone.

But I felt for him. He already shouldered the addiction rumors and breaking away from the horsemen. When I mentioned my worries to him, he'd silenced me with his kiss and told me he was fine.

"Hey, slut," Ian called out as we got up to leave the cafeteria. "Fucking anyone else here? Seems like you get around."

"Ethan, no," I called out as Ethan lunged forward and shoved Ian so hard he stumbled back into the wall.

It was chaos within moments. People gathered to watch, shouting and cheering, as Ethan and Ian tore into one another, Ethan's hits landing more than Ian's.

"Ethan!" I shouted frantically, trying to get to him.

"Rosie," Fox called out, reaching me before I jumped into the fray. His arm wrapped around my waist, and he pulled me back.

Enzo wasted no time joining Ethan, shoving Ethan back so Enzo could beat on Ian. It was over before it started, but Ian wouldn't give up. He took the hits and managed to return some of them.

"You like beating on women?" Enzo snarled, smashing Ian's face into the bricks. "Huh? Who's the tough guy now?"

Ian lashed out with his elbow and caught Enzo in the cheek. It only fueled Enzo's fire because he pulled Ian's face back and smashed it back into the wall.

"Fucking talk to my girl like that again and you'll wish you were never born. She belongs to us. You got that, you fucking piece of shit?"

Ian's nose and lip were bleeding. He glowered at me as Enzo pinned him by the neck with his forearm against the wall.

"Fucking answer me," Enzo snarled.

"I got it," Ian bit out, his glare on me hardening. Absolute hatred hit me with that looked, making me recoil against Fox who tightened his hold on me.

"Fox," Juliet called out through the chaos as people continued to watch and cheer.

"Get the fuck away from me, Juliet," Fox snarled. "Or you'll be next."

I didn't bother to look at her, but I knew she'd left.

Ethan finally tore his gaze away from Ian and Enzo to come to me. He tugged me out of Fox's hold and cinched me to his side, leading me away from the crowd. I didn't realize Fox and Enzo were behind us until we made it to the bleachers.

"Are you all right?" Ethan asked. He lifted me off my feet and placed me on a bleacher, so we were eye level.

"I'm OK. Are you?" I looked over him, frowning. His cheek was bruised, but other than that, he looked fine.

"I'm fine, sweetheart."

"Enzo?" I called out, looking over Ethan's shoulder to him.

Enzo approached me, and Ethan moved aside for him.

"Hey, Sunshine," he murmured, his dark eyes drinking me in. "Sorry you had to see that."

"Are you OK?" I reached out and brushed my fingers against the cut on his chin. Other than the small mark, he appeared fine.

"If there's one thing I can do, it's take a hit. I'm fine. Promise."

"What's important is you, Rosie," Fox said, moving to stand between Enzo and Ethan.

"I didn't get hit."

"I'm not talking just about that. I'm talking about everything. We heard about what happened with your parents."

I averted my eyes from them and stared out at the football field. "It is what it is."

"We're here for you," Fox said gently, giving my hand a squeeze.

"And Juliet."

"Rosalie," Fox sighed. "Let's just finish this, OK? Cole will be back on Friday. We're going to give you the notebook. We want you to read it. *All* of it."

"I don't want the damn thing," I snapped at him.

"It doesn't matter," Enzo said. "You need the truth. The notebook has everything in it. It's a diary we've kept. You know that. But it's more. So when Cole gets back, you'll take it. We'll give you some time with it. Then, you can make your choice. If you tell us to walk, we'll walk. If you decide you want this, we're yours."

"We'll raise the baby together," Fox said gently.

My bottom lip trembled as I finally looked at him. "Why?"

"Because I love you, Rosalie," he murmured, moving in and resting his forehead against mine. "Nothing is ever going to change that. We all do. Even Cole."

"But he left."

"He'll be back. I promise. So can you promise us this is the end of this shit? That you'll read the notebook? Then you'll decide?" Fox pressed.

I wanted more than anything for it to be done.

"And Juliet?" I asked thickly.

"Already on the way out the door," Enzo said gently. "I'm taking care of the loose ends tonight."

I had no idea what that meant, but I supposed the damn notebook would tell me.

"Fine. I'll read it, but only if Ethan wants this." I peered over at Ethan who gave me his sweet smile.

Fox moved aside for him.

"Sweetheart, I've never *not* wanted this. I'm in." His lips brushed against mine. "If you are."

"Guess we'll find out."

Ethan smiled down at me. "Trust me, Rosalie. You're already ours."

CHAPTER 38

No one got into trouble for the fight in the cafeteria except Ian. He ended up with in-school suspension for the remainder of the week, which was fine by me. It meant I didn't have to see him.

When Friday night rolled around, I sat on Ethan's couch, staring up at him.

"Here." Ethan handed me the thick, black notebook, his hands shaking. "Read it. *All* of it. OK? We have a home game tonight. We're going to Cole's after."

"He's home?" I asked.

He nodded. "He got home earlier today. I didn't tell you because I didn't want you worrying all day."

"I-Is he still mad?"

"No. I don't think he was ever mad, Rosalie. Shocked, yes."

"But he left."

"I know," Ethan said softly. "And I haven't really spoken to him to know what's going on in his head. That's why we're going to his place tonight. We're all going to talk and give you some space."

"What if I decide to do this and Cole bails?"

"Then he fucking bails and misses out on the best thing that could ever happen to him. That's on him, Rosalie. We all want you. You know that."

I nodded, my throat tight. "I know."

Ethan leaned down and kissed me. I wanted him so much. We hadn't done a damn thing with each other despite sharing a bed. I reached for the button on his jeans.

"What are you doing?" he murmured against my lips.

"I want you," I replied.

He let out a sigh and clasped my hands. "It wouldn't be right, Rosalie. I want you to know everything before we do this again. OK?"

"What do you mean?"

His lips brushed against mine. "I don't want you to regret me if you decide you don't like what you see in that notebook."

"I'd never regret you, Ethan."

He gave me his sweet smile. "I hope not. When you're done, call me. I'll come home, and we can make love all night long if you want. OK?"

"OK," I answered.

He placed one more gentle kiss on my lips. "I hope that's not the last time I get to do that, sweetheart."

"It won't be," I said thickly, squeezing his hand.

He pulled away. "I'll see you soon."

"Win for me," I called out as he got to the door.

The sad smile didn't quite reach his eyes. "Always."

I STARED at the notebook for over an hour before I got up and paced back and forth.

Did I really want to know the contents? I had to know.

Right? This can't end unless I read it.

Hauling in a deep breath, I sat on the couch and flipped to my name in the notebook.

All the old words greeted me from the first time I'd read it. I flipped past them to a page I hadn't seen and started my journey.

A note to me adorned that first page.

Rosie

Hey, baby. Within these pages you'll see everything, even text messages we decided were important for you to see so you can get the whole picture. Cole, in one of his insane organizational tirades, insisted on the texts being printed and put in this book. Even if he annoys us with his tendencies to be a pain in the ass, we decided they should be included. We wanted you to know everything from our thoughts on you to the reason behind our betrayal. It's important that you get the whole picture. I also have the texts from Juliet. They're here for you to see as well. I didn't get a chance to add them to the notebook. We won't withhold them from you. You can read them and see that we never wanted her. We loathed being with her. We're all so nervous for you to see this. We're fucked up, and we're sorry. We love you, Rosie. I hope to hold you later in our treehouse.

-Fox

I drew in a deep breath and turned the page.

The pages chronicled their thoughts as things shifted from this being a game to them caring about me. I paused as I read words written by Cole.

She's breathtaking. I can't get her out of my head. I want more. This isn't just a game, Fox. I NEED this girl.

I wiped at a tear and continued reading Fox's reply.

I can't. I hurt her too much. Besides, it's not supposed to be this way with her. She's not the girl for us. She'd never want what we're looking for. Especially with me after the way I treated her. She hates me.

I flipped the page to see Enzo's words.

She doesn't hate you. What if I can prove to you she wants it? Will you be game?

Then came Fox's reply.

I don't know. Don't trick her or hurt her. I'll kick your ass if she cries.

Then Ethan.

If any of you pricks make her cry, you won't worry about just an ass kicking. I'll fuck you guys up. You guys don't even realize how special that girl is.

And Cole again.

The last thing I want to do is hurt her. Well, maybe hurt her, but with her consent. I think she might like a little pain with her pleasure.

Then Enzo once more.

Only one way to find out.

I swallowed thickly and continued on, noting all the times they added photos of me to the book and little captions beneath them like, *I love her in black. Her eyes are so beautiful. Do you think she likes flowers or would prefer candy?*

I smiled at their notes as they tried to figure me out, Fox always intervening to correct them on what music I liked or my favorite color. And he was always right, despite the time and distance we'd spent away from one another.

One particular entry by him made me pause and reread.

She's afraid of open water. I told her a story about a monster when we were kids. One of the only wishes I've had over the years away from her was wishing I could finish the story and tell her I got rid of the monster, so she has nothing to fear as long as I was there with her. I don't want her hurt. Not anymore. I love her. I always have. I want to marry that girl. I hope she forgives me someday for becoming one of the monsters I swore I'd protect her from.

I read his passage over and over until I'd memorized it, then I flipped the page to see another entry from him.

I fucked up.

It was dated the day I'd caught Juliet with him. I flipped to the next page. There was a printed screenshot of a group message they'd had on their phones.

Cole: I fucking hate you. You ruined everything! We had her. She was perfect for all of us, and you just couldn't help yourself, could you?

Fox: It's not my fault! Juliet has the videos. She has everything. She's seen the notebook.

Enzo: You didn't need to crawl into the sack with that bitch without talking to us first. I'd have gotten rid of the problem before this shit happened. What the fuck were you thinking? How did I not know Juliet saw everything? Why did you include that bitch?

Fox: I said I fucked up. I was a different person then. And then when Juliet came to my room vowing to release everything about Rosalie and ruin her life, all I could think about was I wanted to keep Rosie safe and would do whatever I had to. I didn't think she'd come over!

Ethan: She's your neighbor and girlfriend, you fucking idiot. What did you think would happen? I'm disgusted. She won't take my calls. I can't handle it if she walks. She was the only bright spot I had in my life.

Cole: Stop being so dramatic, Ethan. We have something bigger to worry besides your inability to stay sober.

Ethan: Fuck you.

Cole: No, fuck you.

Enzo: Enough with this fuck you back and forth shit. What are we going to do?

Fox: I tried to tell her. She threatened to call the cops on me if I kept knocking on her door.

Cole: So let me get this straight. Juliet has everything on Rosalie because you gave Juliet access in the beginning. And that was because you had an ax to grind over something Rosalie had no control over. Juliet was tearing into Rosalie to see how far she could be pushed before cracking, and yeah, we knew that, but I was under the impression you called the bitch off.

Fox: I did call her off after I started waking up.

Cole: Yeah. Nice touch, Romeo. So then Juliet finds out you're falling for Rosie, who she hates, and decides she wants to take her down and trap us?

Fox: Basically.

Enzo: Because the bitch has to be number one in everything.

Ethan: So Juliet has everything on all of us and Rosalie?

Fox: Yes.

Ethan: What does that mean exactly?

Cole: It means the asshole made a deal with Juliet that we'd all be with her instead of Rosalie in exchange for Juliet not spilling the beans. If shit gets out, Fox will lose his football scholarship. The other girls might be like Juliet and be jilted bitches and start shit. This affects so many people. Anyone involved could be fucked over by this.

Ethan: I don't fucking think so. No one barters on my behalf. Fuck Juliet. I'm not doing it.

Enzo: Looks like you are until we get the shit from Juliet. Who fucking knows how many copies she's made and what else she's done?

Ethan: I'm NOT fucking that bitch.

Fox: In order to keep Rosalie safe, you will.

Ethan: I'd rather die.

Cole: Keep using and you will, asshole.

Ethan: Fuck off.

Enzo: Enough already! So we have to lose Rosalie to keep her safe? Seems fucked.

Cole: Welcome to letting Fox run the show.

Fox: We'll just do it until we can clean things up with Juliet. We'll get the videos. We'll get everything. Juliet can be managed.

Ethan: You should've managed the bitch before this, dumb ass.

Cole: Agreed.

Enzo: It doesn't matter at this point. Now, we need to have a plan to fix this shit and get Rosalie to come back.

Ethan: She won't come back as long as we're fucking Juliet. I mean, as long as you guys are, because my dick isn't going anywhere near that slut.

Their argument continued for a few more pages, going back and forth calling one another names and talking about how Fox fucked them all over and him apologizing profusely.

And then the conversation shifted to me and Ian. A photo of us together at my car graced the page. Ian was leaning down and speaking to me. Another slew of texts was printed and glued to the page.

Cole: She doesn't love him. She's doing it to piss us off.

Enzo: It's working. Ethan got so high last night I thought I was going to have to call an ambulance.

Ethan: I'm fucking high right now. Call an ambulance on that.

Enzo: Seriously, dude. Chill. If I find you passed out again in a puddle of your own vomit, I'll call everyone and get your ass committed.

Ethan: Whatever. I want to die. Not like you pricks could stop me.

Cole: Stop being a fucking idiot. It would hurt Rosalie if something happened to you.

Ethan: She doesn't care about me or you anymore. It's over.

Fox: It's NOT over! Stick to the plan. We get the shit from Juliet. We play the part. We keep trying with Rosalie. We'll get her back.

Cole: Fine. But you should let Enzo do what he needs to do. He's who he is for a reason. He's already agreed to take his spot with his father. May as well give him something to start on.

Enzo: I'll do it. Just say the word.

Fox: No. Let's try this first. No one needs to die.

Cole: Yet.

I flipped the pages and watched as Ethan spiraled and how much everyone worried. How he'd been found passed out again. How Enzo had called an ambulance that time because he was barely breathing. My heart ached as I read how Ethan hurt so much and how he wanted to be better but might not ever be.

How he asked for forgiveness if he went too far. How he wanted the guys to know he loved them. How he begged for them to tell me how much he loved me if he never got the chance.

A choked sob escaped my lips as I read his words.

She's everything to me. If I die, tell her I love her and won't ever stop. Not even in death.

"Ethan," I whispered, running my fingers over his neatly printed handwriting.

I pushed forward and turned the pages.

Cole: He's hurting her. She has a bruise on her face. She tried to cover it with makeup.

Enzo: I saw.

Fox: Let's just grab him and take care of the problem.

Ethan: I'll do it.

Cole: Take Juliet out with him.

I flipped more pages. Another printout of texts greeted me.

Fox: I fucking hate you all.

Enzo: Why? Because I fucked her? You're pissed because she let me and not you? You don't own her.

Fox: She was mine first. You pricks are lucky I wanted to share.

Cole: Seems I'm the only one who hasn't had my cock inside her. What the fuck?

Enzo: You're missing out. She's pure heaven.

Cole: Eat shit.

Fox: Looks like our girl isn't as sweet as we thought she was. And now she has Ethan.

Cole: Honestly, I'm not mad. Ethan is head over heels for her and was on his way to a hole in the ground if she didn't come around for him. I'm happy for him.

Fox: He's left us for her. He made his choice.

Enzo: Did he? Because I think we need to have a chat with him.

I turned the page to another barrage of texts.

Cole: I fucked her on the stage. If I wasn't already hooked on her, that would be the nail in my coffin. I'm in love. There. I said it. I did something stupid.

Enzo: You didn't force her, did you?

Cole: Not really. I told her I was going to fuck her. She kissed me back and was a real sweetheart while I did it. Best sex of my life. I just wish it was in my bed so I could actually show her how much I love her.

Enzo: Aw, you're going soft on us, Scott.

Cole: Guess I am. What can I say? She has me. She's all I think about nowadays.

Enzo: Me too. That's love, I guess.

Cole: I like it.

Enzo: That means she's cheated on Ethan.

Cole: Not really cheating when she belongs to all of us.

Enzo: Yeah, but he left us. She's just his now.

Cole: As much as I love Ethan, I think we all know he's still in this.

Enzo: You better hope so.

Cole: You too, you fucking prick. You were balls deep in her too.

Enzo: That was before. I'm in the clear.

Fox: Could you assholes stop messaging? I'm trying to finish this trig homework, but my phone keeps dinging.

Cole: I'd think you'd be more concerned about getting our Juliet issue fixed since you won't let me and the mob prince step in.

Fox: You have a bright future as the future mob boss's right-hand man. Now shut up.

Enzo: I'd hire you.

Cole: I accept the position.

I turned to another page.

Fox: Ethan.

Ethan: Yeah?

Fox: You're in, right?

Ethan: This is a gamble, but yeah. I'm in.

I frowned, wondering what they were doing and continued reading.

Cole: Let me get this straight. Ethan is back and a double agent? He's with Rosalie and back with us?

Ethan: Yes. But if I lose her, you guys will be sorry.

Fox: You won't lose her. You're our way back in. She cares about you.

Ethan: She loves me. Get it right. She even told me she does.

Enzo: Smug bastard.

Ethan: You would be too if the woman you've been pining and practically dying for told you she wanted you and only you. It really did something for my self-esteem.

Cole: Asshole.

Enzo: She tell you she fucked Cole?

Ethan: What?

Cole: I fucked her on the stage. Does that hurt, lover boy?

Ethan: Only you when I punch you in the fucking face, dick head.

Cole: I'm hurt, Masters. I thought we were a team.

Ethan: We are, but don't go fucking my girl then hurling the truth at me like that.

Fox: She hasn't told you then?

Ethan: No. She's been acting weird though. Guess that explains it.

Enzo: Guilt. She's feeling guilty, and it's making her sick.

Cole: You sure didn't act guilty when you went behind our backs and fucked her.

Enzo: That's because I didn't feel guilt. I felt fucking amazing that she wanted me. So eat shit, Cole.

Fox: Can we agree to stop playing the games and just be honest? I don't want to hear about her having to do this shit. She's trying to tear us apart by doing it. She may feel guilty, but she's also still pissed. If we're going to get her back, we need to be united.

Enzo: Agreed.

Cole: Fine.

Ethan: Whatever. But if I lose her again. . .

Cole: You won't. Not if she already told you she loves you.

Ethan: I hope so. She's my entire world right now.

Enzo: Do you forgive her? And us?

Ethan: Yes. Always. I hate to get mushy, but I love you guys and her. We're a family. If I have to eat shit to get us all back on track, I will.

Cole: Ain't that sweet. We love you too, buddy.

Enzo sent a kissy face.

Ethan: You wish, De Luca.

So Ethan had known. In fact, he'd gone back to the guys and was being a double-agent. Not out of ill will, but because he took the risk hoping to fix everything. I didn't like that he'd lied, but at the same time, so did I. And he forgave me for mine.

I flipped more pages.

Fox: Ethan. Are you home?

Ethan: Almost. Just picked my car up from my parents.

Fox: There's something wrong with Rosie. She's in bed crying. She won't answer my calls. I don't want to piss her off. Can you go to her and check to make sure she's OK?

Ethan: She didn't answer me. I'll be there soon.

That was the night Ian had cut my hair and hurt me. Fox had called Ethan to come to me.

My eyes misted over as I flipped more pages.

Ethan: She told me she cheated.

Cole: You OK, buddy?

Ethan: It was with you, asshole.

Cole: Did she tell you I rocked her fucking world?

Ethan: She said she called out my name because she wished it was me.

Cole: Fuck you, Masters (laughing face)

Fox: Ethan, you good? All sober and shit?

Ethan: Yeah. I feel great, actually. I hit some weed, but it was enough to keep me chill. Better than methadone.

Enzo: Weed is a gateway drug.

Ethan: It's a lifesaver for me. It keeps me from completely losing my shit.

Cole: Leave him alone. It beats heroin and whatever the fuck else he can get his hands on.

Fox: No thanks to you.

Cole: I only gave him the small shit to keep him from totally fucking up. I was trying to help.

Fox: Wasn't helping.

Ethan: Let's not argue about it. I'm better, or at least on the road to it. I want to be better because I have Rosalie. I can't disappoint her. That alone would kill me. I'd die for that girl.

Enzo: Well, now you don't have to. You got your shit together. All's well.

Ethan: Yes.

Cole: What are we going to do about Ian?

Enzo: You already know what I think.

Ethan: She got the flash drive. She's free.

Fox: WHAT?!

Ethan: Yeah. She deleted everything. He called her, and I put him in his place. But be prepared for his retaliation.

Cole: Fuck him. He can bring it. He's got nothing now.

Enzo: I agree. Maybe he needs another beating.

Fox: Maybe we should give it to him.

Ethan: Just chill. I'll handle it.

I moved forward more pages, skimming their conversations before stopping on another one I reread.

Fox: Cole, you gotta talk, buddy.

Enzo: Cole, man, Rosalie is worried. Where are you?

Fox: Don't do this. Don't run.

Enzo: She needs you, man.

Ethan: She's terrified you aren't coming back. At least let us know what's going on.

Fox: Cole, I swear I'll go to your parents and talk to them if you don't answer.

Cole: Fuck off.

Enzo: Ah, there he is. Man, what the fuck?

Cole: Leave me alone.

Fox: Where are you? Are you coming back? We talked to Rosalie. She wants us. ALL of us. She's scared you're running. It's fine if you are, man, but it's not like you. So what if she's pregnant. If we all stayed together, it would've eventually come to this.

Cole: Yeah, maybe ten years from now! I've ruined her fucking life. She's going to graduate pregnant. Everyone will talk even more shit about her. Hell, she might not even go to college. I fucked up. Bad. It's better if I just leave. She doesn't need me. She has you guys. You'd all make better parents than me. I don't even know how to be a good dad since my own old man won't even talk to me.

Ethan: Don't be like this. Give yourself a chance. She needs you.

Cole: I gotta go. I've disappointed enough people.

He was scared of disappointing me? I bit my bottom lip and reread the message before turning the page.

Cole: I'm back.

Fox: About damn time.

Cole: Is Rosalie pissed at me?

Ethan: She's worried and hurt. I wouldn't say pissed. I'm giving her the notebook. She'll be able to see everything. Then she'll make her choice.

Cole: Fine. My place after the game. We can all wait like bitches together, and you guys can listen to me practice my apology speech.

Enzo: It sucks. I don't even need to hear it to tell you that. Just kiss her and say, "I'm sorry for being an asshole."

Cole: That's basically my speech.

Fox: Well, I guess we just sit and wait now.

Ethan: I still get the girl. I'm not worried. Not really, anyway.

Enzo: Lucky bastard.

Fox: It'll be OK.

Cole: Hopefully, one of these times you'll be right, Evans.

I turned to the last page and saw their scribbled notes to one another.

Fox: Juliet still has the videos. I got what I could. I'm sorry. I tried.

Enzo: I did too. You know there's one way to shut her up.

Ethan: She's a supreme bitch, but has it really come to that?

Enzo: You wanted to do it to Ian.

Ethan: That's different. He was abusing Rosalie and deserves it. Juliet is just a dumb bitch.

Cole: Mark my words, she's going to be a problem. If something happens to my kid and my girl, I'll lose my shit. I've always been barely hanging on.

The messages ended. The very last thing was a handwritten note from Fox.

Rosie,

If you're reading this, I'm sorry. I tried. Juliet still has a lot of things. She made copies. I don't know exactly what's left. All I know is I can't go on with her, doing this shit with her to protect you without your OK. I need you to tell me to. That you'll want me despite me continuing. I'd do anything for you. If you want me to keep going, I will. We all will. Please, Rosie, tell me what to do. I love you.

-Fox

I breathed out and swallowed hard. All this time, everything had been for me. He thought he was protecting me. Sure, he lied, and that really pissed me off. He could've been honest about it. And maybe he would've been. He did say he wanted to talk to me about something all those weeks ago. But we'd been too caught up in the excitement that it hadn't happened.

But I didn't want *this*. I was already in shit, so I may as well full tilt through it. I took the pen on the table and scribbled a note beneath Fox's.

Let it go. All of it. Be with me and let her do what she needs to do. Together, we'll get through anything. I love you all so much.
-Rosalie

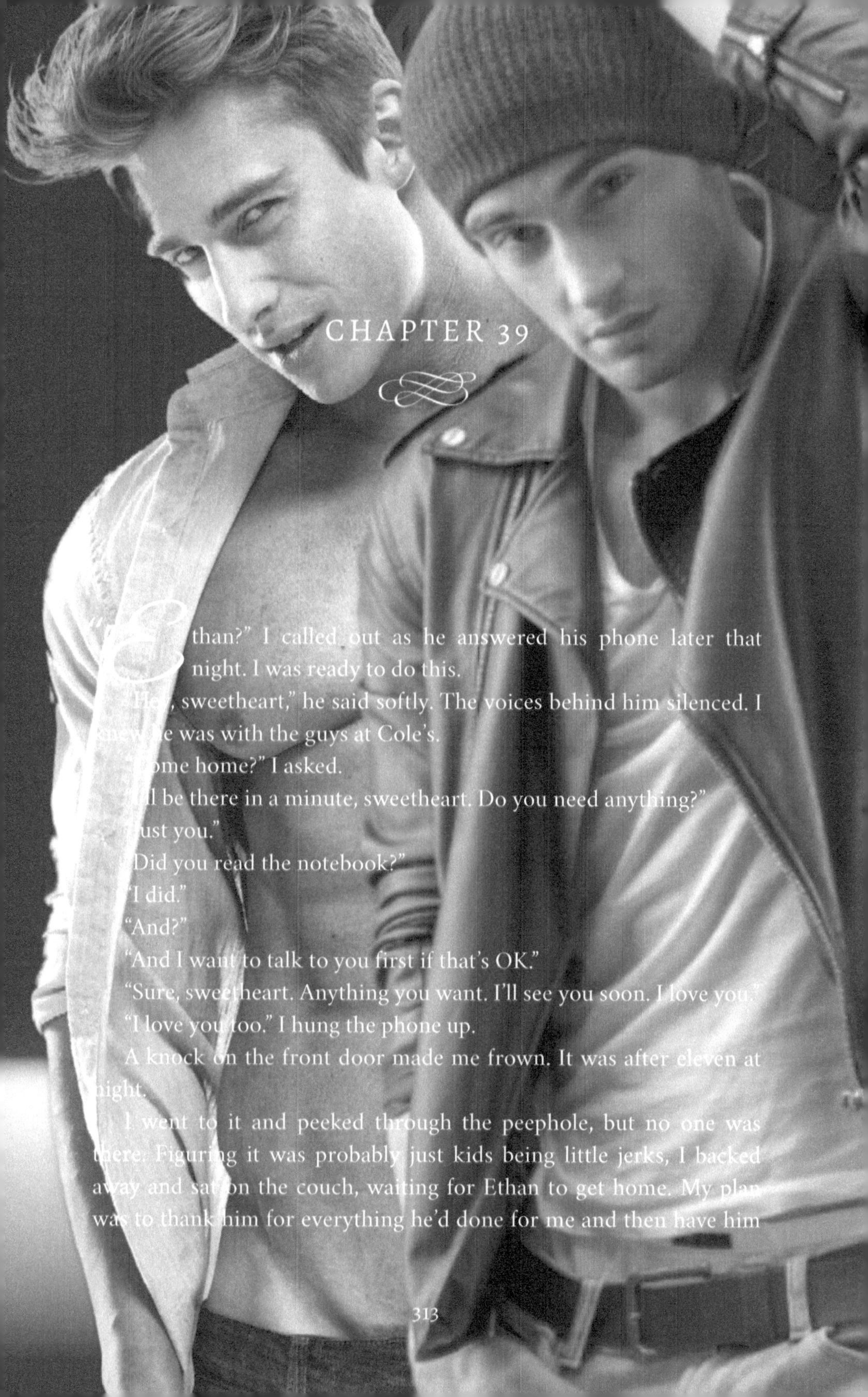

CHAPTER 39

"Ethan?" I called out as he answered his phone later that night. I was ready to do this.

"Hey, sweetheart," he said softly. The voices behind him silenced. I knew he was with the guys at Cole's.

"Come home?" I asked.

"I'll be there in a minute, sweetheart. Do you need anything?"

"Just you."

"Did you read the notebook?"

"I did."

"And?"

"And I want to talk to you first if that's OK."

"Sure, sweetheart. Anything you want. I'll see you soon. I love you."

"I love you too." I hung the phone up.

A knock on the front door made me frown. It was after eleven at night.

I went to it and peeked through the peephole, but no one was there. Figuring it was probably just kids being little jerks, I backed away and sat on the couch, waiting for Ethan to get home. My plan was to thank him for everything he'd done for me and then have him call the guys over. But I just needed those last few moments alone with him to make sure *this* was what he wanted. After all we'd been through lately, he had to be my first priority.

A creaking of floorboards sounded out behind me. Frowning, I peered down the darkened hall. I stood up and walked toward the noise, my pulse roaring in my ears.

"Hello?" I called out softly, my voice shaking. I stepped into Ethan's room and noted his open window. Quickly, I crossed over to it and closed it, rubbing my arms from the brisk night air. When I turned to leave the room, I let out a shriek.

"Hello, Rosalie," Ian said, giving me a dark smile, his eyes glittering with cruel intentions.

"Get away from me," I shouted, rushing to the other side of the bed.

Ian advanced quickly. I tried jumping over the bed to get away from him, but he caught my ankle and tugged me roughly backward. I screamed bloody murder as we fought, me kicking and hitting him until he straddled me with my hands pinned over my head. I still tried bucking beneath him, but he was so big, I didn't stand a chance.

With one hand, he fumbled with a roll of duct tape and tore a chunk off with his teeth. I stared up at him wide-eyed, knowing if Ethan didn't get there soon, I'd be toast. He pressed the tape over my mouth, effectively silencing me.

"Shh, shh, shh," he tutted softly before turning me roughly onto my stomach.

I fought against him, screaming behind my muzzle, as he bound my hands and then my feet. When he had me sufficiently tied, he flipped me back over and sneered down at me.

"That's better."

Another scream faltered on my tongue as he pulled a gun out of his back pocket and pushed it beneath my chin.

"Now, I have a request," he said easily, like he hadn't just taken me hostage.

I stared up at him fearfully.

"I don't want you to have that piece of shit's baby. I figured you'd have mine, but that won't work if there's already a bun in the oven, will it?" He cocked his head at me. "So I was thinking. *Abortion.* But then I realized I have nothing on you to make you do that for me because you decided to fuck me over." He traced the gun along my jaw and leered at me. "And wouldn't you fucking know it, Juliet isn't cooperating with me. So then I thought, why not help you out with that. *I'll get rid of that thing inside you then fill you with mine.*"

He was nuts. Certifiably insane! Ethan, oh god, Ethan! He was on his way home. Ian would kill him.

"It'll only hurt for a minute. If you end up dying, I guess that's OK too. I'll follow you into the afterlife. I said I wanted you forever. I meant it."

I shook my head vigorously at him as I squirmed beneath him. He ran his hand up beneath the sundress I was wearing.

"You're a stupid girl, Rosalie. Always giving it away to men who don't care about you. I gave a damn about you. *Me.* You shoved me aside because I wasn't one of *them.* You'll pay. All of you will. And being mine forever will be a nice way to start."

No. No. NO!

The rumble of the garage door filled the air as Ethan pulled his car in. Ian snapped his head in the direction of the door. In an instant, he jerked me off the bed by my feet and dragged me down the hall, my head hitting the floor with a loud thump.

He dropped my legs unceremoniously behind the couch and moved to a corner.

Shit. He was going to ambush Ethan.

The door opened, and Ethan stepped into the house. Tears rushed down my cheeks as I stared at him. He hadn't seen me yet.

"Rosalie? Sweetheart? Where are you?" Ethan called out. His gaze swept through the room before coming to rest on me. His lips parted before he rushed at me.

"Rosalie! What the fuck? What happened?" He tugged the tape off my mouth.

I cried out, "Behind you! Ian!"

But it was too late. Ian moved forward and smashed his gun into the back of Ethan's head.

Ethan crumpled to the floor beside me, blood trickling from the blow.

"Now *that* was fun." Ian let out a bark of laughter. "But we're only getting started."

CHAPTER 40

Ian smashed me in the face with the butt of the gun next, and it was lights out. When I woke up, I was still on the floor, and Ethan was tied to a chair, his head lolling to the side, blood running down the side of his face.

"Ethan," I whimpered, trying to break free of my bonds to get to him.

"Easy there, Rosalie," Ian called out, rising from a dark corner like the fucking creeper he was. "We're waiting for Prince Charming to wake up." He tossed the notebook aside and smiled down at me. "Interesting read there. They've added to it since I saw it last."

"You're a fucking piece of shit," I shouted at him.

"Aw, babe, you sound upset."

"Eat shit, Ian. Let us go."

"Why would I do that? I told you what I was going to do. I'm just waiting for Masters to wake up from his nap to do it. Figured I'd let him watch."

I struggled against my bonds, making Ian laugh maniacally. He went to Ethan and nudged him.

"Wake up, you fucking piece of trash." He poked Ethan hard in the chest with the gun over and over until Ethan's eyelids fluttered open.

He stared up at Ian confused before things seemed to click into place. Ethan let out a snarl and struggled against his restraints.

"Listen, I want to make this fast, OK?" Ian said conversationally.

Ethan didn't stop struggling, which only made Ian laugh.

"Rosalie," Ethan choked out, his gaze landing on me still on the floor tied up. "Fuck. Rosalie!"

Ian smashed his gun across Ethan's face, snapping Ethan's head to the side. Ethan let out a grunt of pain as I called out for him through my sobbing.

"Listen, Masters. Here's the plan, OK? Are you listening?" Ian got right in Ethan's face. Ethan's chin trembled, the blood pouring from his nose.

"Good. Here's the plan. I'm going to cut out that fucking abomination you put in my girlfriend's belly. Then I'm going to put my own in there. After that, I'm going to let you kill yourself since everyone knows what a fucking messy time bomb you are. It'll be perfect."

"It won't work. I'll tell everyone!" I shouted at Ian.

He moved away from Ethan and kneeled in front of me. Slowly, he pulled out a knife and ran it along the barrel of his gun.

"No. You won't. You won't be able to talk once I cut out your tongue. Shame, really, since you're a great kisser. But a man has to do what he has to do. Right, Masters?" Ian let out a cackle and looked over his shoulder at Ethan.

"Don't," Ethan choked out. "Please. I'll do anything. Don't hurt her."

"And why would I do anything for you? You stole my girlfriend from me. You got her pregnant."

"I'll give you whatever you want," Ethan continued, his body trembling. "Please don't hurt her. Kill me. I'll kill myself if you swear you'll leave her alone."

Ian cocked his head at Ethan. "You'd kill yourself and take the heat off me?"

"Anything for Rosalie."

"Ethan, no!" I shouted, desperate to break free. I struggled and tried to kick the bonds off to no avail. Ethan didn't cast me another look.

"There are pills in my dresser. I'll overdose. Get them. I'll take them all. I'll die willingly if you free Rosalie. You can tell everyone we fought over her, and I couldn't take the stress of her choosing you over me. Just free her!"

"No," I wailed. "Ethan, no!"

Ian stepped back and surveyed Ethan.

"Will you record a goodbye message?"

"Yes," Ethan rasped. "M-My phone is in my pocket. Get it. I'll say anything you want me to say. Just promise that Rosalie goes free and unharmed."

Ian analyzed him for a moment before nodding and moving to get Ethan's phone from his pocket. After a moment, he held it in his hands. He opened it, and I assumed turned on the voice recorder.

He held it in Ethan's direction and raised an eyebrow at him.

Ethan licked his lips as I stared up at him, tears rolling down my cheeks.

"This is Ethan Masters. I'm sick. I have been for a long time. The world doesn't need a monster like me in it. I want my friends and family to know I'm sorry and I love them. And Rosalie, I said I'd die for you. I meant it. I fucking love you so much. Be brave and strong. I'll always be with you. I'll be your guardian angel, sweetheart." He let out a soft sob.

Ian ended the recording and smirked at me. "You hear that, *sweetheart*? He said he'd die for you. Guess he really loves you, huh?"

"Ian, please. Please don't do this. Don't hurt him. Please! Whatever you want, I'll do it."

"It's so strange to me that you two are willing to sacrifice so much for one another. It almost makes me feel bad."

"You're a rotten piece of shit, Hall. Just like your father," Ethan spat, glaring at him.

Ian laughed wildly. "Thank you, Masters. That's the nicest thing you've ever said to me. Tell me, how was Rosalie's pussy? Is it still tight?"

A muscle popped along Ethan's jaw.

"I bet it is." Ian licked his lips. "You know, she never let me in. Always fought me even when I jammed my fingers into her cunt. Being such a slut, you'd think she would've fucked me but *no*. Always telling me no." He shook his head at me. "You know, I thought that baby would be mine. I switched out your birth control, hoping you'd tell me yes. Do you remember our conversation?" He cocked his head. "What did I tell you, Rosalie?"

"You'd give me a chance to say yes," I whispered hoarsely.

"Well, now is your chance, but I want to make this really fucking beautiful."

I watched as he got up and stood over Ethan. My pulse roared in my ears. Time seemed to stand still.

"I don't want you to just go to sleep, Masters. I want you to watch as I take it from her, baby and all, while you bleed out. It'll be a nice little memory to keep her in line for me, so she knows what I'm capable of."

"Don't, Ian." I wept, watching as Ian kneeled beside Ethan and adjusted his bindings to get to his wrists.

Ethan let out a shrill cry as Ian made a long, jagged slit down his wrist. Blood trickled onto the floor.

"Ethan!" I screamed his name over and over as Ian made quick work of the other wrist. Ethan's jaw trembled, his face pale as Ian stood and grinned down at him.

"Death is a nice look on you, Masters. Better than anything else you've ever worn."

"Ethan," I sobbed out again, my wrists and legs raw from twisting in my bindings.

"I've had enough of you, Rosalie." Ian stalked over to me and kicked me in the stomach. "I read that blunt force trauma to the abdomen can induce a miscarriage. I think that would be easier on you than me cutting the baby out of you. What do you think, Rosalie?" He dragged the tip of the knife along my stomach making me flinch.

I let out a gasp as Ethan called my name weakly.

"Masters, pay attention. I want the last thing you see is me taking what's yours." Ian cut the bonds on my legs. Before I could kick him away, he was between my legs, unzipping his pants. He ran the knife along my bare thighs beneath my sundress. The blade bit into my skin, making me jerk away. When he brought the blade against my panties, I froze, not wanting him to stab me down there and hurt the baby. Though how me or the baby would ever survive this I didn't know.

Ethan's eyes grew wild as Ian rested his hand on my belly.

"Don't. Don't fucking do it. You said you wouldn't hurt her!" Ethan choked out. "Rosalie. Rosalie, sweetheart."

"I don't recall saying *that*, Masters. Blood loss is fucking with your head." Ian licked his lips and glared down at me.

I trembled beneath his touch, bile burning my throat at the knowledge of what was to come.

I locked gazes with Ethan. He struggled against his bonds, terror in his eyes. Ian let out a wicked laugh and shifted forward, touching me.

"Look at me, Rosalie!" Ethan shouted, spit flying from his mouth as he struggled. "Don't look at him. Look at me. Me and you. Us, baby. Always us. I love you. I love you so fucking much. Look at me, Rosalie!"

I kept my eyes on Ethan as terror tore through me. I didn't look though. Ethan was my anchor between this world with him and the one of pain Ian was bringing me to.

"Rosalie," Ethan wept as Ian grunted. My skin burned with eat bite of the knife as he tested my flesh.

"Ethan," I whispered, a tear falling from my eye as Ian made to push forward.

And then somehow Ethan was free. He stumbled forward and knocked Ian away from me. The knife nicked my arm, making me see stars for a minute. They both tumbled to the floor in a heap of arms and legs. The gun went sliding away, the knife beside me. Weakly, I reached for the weapon and managed to cut myself free, fumbling many times before I achieved success. Blood ran down my thighs. My stomach was wet with it. I didn't dare look at the damage, opting to hold my abdomen as I staggered forward, knife in hand.

But I wasn't fast enough, and Ethan had lost too much blood. Ian overpowered him and grabbed the gun, triumph on his bloody face. He aimed it at Ethan who sat up on his elbows, his face pale and sweaty, blood still oozing from his wrists.

"I've changed my mind. Fuck letting you take the glory in your sentimental fucking goodbye. Sorry, Masters. Sometimes the bad guy wins. Tell the devil I said hi."

And he pulled the trigger.

CHAPTER 41

I stared in horror as blood blossomed from Ethan's chest. His mouth fell open, and his gaze locked on mine.

"Rosalie. . .I-I'm sorry," he choked out, falling to his side. Blood began pooling around him as his eyelids fluttered.

"Ethan! NO!" I screamed, staggering to him.

Ian caught me around the waist and hauled me back. I turned, and with all the strength I had, I thrust the knife at him.

But Ian was fast and knocked it away before it hit its mark, clattering to the floor. He pointed the gun at my face as I clutched my stomach, my breath coming in sharp gasps as I struggled to remain upright. Fear flooded every fiber of my being as I stared down the barrel.

I can't lose Ethan! Please, God! The baby!

"I'll fucking shoot you in the face, Rosalie. Don't try me. It would be a terrible loss, but I've lost plenty already in my life." He glared at me, his eyes filled with hatred.

And then he struck me across the face with the gun, sending me flailing to the floor. He was on me in minutes, his fingers in my hair, as he dragged me across the floor, kicking and screaming, my face bleeding.

"Ethan! Ethan!" I screamed, reaching for him. He lay on his side, his eyes glassy, his chest barely moving.

Please, God, don't let him die! Please!

"Ethan!" I cried out one last time before Ian bent over and smacked me in the face with the gun twice.

My world went black. My last image was of Ethan's lips parting and his soft voice choking my name as the blood tickled from his mouth.

"You think she's going to want us?" I asked, settling back on the leather couch in my living room.

"Yes." Fox paced the room. "Ethan said he'd text or call or some shit. It's been over an hour. What the fuck is going on? This isn't like him."

"Maybe he's getting some," I grunted, swallowing the rest of my whiskey. I knew I shouldn't be drinking, but life had me by the balls. I wasn't an anxious guy, usually opting to leave that shit to Ethan. But fuck, I was fucking shit up bad. Walking out on Rosalie when she needed me ate at me like a fucking hungry animal.

I'd be surprised if she didn't kick me in the nuts when she saw me again.

If she ever wanted to see me again.

I shoved the ugly thought out of my head. If Fox could worm his way back in after his bullshit deal with Juliet, so could I. If I didn't have a little shred of hope, I didn't have shit.

I had to make this work. I was so in love with that girl.

And she's having my baby. Our baby. I was going to be a father.

I cleared my throat as Enzo's phone buzzed.

He lifted a brow at us before answering.

"Ethan. Man, what's going on—" His brows crinkled, and he dropped the stress ball he'd been squeezing.

"We're coming." Enzo nodded for us, and we were on his heels in moments as he raced out the door.

Worry coursed through me. Enzo rarely got upset, but I could feel the fear rolling off him as he ran to his car.

Wordlessly, we piled in. The Bluetooth connected as we peeled out of the driveway.

"I-Ian took her. I-I tried," Ethan's voice was weak and choked.

"What the fuck is going on?" Fox demanded.

"S-Shot me. S-Sorry."

I stiffened as Fox let out a surprised choke. Enzo punched his steering wheel. Fox immediately pulled his phone out as I sat staring at the dashboard, my body numb inside.

"Ethan, are you home?" Fox called out.

"F-F-For now. N-Not m-m-much lon-longer."

"Fuck," Enzo growled. "Don't talk man. Don't move. We're coming. Save your energy." Ethan's breaths came in short, sharp gasps. It was agony to listen helplessly as one of my best friends lay dying over a fucking phone call.

And Rosalie. That prick had my girl. If Ethan was this hurt, I shuddered to think about the condition of Rosalie.

"There's been a shooting," Fox shouted into his phone. "My friend was shot." Fox rattled off Ethan's address to 9-1-1 as I continued to sit in the backseat. Every possible awful scenario rushed through my head.

Moments later, we piled out of Enzo's car and rushed into Ethan's house. It looked like a tornado had struck. Blood was everywhere.

"Fuck," Enzo snarled.

We rushed to Ethan, lying on the floor in a pool of his own blood.

"Ethan," I rasped out, my throat tight as I took in my friend.

He'd lost a lot of blood. Too much.

Fox shared a look with me. We were both thinking the same thing. *Ethan wasn't going to make it.*

Enzo dropped to his knees and gently pulled Ethan onto his lap, putting pressure on his chest wounds. "Get something for his wrists!"

Fox ran to the bathroom and came back with an armful of towels.

Enzo snatched one and pressed it to Ethan's chest as Ethan tried to drag in gasps of air.

"Fuck!" I sobbed, yanking at my hair as Ethan's breathing became more strangled. "Fuck!"

"We can't leave room around the wound," Enzo grunted. "Sucking chest wounds shouldn't suck."

Fox ripped a towel into strips and moved to Ethan's wrists. Enzo shouted commands to him.

"Tie above the wounds. Tight. I don't give a fuck if he can feel his fingers. We've gotta slow the bleeding."

Fox tied the bands of towel tightly around Ethan's torn wrists and stepped back.

"T-Took her. H-hur…" The words faltered on Ethan's lips.

"Stay with me, Ethan," Enzo murmured, pressing tight against Ethan's chest. "The ambulance is on the way. Any minute."

"F-Fin-Find h-h-h-her," Ethan choked out. "P-P-Please."

"I love you, Ethan," Fox said in a wobbly voice. "Cole, let's go."

I sank to my knees and kissed Ethan's forehead. "We'll find her. You better fucking be alive when we get back."

Ethan gave me a weak smile, his face waxy and gray. I got up and locked eyes on Enzo's.

"Do what needs to be done. I'll make sure it gets cleaned up," Enzo said, darkness oozing from him.

Enzo started coming into his own weeks ago, taking on new roles within his father's organization. We all knew what he was destined for. And I trusted him completely.

I gave him a nod and followed Fox out to the car. We climbed in, Fox behind the wheel, and drove off, scouring the area for signs of them. It was dark, and we had no idea where to even fucking look.

"Are you scared?" I asked Fox as we drove well over the speed limit down a side road. "Terrified," he whispered.

"Ethan's going to die."

He nodded tightly.

"We can't lose Rosalie and the baby too," I continued, my heart hurting. *I hadn't even gotten to tell her I was sorry.*

"We won't." Fox didn't sound like he believed it. His hands trembled on the wheel as he made a hard right.

We were out of town now. Ian's place was dark. No one was there.

"What the fuck is that?" I called out as I caught sight of a fire blazing ahead on the side of the road.

"An accident." Fox sped up.

The night was dark, too dark. The flames from the burning vehicle lit up the deserted side road.

"That's Ian's car," I shouted. Fox hadn't even put the car into park before I was already out, racing to the scene.

The car rested inside a tree. Most of the damage appeared to be on the driver's side, but the front end was on fire, flames and smoke blanketing it. Inside, I could see Rosalie's lifeless body in the passenger's seat, the deflated airbag in front of her.

"Fuck!" Fox shouted, throwing himself against the window when the door wouldn't open.

I watched in horror as he repeatedly banged and pounded on the glass. Then I raced back to Enzo's car and opened the back hatch. After a moment, I found what I was looking for and darted back to the burning car.

"Get back," I shouted at a hysterical Fox.

He stumbled back as I smacked the window with the tire iron. On the third hit, the glass shattered. I reached in and unlocked the door. I pulled Rosalie out.

Ian groaned from his seat, his face so covered in blood that he was nearly unrecognizable.

"Leave him!" I screamed at Fox who ran to Ian's side after unlocking the doors. Fox didn't listen. He dragged Ian out of the car and tossed him into the road. Fox grabbed the gun from the console before returning to me.

"Rosalie?" I whispered softly, my voice trembling as I held her limp body in my arms. "Baby. Please. Don't go. Don't leave. I didn't even get to tell you how excited I am about the baby or how much I love you." I pressed a kiss to her battered and bruised forehead, noting she wasn't breathing like she should.

"S-She's dying," I choked out, sobbing. My tears fell on her face. I rested my hand on her abdomen. There was so much fucking blood. "Don't fucking do this, Rosebud. We have a whole life to live together. Us and the baby."

Fox was on the phone again. He was the fucking ambulance whisperer, calling them to every scene.

He dropped to his knees beside me and took Rosalie away, cradling her in his arms. "I love you, Rosie. I love you. I love you." He repeated the words over and over as he held her, tears streaming down his cheeks. "Don't you fucking leave me. Don't leave me. God, please don't take her. Please, Mom," he cried out. *"Please, Mom.* Anyone listening. Help me. Fucking help me!" he bellowed the words loudly, his bottom lip trembling. "Rosie. I need you. I need you." He pressed his lips to hers and breathed into her. And he did it again and again, offering his breath to save her.

I swallowed hard as Fox wept between breaths.

Then I turned to Ian in the road. Numbly, I staggered to my feet and made my way to him. He stared up at me as I loomed over his body.

"Is she dead?" Ian asked, his voice barely above a whisper. He was burned badly. His shirt was seared to his chest.

I shook as I sank to my knees next to him.

They say there's a turning point for everyone. A point where you're faced with two different paths. One of good. One of bad. Based on your choices, it determines how your life will end up. Every fork in the road, every choice I'd made, led me to my knees on the center of that old road in the middle of nowhere, staring down at the monster who'd tried to take my world from me. Whose father had already started an ugly domino effect five years prior.

"I hope I killed that fucking baby. And she's next. She won't live." He let out a rattled cough. "I hope Masters makes it, so he can live with knowing I killed that bitch and his kid."

I leaned closer to Ian, my eyes locked on his. "The baby was *mine*, not Ethan's, you fucking maniac. I was the one she chose. Not you. I hope that fucking eats your soul all the way into hell."

Ian let out a strangled laugh. "I don't believe you."

"Doesn't matter. In the end, she chose a horseman, not you."

I looked away from Ian over to Fox, who still wept and breathed for Rosalie.

My best friend was losing his best friend. The mother of my child. The girl who meant everything to all of us.

"Juliet is going to take you down. I know she will. It doesn't end with me. Not even fucking close." He let out a sputtered laugh, blood on his lips. His breath rattled in his chest. "She'll finish what was started," he rasped, turning his head to where Fox cradled Rosalie in his arms, his mouth on hers as he tried to give her life.

A tear trickled out of Ian's eye, his breathing becoming more labored. "None of you will ever love her like I fucking did. Rosalie will follow me in death. I'm not sorry."

I ripped my gaze away from Fox and Rosalie and glared down at Ian.

"Me either," I answered softly. I reached down and placed my hands on Ian's chin and the top of his head then twisted.

The crack of his neck echoed in the night, the vibration coursing through my body as he let out his last breath.

More than one person died on that old cracked, paved road that night.

Some of us would just wake up the following morning, reborn into something else entirely.

Thank you for reading In Silence. Please consider leaving your review.
To Be Continued in *In Pieces: A Black Falls High Novel*
Flip ahead for a sneak peek at In Pieces, the novella from Cole, Ethan, Fox, and Enzo!

ACKNOWLEDGMENTS

Huge thank you to my alpha readers.

To my editor, thanks for putting up with me and all my unputto-getherness (that wasn't a word until just now).

Here's to my husband for taking those midnight strolls with me and listening as I vented about this book. Seriously, the guy deserves a gold star or something.

To Kiki. I started writing this series for you because I knew you needed the perfect book to take you on an adventure. I may have gotten carried away.

And finally, to my survivors. I see you. May you all rise from the ashes and kick some ass.

ABOUT THE AUTHOR

Known mostly for being strange, USA Today bestselling author K.G. Reuss knows what it takes to wear the crown of town weirdo. A cemetery creeper and ghost enthusiast, K.G. spends most of her time toeing the line between imagination and forced adulthood.

After a stint in college in Iowa, K.G. moved back to her home in Michigan to work in emergency medicine. She's currently raising three small ghouls and is married to a vampire overlord (not really but maybe he could be someday).

Come join the Facebook group! Facebook: K.G. Reuss's Renegade Readers

IN PIECES

ENZO

"How was Rosalie this morning?" My father, Anthony, asked as he straightened his tie in the back of the black SUV which was taking us to the funeral.

"Alive," I answered, sighing.

He nodded. My mother patted the top of my hand reassuringly, but said nothing. Mom liked Rosalie, at least what she'd met of her when I'd brought her home that one time. Father never had the pleasure.

"I'm impressed with how you've handled everything. And how you cleaned it up," Father continued.

"Learned from the best." I glanced at Emilio who winked at me. Emilio was Father's righthand man. The guy he trusted with his life. He was a second father to me, teaching me all the ways to take care of business, including cleaning up a crime scene. Six months ago I'd have laughed at it, now, I knew all those hours sitting in a car watching my father's men work with Emilio at my side had been worth it.

As much as I tried to deny it, this was my life. I was the son of a mob boss, not some rich kid from the 'burbs. Playing the part was tiresome. If anything from this entire shitty situation taught me anything, it was that I needed to handle shit. I'd watched my friends fall apart the past week. Hell, I'd watched them fight for their lives too.

"The world is an ugly place," Emilio said. "Too bad you have to see it, kid."

Father studied me with his dark eyes. "Can you handle it, Lorenzo?"

I locked eyes with my father. "I wasn't made for this job, Father. I was born for it." "That's my boy." He patted my knee.

Something snapped inside me that night nearly a week ago. Holding Ethan in my lap as we

waited for an ambulance to come kept replaying in my mind.

"Hang on, E," I encouraged, pressing down on his wound, his blood soaking my hands and clothes. "Fox and Cole went to get Rosalie. They're going to find her. She'll be fine."

"He h-hurt her."

"Shh." I swallowed hard at the information. What kind of sick prick hurts a woman like that?

"H-He t-t-tried to t-take the b-baby."

My guts twisted at the thought of my poor Rosalie becoming the victim to such a fucking lunatic. Anger boil low in my guts as I tried to keep myself focused, but all I wanted to do was turn the knife on Ian and send him to hell.

"H-He t-tried to r—"

"Don't you dare finish that sentence," I choked out. "Think of happy thoughts. Think of Rosalie's smile. The way she always smelled like lavender and a summer's breeze. How she kissed and touched. The way she loves you."

A smile touched Ethan's lips. My hands shook as I continued the pressure on his chest. His skin was so pale and waxy. He looked like a corpse in my lap.

"Yes. Just like that," I murmured. "Do you remember when you saw her for the first time?"

Ethan nodded, the smile still on his lips.

"She was the most beautiful girl in the room. Remember when you told us about the first time she talked to you?"

He shook in my arms, the light fading in his eyes.

"Come on, stay with me, E. You need to be here for when she gets back," I said, my voice shaking. Sirens wailed in the distance. "She needs you. We all do. You'll break her heart if you leave."

"I-I drew her a p-picture. Make sure s-she gets it?"

"You give it to her your damn self," I grunted, holding him tighter as I fought my tears off. A banging on the front door signaled the arrival of help.

"In here!" I shouted. The door burst open and the police came in before the medics.

Ethan was taken from me immediately as the medics began working on him. I stumbled to my feet as law enforcement swarmed in. I was covered in my best friend's blood.

"Lorenzo De Luca. What a surprise," one of the officers called out.

I didn't bother saying a word, intent on watching Ethan as they clicked the belts into place over him and carted him off to the back of the ambulance.

I made to follow, but someone called out to me.

"De Luca. We have some questions for you."

"Did you hear what I said?" Father's voice brought me back to the moment. "Sorry," I muttered.

He sighed and repeated himself. "I said, look the part. Say nothing. If anyone says

anything to you, don't show your feelings on any of it. We're here for looks only. Got it?" "*Capito*, Father," I said, sitting straight. Father didn't like to see weakness. No tears. No

slouching. No emotion. Only cool, calm restraint.

He nodded as the car pulled up to the church. Benny, our driver, got out and opened the

door. Emilio stepped out first followed by my father. I got out next and buttoned my black suit jacket, designer aviator glasses in place, and held my hand out for my mother. She took it and stepped out in her black dress.

Fall was in full swing, the trees surrounding the church lit in varying shades of gold, red, and yellow.

The season of death. I scoffed at the fitting notion.

We walked together into the church and took a seat near the middle. I wasn't surprised when Cole slid into the seat next to mine.

Father liked Cole. To be fair, he liked all my friends, but he always told me Cole would make a great addition to the family and had encouraged me to recruit him. I never thought it was a good idea until I learned of Ian's fate and the reaction it got from Cole.

He'd wept in my arms for all of a minute before he drew himself up and wiped his eyes. He'd never cried over the moment since, at least as far as I knew. And I don't think he wept over killing Ian. I think he wept because he knew what Ian had done to Rosalie.

"Fox will be here soon. He's taking a call outside. Mrs. Bishop called and wanted to talk to him."

I nodded, not saying a word.

Cole continued in a whisper. "Docs say they might let Rosebud off the meds soon, so she'll wake up from the coma they have her in."

I nodded again.

"I want to be there when it happens."

"You will be," was all I said.

We sat in silence as students from school filled into the empty seats. I could see Ian's mom

and brother sitting in the front. His father stood off to the side, his eyes raking over the crowd. "My parents are in the back," Cole grunted. "Think Daniel will cause a problem?" "Doesn't matter if he does," I answered. "We'll solve it."

Time past quickly and it wasn't long before Fox was sliding in next to us.

"How's Rosalie?" Cole asked, clearly worried something had changed in her condition in the last thirty minutes.

"Still a sleeping beauty," Fox said.

"And Ethan?" Cole pressed.

"The same. Docs said if he continues to improve, they'll try to take him off the ventilator

tomorrow morning."

"And if he doesn't?" I glanced to Fox. A muscle feathered along his jaw.

"Then we just try again later. His parents are positive he'll pull through. So are the docs last I knew an hour ago."

"It's been almost a week," Cole grumbled.

"He needed the rest," I said, hoping they'd at least appreciate some humor. Fox's lips twitched up. "I'm going to tell him you said that."

"Good. I hope he kicks my ass." I fucking meant it too.